THE GIRL AND THE DEADLY SECRETS

A.J. RIVERS

The Girl and the Deadly Secrets
Copyright © 2023 by A.J. Rivers

PROLOGUE

Thursday, August 12

Present day

X AVIER PICKS UP THE REMOTE AND PROMPTLY TURNS THE MOVIE off.

"I need to start from the beginning," he says. "Why would you start me at the end that isn't the end of a series that wasn't supposed to have a beginning because it wasn't a series?"

Dean looks at him for a silent moment. We're already off to a fantastic start with this '80s slasher movie marathon we've been planning. With Friday the 13th looming right on the other side of midnight, it just seems appropriate to do it tonight. I should have known it wasn't going to go nearly as smoothly as finding the right film streaming and letting it play. Xavier has just found out that Dean tried to pull a fast one on him by starting with the fourth movie of the series rather than at the actual beginning. No one who has ever encountered Xavier should be surprised by his reaction.

"You're right," my cousin replies flatly, still staring at Xavier. "Why would I do something like that?"

While Xavier searches for the first movie, I go to the kitchen to refill my drink and contemplate the possibility of snacks for the movies. I look into the freezer at an assortment of ice cream pints and nearly grab one, but reconsider. The pizza we ordered should be here any minute and I intend on eating several slices. I don't want the ice cream in the way. I get back into the living room just as Xavier is starting on a fresh set of questions.

"Is that a real full moon or a stunt moon?"

In our intermission between the first and second movies a couple of hours later, I clean up the dirty dishes from around the living room and bring them back into the kitchen. The ice cream is still calling my name and I'm deciding which flavor to choose as I'm wrapping leftover pizza when my phone rings. A glance at the screen tells me it's my husband.

"Hey, babe," I answer. "How are you doing?"

I do my best not to let my voice divulge how much I miss him. It feels like he's been in Michigan for far too long, but I know he's doing the right thing being there. His aunt is going through hell and needs him with her now.

"Good," Sam says. "It's a lot, but I'm glad I'm here."

"I know you are," I say. "How is Rose?"

"Getting through it a lot better than I thought she would. Though, honestly, I should have expected that. She already got through the hardest part. This is just the formality."

"I miss you," I tell him. I almost feel guilty saying it. Sam is by his aunt's side as she copes with the loss of her only child, the cousin Sam was extremely close with growing up. The last thing he needs to be thinking about is me sitting at home wishing he was here with me.

"I miss you, too. Are the guys there?"

There was a time when this probably would have frustrated me. My mind would have immediately gone to the idea that he thought I couldn't manage alone, or that I needed the two men to be there with me because he wasn't. A few years of marriage and getting to know Dean and Xavier have mellowed me in recognizing that Sam just wants to know I'm safe and happy while he's not around.

"Yeah. We're getting ready to start movie number two of our marathon. Well, actually, movie two and a half. Xavier found out that we started on the fourth one, and we got over an hour in before we had to find the original," I tell him.

"Why would you do that?" Sam asks, sounding almost shocked. "Even I wouldn't try to do that."

I would laugh if my first instinct wasn't a self-reflective nod he can't even see.

"I know. The mistake has been rectified," I say.

"Make sure you get some sleep. I know you have work tomorrow," Sam says.

It's not so much that he knows I have work as he just assumes I do. Essentially, I always have work.

"I will. You get some sleep, too. I love you," I say.

"I love you. Goodnight, babe."

"Goodnight."

I'm smiling as I end the call and tuck my phone back into my pocket. There are some moments in my life when I can't help but acknowledge how damn lucky I am.

The movies keep rolling and I'm fairly awake through the second and third. By the middle of the fourth, I'm curled up in my favorite corner of the couch fading quickly. I enjoy a good gory slasher as much as the next person, but after a few hours of it, my brain clicks off and the rest of the day catches up to me. And Sam's right. I do have work tomorrow. Come way too early in the morning, I have a meeting with a fellow agent who I'm working with on a particularly sticky and twisted serial mass murder case.

Generally speaking, I don't partner with other agents if the crimes involved use just one of those modifiers. A mass murderer I can handle. A serial killer I've got. But it's when the two start getting combined that things get tough.

I'm not one to crave working alongside a partner. I'd call myself a lone wolf if just the thought of that phrase didn't make me want to roll my eyes so hard it threatens to tip me over backward. I'll just stick with saying I do better on my own or at the helm of a team and leave the flowery sentiments alone.

I don't realize I've fallen asleep until something wakes me up. I don't know how long I've been out, but a quick look at the TV screen shows the movies have stopped playing. That means the guys are asleep, too. The splash screen on the streaming menu for the sixth movie is up, so they lasted a good while longer than I did. It also means they aren't the ones who made the sound that jostled me awake.

I don't know what it was that woke me. It shocked me out of sleep suddenly and sharply, making me think it was something loud, but neither of the guys has woken up and everything around me is quiet and still. I'm wondering if it's possible I was having a dream that startled me awake when I turn my head and feel something warm trickle down the side of my face.

Touching my fingertips to the warmth, I shift my position and feel a wave of dizziness and pain come over me. My vision blurs slightly as I lift my hand in front of my face to look at my fingers in the light of the TV. Red liquid glistens on my skin. My head is bleeding.

Before I can fully process what that means, something crushes against the back of my head, sending me falling forward off the couch so my face smashes into the coffee table. I sag down between the two pieces of furniture, my body caught so I am partially still on the couch while the rest of me remains suspended. Pain pulls at my muscles and the areas of skin being stretched and compressed.

Time is slow and murky. I try to look for Dean and Xavier, but don't see either of them. The nest Xavier made out of pillows and blankets on the floor in front of the TV is empty. Out of the corner of my eye I can see the recliner where Dean was sprawled, but he's not there.

Fighting to get my body upright and in control again, I call out for them. Another blast of hard, blinding pain across my head dislodges me from my position and I hit the ground. The force of my body falling pushes the table a few inches away from the couch, giving me enough room to maneuver myself. Dizzy and squinting with the lingering pain going through my head and down my neck, I push back and onto my knees. My toes tucked under, I brace myself before finally looking up.

An ominous figure looms over me. In the darkness of the room I can't make out any of the features hidden deep in a sweatshirt hood. But it isn't a question of who they are that's running through my mind. It's how they got inside.

The light coming from the TV is enough to illuminate an object in the person's hand. It must be what they hit me with, and they're lifting it again. I force myself up and barely manage to dodge what looks like a piece of metal pipe as it whizzes mere inches from where my head was a second ago. The person lunges at me, but I move around to the other side of the coffee table.

My shout for Dean barely gets past my lips before the figure dives at me. There's nowhere for me to go. I can only duck to the side a few feet and it's not enough for me to escape the impact of their body crashing me into the TV.

Sharp pain and heat sting the back of my neck and my arms. The weight of the person comes down in the middle of my chest, making it hard to breathe. I grip my assailant's arm as hard as I can to hold it back and prevent them from swinging the pipe again, then pull my knee up sharply. I'm aiming to dig it in the center of their gut, but I can't move enough, and my knee hits a hip bone. It doesn't have as much of an effect as I want, but they grunt and shift, giving me space to roll to my side.

"Dean!" This time it comes out fully, almost more like a shriek. The taste of blood rolls across my tongue. Drawing my elbow back as hard as I can, I plant it in the person's face and follow it with a backward kick to their chest. It stops them from coming down on me again and I'm able to get to my feet. They're blocking my way to the front door and the steps, so I go back the way I came. The person moves to the side to come around toward me and I step up onto the table. Kicking aside the remnants of snacks and drinks that still clutter the surface, I throw myself off and tackle them.

The force of my body hitting them causes them to stumble back. They try to stay on their feet, but the impact sends them to the ground. I maneuver myself to get my knee onto their throat, but they shift. An instant later I'm in the air. My head hits the side table first and the rest of my body sinks to the ground. I no longer have control of my limbs. I can only watch as the pipe rises up above me one more time. Somewhere in the distance, I think I hear footsteps. Maybe Dean's voice. Maybe just wishful thinking.

Dean Steele stood in the middle of the street waiting for the flash of lights. When the corner in front of him glowed red, he ran forward toward it. The ambulance crew knew where they were going. They were all from Sherwood. They knew the small town and its neighborhoods. They'd been to Emma and Sam's house. But Dean didn't want to risk wasting even a second.

When the truck turned the corner and caught him in its headlights, Dean jumped onto the curb and pointed down the street toward her house where Emma lay on the living room floor. She'd been sleeping on the couch when he woke up in the last few minutes of the sixth movie. Xavier had been sitting upright in his blanket nest but was staring at the TV with a blank expression on his face, not giving Dean much confidence he was actually fully awake. Dean convinced him to go up to their bedrooms for the rest of the night and he'd woken up Emma on the way up the stairs.

He thought she was awake. He thought she was following right behind them.

He didn't know she wasn't until he heard her screaming.

Dean chased the ambulance back down the street and ran up into the yard as paramedics spilled out onto the grass.

"Where is she?" one asked.

"Inside," Dean said. "It's my cousin. Emma Johnson."

He used her married name rather than the one she used when she was in the field. When she was investigating a case she was FBI Agent Emma Griffin. When she was home, she was Emma Johnson, wife of Sherwood's sheriff Sam Johnson, Dean's cousin, and Xavier's devoted friend.

"And what happened to her?"

They were on the steps now, going up onto the porch that Sam built for Emma so she could sit and read in the evening.

"I don't know. I was upstairs sleeping and heard her screaming. When I came downstairs someone was hunched over her. I yelled at them and they took off running," Dean said.

"They?" the paramedic asked as he went through the front door and into the living room. "You couldn't tell if it was a man or a woman?"

"No. They were wearing baggy clothes and a hood," Dean said.

He stopped a few feet from where Emma was lying. He'd turned on the lights in the living room and now the glow of the lamp bulb over her illuminated the ghastly injury on her head. A gash across her forehead and another injury on the side of her head both poured blood across Emma's face and down onto the carpet beneath her. Xavier kneeled beside her, his face stoic, one hand resting on her back.

He'd wanted to pull her onto his lap but Dean stopped him. They didn't know the full extent of her injuries and didn't want to hurt her further by jostling her. Instead, Xavier looked like he was guarding her. Standing vigil.

The thought made Dean's stomach turn. She was breathing. But just barely.

"Emma," the paramedic said as he crouched down beside her, taking tools out of his bag. He leaned closer. "Emma, can you hear me? If you can hear me, open your eyes. Come on. Open your eyes for me."

Dean had already tried that. He'd tried to get through to her, to get her to respond, but there had been nothing. He wanted to tell the team that, to force them to get her onto their gurney and to the hospital where there were people who could do something to help her. He forced his mouth to stay closed. They knew what they were doing. This was what they did. It was their occupation but had to also be their passion. He couldn't imagine anyone doing anything like this without it being deeply important.

He knew. He'd done unthinkable things while haunted by unspeakable memories because there was a burn inside him that wouldn't go away, pushing him to continue to serve.

"You said you didn't see what happened to her?"

Dean did his best not to let the questions frustrate him. They were trying to help. They had to try to figure out what caused Emma's injuries so they knew best how to treat her.

"No. I was sleeping upstairs and heard her shouting my name. I came down the steps and she was already on the floor. The person was over her with something in their hand. It looked like they were about to hit her, but then they heard me coming and ran out through the front door."

The paramedic had taken Emma's vitals and peeled an eyelid back to try to get any kind of reaction out of her, shining a pin light against her pupil and moving her hands to garner any response. When there was nothing, he moved out of the way and instructed the rest of the team to load her into the ambulance. The front door was still standing open and Dean noticed new lights had joined those of the ambulance. The blue splashed across the walls and bounced off the glass of framed pictures. He looked out over the grass to the sheriff's department cars pulling up frantically.

Sam should have been among them, but he wasn't. He was still in Michigan handling the situation with his cousin. Dean knew it was irrational to feel the surge of anger and frustration he did at the thought of Emma's husband, the sheriff, not being there when she was in such obvious need. He should be the one responding, figuring out what happened, being by her side.

Dean followed the gurney with Emma strapped to it down out of the house and met the deputies in the middle of the lawn.

"What happened, Dean?" asked Seth, one of Sam's deputies.

"Someone came into the house and attacked Emma. I didn't get a good look at them. I couldn't tell anything about them," Dean said.

He ran his hands down his face then clawed his fingers back through his hair. He hated that answer. Emma had been calling out for him and he didn't do anything. He didn't stop the person. He didn't protect Emma. And now he couldn't even give a basic description that might help them narrow down who could have done it. He had no information to give them other than that the person seemed to be of medium to slightly larger height and build and was dressed in baggy dark clothing. He couldn't even say for sure it was black.

"They attacked her? What did they do?" Seth asked.

"I don't know. I was upstairs in my room with a fan on. I sleep with it to drown out noise."

"And it drowned out the sound of an attack?"

Dean couldn't help but pick up on the note of suspicion in the deputy's voice.

"Are you suggesting I heard something and didn't bother to go see what it was?" he asked.

"It was just a question, Dean. I'm just trying to figure out what happened here."

"I don't know what went on before hearing her shouting my name woke me up. I guess I was just in a deep sleep. I honestly can't tell you. I wish I could, but I can't," Dean said tersely.

"What were you doing tonight?" Seth asked.

Dean felt like he was being interrogated. The sound of the ambulance door slamming rattled through him. He should have been in the back of it with her. He looked around. He didn't see Xavier. Seth was about to say something else, but Dean held up a hand to stop him.

"Where's Xavier? Do you see him?"

The officers glanced around and shook their heads. Dean went back into the house, but Xavier wasn't there. He came back out as the ambulance was pulling away. Through the back window he could see Xavier perched on the seat beside the secured gurney, staring down at Emma. His heart sank. He shouldn't be in there alone. He shouldn't be at the hospital alone when they took Emma into the back.

"I have to go," he said to Seth as he made his way toward his car.

"We need to get some more information from you," Seth said.

"Then you're riding with me because I'm going to the hospital."

Dean got behind the wheel and started the engine. He was about to pull out of the driveway when the passenger door opened and Seth hopped in. They were skidding away before the deputy's seatbelt was latched.

"Dean, you need to keep it together. Being out of control when you're behind the wheel isn't going to do anything but put both of us in danger. We don't need you getting hurt tonight, too," Seth said, sounding more compassionate.

Dean lessened the pressure of his foot on the pedal but didn't take his eyes away from their intense focus on the windshield. A thick fog had rolled in, and even his high beams couldn't quite penetrate them. He could only faintly see the outline of the ambulance's brake lights just ahead of them.

"We were watching movies," he said.

"What?" Seth asked.

"You asked what we were doing tonight. That's what we were doing. Watching movies. Retro slashers."

"Seems appropriate," Seth said. Dean's eyes flashed over and burned into the deputy. "Considering the date."

"Yes."

"Was there any alcohol?"

"No."

"Anything else?"

"We weren't on drugs. We weren't partying. This wasn't a hallucination and I didn't go into a rage and attack my cousin then use a hooded figure as a cover for it. I know what you're thinking and that's not how my blackouts work. This wasn't me. And it wasn't Xavier. I came downstairs, Xavier was right behind me, and I saw the person first. Then I realized Emma was on the floor and they were holding something over her like they were going to hit her with it," Dean said.

"What did it look like?" Seth asked.

"I'm not positive. A piece of pipe, maybe. They put it down by their side when they ran out of the house."

"Did you chase them?" Seth asked.

"Yes. I went after them, but they went between two houses and I lost them in the mist," Dean admitted.

"Did they unlock the door?"

"What?"

"Did they unlock the door? When they ran out of the house, did they have to stop and unlock the door?" Seth asked.

Dean glanced over at him and shook his head. "I don't know. I was more concerned about Emma than I was about what they were doing."

"Sam installed several locks on the house a couple of years back," Seth explained. "It would stand to reason if the attacker had to unlock each of those before leaving the house, it would have slowed their progress considerably and you should have been able to catch up to them."

"What are you saying?" Dean asked.

"That they probably didn't have to unlock the door before leaving."

Dean pulled into the hospital parking lot and the first parking spot he could find near the emergency room. He didn't care if he was all the way in or if Seth got out. He flung the door shut behind him and ran for the sliding doors.

His phone ringing at this kind of time meant nothing good in Sam's mind. It was so late at night that it was early in the morning, a few hours before he would usually wake up for the day. Despite that, he never put his phone on silent at night. Precisely for moments like this. When the sound of the ring brought him, disoriented and jumpy, out of his sleep. His heart already pounding in his chest and his skin tingling from the surge of adrenaline, he sat upright and snatched the phone.

He expected it to be Emma. He wanted it to be Emma. If he saw her name on the screen it would mean she probably couldn't sleep. Sam could imagine her sitting in the office, cross-legged in her chair, sifting through case files and trying to put the puzzles together. She always liked to joke that some people counted sheep when they were up in the middle of the night. She counted blood droplets.

That usually made him laugh. Until now. Until he saw it wasn't her name on the screen. Instead, it was Seth's. The deputy knew where he was and that unless there was an extreme emergency, Sam wasn't to be disturbed. It was the only way he was going to be able to fulfill his responsibilities in Michigan. He didn't need to worry about Sherwood and anything happening there. Technically, he wasn't even the sheriff right now. He'd taken a leave of absence in order to focus his attention fully on his cousin's disappearance and murder.

But that reality didn't provide him any comfort. If anything, it made it worse. That only meant the emergency was dire.

"Hello?" he answered.

Twenty minutes later, Sam was out the door and in his rental car, driving toward the airport as fast as he could make the vehicle move while keeping it on the road. A call to Eric was enough to have a private plane waiting on the tarmac for him. Sam didn't know what strings were pulled or how, and he didn't care.

The flight felt like the blink of an eye every other time he took it, but that night it was drawn out like torture. Every minute stretched on impossibly until the anger bubbled up inside him and he wanted to break apart the plane with his bare hands just to get the anxious, furious energy out of his system.

Finally the plane was on the ground and he raced for another rental car that would get him to the hospital. It wasn't fast enough, but finally he stormed through the doors and found Xavier and Dean. He hugged each of them.

"What the hell is going on?"

He was barely listening as they recounted the events of the night. Sam felt like someone had taken an open pair of scissors right down his forehead and pushed until he split like a zipper into two perfectly symmetrical halves. One side needed every detail of what happened to his wife. The other could only think of the reality that Emma was hurt somewhere in the building and he didn't know where. Finally, he broke away from Dean and stalked up to the first doctor he saw.

"Where is Emma Johnson?" he demanded.

The doctor shook her head. "I don't know, sir. I'm sorry. She isn't one of my patients."

Sam dodged around her and headed for the next. Dean came up beside him and grabbed his arm, yanking him out of the doctor's path.

"They're doing tests right now. The doctor said he would come out and talk to us when he was finished," Dean said.

"I want to be with her. I need to be with her," Sam insisted.

"You can't," Dean said, shaking his head. "I understand, but you can't. No one can go back to see her until they've gotten through all their tests and she's in her room."

"So, I'm expected to just sit here and wait?" Sam asked.

Dean nodded. "Now we wait."

Waiting wasn't easy for Sam. It could have been for ten minutes. It could have been days. The time didn't matter to him. All that mattered was the doctor hadn't come back out into the waiting area to tell him what was happening with Emma. He gripped a cup of coffee Xavier made for him. If he'd taken a sip of it, he'd have known it had gone cold. He'd know how much time had passed.

He'd seen doctors come through the door leading to the treatment areas several times while waiting and stepped toward each one of them, but they hadn't come to him. Finally, one did. Sam recognized the man's eyes when they met his. He'd seen him before. He'd worked with him, looked at those eyes over victims. Sam searched for anything in those eyes that might tell him what the doctor was going to say before he opened his mouth. Even if he got only a fraction of a second, he wanted to know.

"Sam," the doctor said, reaching his hand out toward him. "I'm glad you made it back."

"Connor," Sam said. "What's going on? How is Emma?"

"Come with me. Let's talk."

Sam looked over at Dean and Xavier where they perched at the edge of hard blue cushions on the waiting room chairs.

"Come on," Sam said.

Connor paused and held a hand slightly up to his side. He shook his head once.

"Maybe it should just be the two of us," he said.

"They're family," Sam said. "They're coming."

There was no point in arguing. The two men had already come to Sam's side and weren't going to leave it. Connor turned and led them down the hallway away from the entrance to the treatment area and into what would have seemed like a lovely parlor had it not been for the context. This was the kind of room where ladies drank tea and talked about their days. It wasn't somewhere Sam wanted to be brought by a doctor to talk about his wife.

"We've been running some tests on Emma," Connor started when they sat on the floral furniture around a highly polished table holding only a box of tissues. "I have to be honest with you. She wasn't in great condition when she got here."

"Dean told me she was attacked," Sam said.

The doctor nodded. "It looks like she put up a hell of a fight. But there were blows to the head and it looks like when she fell, she hit her forehead."

"She was right next to the side table," Dean said to Sam. "There was blood on the corner."

Sam drew in a breath and nodded. "Was she able to tell you anything?"

Connor pressed his lips into a tight line. "That's the thing. She hasn't regained consciousness. We ran a series of scans to find out what is affecting her. There's a portion of the brain called the reticular activating system that's responsible for arousal and wakefulness. Emma has suffered damage to this system, which is keeping her from being able to wake up."

"So—so you're telling me she's in a coma," Sam said, not believing the words coming out of his own mouth.

Connor simply nodded. "Yes. I'm sorry we don't have better news."

"Well, what happens now? How long is this going to last?"

"There's no way to know, Sam."

A flash of anger ran through him. It wasn't the doctor's fault, but that was his wife. He calmed hands that he hadn't realized had been shaking and took a deep breath. "That's it? There's nothing you can do?"

"That's not what I said. But I want to be honest and upfront with you. I'm going to talk to you as a friend. A patient in a comatose state is a very delicate situation. There are different kinds of these states with different causes. There's a common belief that there's no form of treatment for being in a coma, but this isn't entirely true. Treatment is based on what caused the state and if there is any kind of intervention that can be done to help alleviate that cause. But in most situations, the majority of what we can do is provide support and care for the duration."

Sam started shaking his head, his eyes closing as he tried to block out the sound of the words. If he didn't hear them, maybe they weren't true.

"No," he said. "Emma is stronger than that."

"Sam, I need you to listen to me. I understand this is really hard to hear. But it's where we are right now. You're right. Emma is strong. She's dealt with a lot before. But this is a challenge we're all going to have to deal with one step at a time. I can promise you we'll be there for her. We'll make sure she gets everything she needs to avoid infections, keep her muscles strong, breathe effectively. Everything that will take stress off her body and preserve her health as much as possible," Connor said. "And we'll keep exploring options for further treatment if they become available."

"What can I do?" Sam asked.

"Talk to her. Hold her hand. The reality of these kinds of cases is still not fully understood. But there is some evidence that suggests a patient in a comatose state can still absorb and benefit from ongoing attention. She is unconscious, but her brain might be able to detect the sound of your voice and what you're saying to her. Stimulating her senses could help her brain to heal itself more effectively. Hold her hand, touch her hair and her face, play music for her, bring things with familiar smells. Be here with her. We'll do everything we can. And even if there isn't scientific proof Emma will do better with you doing those things, if you do them while you're here visiting her, it will make it easier for you," Connor said.

"I'm not visiting her," Sam said.

"I know it's hard to think of seeing her hurt, but it's really important that…"

"No, I mean I'm not just visiting her. I'm not only going to be here during certain hours of the day. I'm going to be right here with her. I'm not leaving," Sam insisted.

"She's in good hands, Sam. You need to make sure you're taking care of yourself as well."

"Emma is my *wife*," he replied. "She is my priority. She's what matters. I'm not leaving. If there's even a small chance that having me near her will do anything, I'm going to stay by her side every second I possibly can."

Two days later Sam released Emma's hand and kissed her forehead, being careful not to disrupt the bandage covering the gash. He walked out into the hall to find the nurse assigned to Emma for the day.

"Hey, Lucy," he said as he approached a cherubic woman in pink scrubs. "I need to dip out for just a short time. Dean brought me some stuff, but there are a couple of other things I need from home. He had to leave town, so I'm going to run to the house and be back as fast as I can."

Lucy shook her head and smiled the kind of smile that was inborn to put people at ease.

"No need to rush. We'll take good care of Emma. Go on home and relax a bit. Take a shower, eat. It's important to make sure you're taking care of yourself, too. It's not going to do anybody any good if you wear yourself down before she can have a chance to wake up," she said gently.

"Thank you," Sam said.

He walked down the hallway to the elevator and left through the lobby. It had only been a couple of days since he arrived, but he hadn't stepped foot out of the hospital in that time and it was slightly disorienting walking out into the sunlight. For a moment he walked around the parking lot trying to find his squad car, then remembered he'd gotten a rental car from the airport and it was parked in the emergency room lot. Rather than going back into the building, he walked the sidewalk going around the perimeter, trying to remember as he went what his rental car looked like. He'd been so frantic the night he came he hadn't registered the details.

Sam found the car primarily by the way it was parked, at a diagonal and barely in the spot. He used the key fob to unlock it and had just slid behind the wheel when he realized he didn't have his phone. He searched his pockets, but it wasn't there. Muttering profanities to himself, he got back out and jogged toward the entrance. He couldn't leave without his phone. He needed to make sure the hospital could get in touch with him if they needed to.

Entering through the emergency room meant Sam had to weave his way through the maze of hallways and lobbies to find the elevator to bring him back to the floor where they had admitted Emma. As the elevator chimed and the door opened, an unsettling feeling came over him. He could hear frantic voices, but he couldn't see anyone. None of the staff was in the nurse's station or milling around as they generally were.

He took off toward Emma's room, his heart sinking when he saw the door closed. The door wasn't supposed to be closed. It was open when he left. They promised him they would watch over her.

He shoved it open, calling out to Emma as he did. The closed door concealed a large figure in a black ski mask straddling Emma on the bed. Gloved hands held a pillow over Emma's face, the pressure enough to compress her down into the mattress.

"What the hell?" Sam shouted.

He lunged toward the bed as the figure scrambled off and headed for the door. Sam wanted to go after them, but the machines attached to Emma had started going off and their scream pierced through his mind, obliterating all thoughts of anything beyond his wife's safety.

Emma lay limp on the bed, her face pale and ashen. Her lips were the only thing with color. Bruised from the pressure of the pillow and streaked with blood from where the skin cracked, they stood out horrifically against her colorless skin. Sam cupped his hand around her cheek and pressed the other to the center of her chest feeling desperately for any sign of life.

He realized her chest wasn't moving as footsteps pounded outside the door and the medical team swarmed the room.

"What's going on here?"

"What happened?"

"Get out of the way, we need to check her."

"Sam, you need to step out. Let us take care of her."

The voices didn't seem to be coming from any of the people in front of him. Sam knew they had to be, but he couldn't attach them to the faces. The doctors and nurses were moving too slowly. They couldn't help her if they didn't move faster.

The scream of the monitors wouldn't go quiet.

"Save her!" he screamed.

His head snapped to the door and he shot out of it, racing the passing seconds to catch up with the man who had assaulted Emma. Sam knew whoever it was wouldn't have gotten into the elevator. It was too risky. Too slow. Too constricted. There would be nowhere to go, no ability to change directions or avoid someone going after them. They would rely only on their own feet, their ability to run up or down, to leave through any door.

Sam slammed his hands against the brushed metal bar at the center of the stairwell door. The sound crashed through the floor and reverberated against the walls of the stairwell. He could hear footsteps thundering beneath him and chased after them. Holding onto the railing, he launched himself over the corner to land in the center of the partial flight below. Even with cutting out these steps, he couldn't catch up. Sam heard the clattering of a door opening and slamming below him. He got to the next flight and ran through the door.

Confused, frightened-looking nurses watched him with wide eyes as he stalked toward them.

"Where is he?" he demanded. "Where did he go?"

One of them pointed down the hallway, her hand visibly shaking. Another started to say something, but Sam didn't pause long enough to hear. He ran down the hall, his shoes squeaking against the polished marble floor, and took a sharp turn around the only corner. A doctor stepped out of a room into his path. His hand went to Sam's chest.

"Sir, I'm going to have to ask you to stop. There are patients trying to rest."

"Get out of my way," Sam growled as he grabbed the doctor's wrist and wrenched his hand away from him, tossing the man to the side.

He ran again, turning another corner, but there was no one ahead of him. He backtracked, going back down the other way, but he could only watch as the stairwell door shuddered closed.

"Put the hospital on lockdown," he shouted. "Do whatever you need to do. No one leaves. No one comes in."

He didn't know if they would listen to him. They didn't know who he was or that there was a federal agent lying floors above them, fighting for her life because of the man Sam was chasing. But he couldn't stop to explain it. He ran into the stairwell and continued spiraling down. He'd gone another flight before he realized he couldn't hear any footsteps. He couldn't hear the man descending, but he also couldn't hear him going up further into the hospital.

Either way would have been an option. Down would have brought him to the main entrances and out into the surface parking lots. Up would have brought him to the roof and to the access point of the small parking deck. Sam ran back up a couple of flights, changed his mind, and ran down again. His mind started to blur. He couldn't think clearly in his rage and panic. He walked to the nearest door and stepped through it. His heart pounded heavily and his breath gasped from his lungs. He could feel sweat running down the back of his neck and stinging his eyes.

Not paying attention to anything around him, he walked slowly along the hallway. He stopped only when his downcast eyes saw the bottom of a wall steps away and he realized he'd reached the end of the hall. Looking up, he saw a pane of glass stretching nearly the size of the wall. Beyond it were rows of bassinets, many of them holding tiny babies swaddled in white hospital blankets.

Sam stumbled forward toward the glass. He pressed his hands to it, his breath coming in sobs as he stared through the glass at the newborns. His forehead fell forward to press to the cool pane and the sting in his eyes deepened. Squeezing them closed, he fought to control his breathing and the buzzing in his ears that blocked out everything else around him.

Images of Emma's limp, pale body and the blood on her lips overwhelming him, Sam slid down the pane of glass and onto his knees. His heart felt like it was splitting and from the rupture poured a silent, desperate plea for help. He cried out to anyone who was listening, anyone who could do anything.

The feeling of a hand wrapping around his upper arm sparked his defensiveness and he wrenched himself out of the grip, rearing back to attack whomever it was who dared touch him.

"Sam, calm down. Sam, it's me."

Despite the words, Sam couldn't place the voice. One hand was still gripping the ledge of the wall at the bottom of the window and gripped harder as he pulled his shoulder away from the touch that landed on him again.

"Sam, get up. I need you to come up and talk to me."

Those words cut through the fog and Sam looked up. Connor's face was gray, his eyes bloodshot. His hair stood on end at odd angles as if he'd run his hands through it while it was damp with sweat. The doctor hesitated for a second before reaching down toward Sam again. Sam gave him his hand and let Connor pick up him off the ground.

"We couldn't find you. We've been searching for you. Come on," Connor said.

Sam dug in his heels, refusing to move even a step without knowing what he was walking into.

"Emma," he said. "Is she…how is she?"

"Come on. Let's go to my office and talk," Connor said.

He gave Sam's arm a tug, but Sam didn't move. His jaw set and his eyes flashed with defiance and fear.

"Tell me now," he said.

Connor took a breath. "She's alive. The team managed to get her heart beating again and she's breathing on her own."

Relief washed over Sam, making him sag against the wall. He turned his head for another look at the babies lying in their tiny plastic beds. Something about them was as comforting in that moment as it had been painful in the last. It wasn't that he longed for one of his own or even that they represented some possibility for him. Those conversations and final decisions had been made years ago. He and Emma loved having Bellamy and Eric's daughter Bebe in their lives. And they both held onto the thought that maybe one day Dean would settle down with someone and have a child of his own. They welcomed the thought. But both of them were at peace with the choice that those were the only ways their family would grow. Emma and Sam's lives were on a different path.

And maybe it was as simple as that.

Those little babies represented not just new lives, but potential. Possibility. Opportunity. Everything that could be. For those little ones, life had just begun and there was so much ahead of them. Right now, what they could be and do was limitless. Their lives were spread open in front of them. There was so much out there for them to see, so much for them to experience in the world.

In so many ways, Sam still felt like them. He was obviously far older and had already lived through so many of his possibilities and opportunities. But there were more. He knew there were years to be lived and experiences to be had. There were things that needed to be done. And every one of them involved Emma. He couldn't even begin to imagine his life without her. He hadn't been able to since he was nine years old and saw her for the first time. From the moment he saved her ball from rolling across the street and looked into her eyes as he handed it back to her, Sam knew Emma was a permanent fixture in his life.

Even if he didn't fully understand it at the time, and even if he had to wait for far longer than he ever thought he would, even facing a stretch of time when he thought he had lost her, that little boy version of himself knew he wanted every adventure in his life to be shared with her.

Finally able to catch his breath and feel like he could move one foot in front of the other, Sam followed Connor to the stairwell door. He took out his badge and scanned it over a panel, disengaging a magnetic lock embedded deep within the door.

"The hospital has gone into lockdown. The elevators are disabled and all access to stairwells and each of the individual wards of the hospital must be accessed using an authorized personnel ID badge," he explained.

Sam was relieved to hear about the precautions, but it wasn't enough. If the hospital was still on lockdown, that meant no one had been able to find the man responsible for Emma's attack. Most likely, he'd escaped the hospital and was already gone. He followed the doctor to his office and sat down as Connor closed the door behind them.

"Can I get you some coffee?"

"No," Sam said. "I just want to know what's going on."

Connor's eyes glanced over toward the coffee maker sitting on a marble counter in front of the window as if he was considering making a cup for himself, but he thought better of it and sat across from Sam. Folding his hands on the desk in front of him, he leaned slightly forward to show his engagement.

"Emma was without oxygen in her brain for about two minutes. We were able to bring her back and we are going to run further tests to determine if there was more damage."

"Who did this? How could any of you have let this happen?" Sam asked.

Connor looked startled by the questions. "We didn't let this happen, Sam."

"Yes, you did. I talked to the nurses before I left. I was gone only long enough to go downstairs to the parking lot. I was just going to go home and get a few things and I specifically said to make sure she stayed safe. Not anybody in that room. I was gone for less than ten minutes and when I came back there was somebody smothering her. How the fuck does that happen?" Sam asked.

"There was an emergency on the floor…"

"Emma being in the hospital at all is an emergency. Do you not understand who she is? What she's done? Did it somehow miss you how she ended up here in the first place? She was attacked in our home. Somebody beat her into a coma and nobody has been able to figure out who it was."

"I understand that."

"Do you? Because it seems like you aren't taking it particularly seriously. She was supposed to be safe here. You were supposed to be watching her."

"Like I said. There was an emergency with another patient. I'm sorry this worked out the way that it did. I'm sorry that there was a miscommunication among the team and Emma's room was left unattended. None of us wanted this to happen, Sam. All of us take our jobs very seriously and we are well aware of not only who Emma is, but how much she means to a lot of people. Including us, I'll point out. I'm sorry. I can't say it enough times, I understand that. But what matters right now is that she is alive and we have to figure out how we are going to keep it that way."

"I'm going to put in a call to Eric Martinez at the Bureau. I want an agent guarding her door twenty-four hours a day. No one has access to her unless I have given you their name. Emma will fight through this. She has to. And whoever did this will not get away with it."

CHAPTER ONE

Two weeks later

ANYONE PLANNING TO BOARD A PLANE THAT NIGHT WHO SAW THE thick mist rolling down the streets of Sherwood would immediately expect their flight to be delayed. It was the kind of fog that kept you from being able to see more than a couple of feet in front of you. No pilot would want to roll to the end of a runway with a commercial flight full of passengers and take to that sort of sky, responsible for all the souls sitting behind them.

But the woman who walked up to the glass doors of the terminal, briefly looking at her own reflection against the dark backdrop of the night sky, hadn't come from Sherwood. She didn't see the mist. Even if she had, it wouldn't have stopped her. She still would have walked through those doors and into the biting chill of the cavernous airport.

It was the strange window of the late night when the airport temporarily came alive again, if only for an hour or two. International and red-eye passengers milled around the terminal in search of coffee and snacks and crowded at the gates wanting to get onto their plane as quickly as possible so they could settle in and attempt to get some sleep. Those arriving shuffled off their flights and moved around in an effort to loosen travel-stiffened joints while blinking away the sudden brightness.

This kind of energy and crowd didn't last all night. It was a specific sliver of time that would fade back into silence for a while before the daytime rush started up again. That was why she chose it. She needed to blend in.

Not showing any thought or care on her face, she walked purposefully, but without rushing through the open atrium and toward the self-check-in kiosks at the far end of the space. Several people were crowded around the machines positioned on an octagon of bright blue carpet. She stepped up to one of the machines and set her rolling suitcase to the side. Shifting the large bag over her shoulder, she reached in and rummaged around to find her phone. It was at the very bottom of the bag, tucked into the corner and under the assortment of clothing, size-approved toiletries, and basic ephemera that seemed to find its way into every bag.

She took out her phone and scrolled through several screens until she pulled up her confirmation email. Out of the corner of her eye, she saw a man in a dark, meticulously tailored suit step up to the machine beside her. He didn't need to rummage in anything to find his phone. It slipped from his pocket and swept under the red lights of the scanner seamlessly. This was the type of man who traveled frequently. Boarding a plane was as second nature to him as climbing the steps to a corporate office each morning was to others.

The woman took her time reading through the prompts that appeared on the screen. She considered each option and made her selections thoughtfully, occasionally changing her mind once or twice before settling on her response and moving to the next screen. With each measured moment, she could feel the time clicking past. She counted the number of heartbeats that needed to pass, slowing her breathing and her reading to ensure she'd been standing there long enough.

The man beside her moved much more quickly. His boarding pass printed out of the kiosk and he grabbed it before reaching for his bag. No one around them noticed the deft way his hand slipped past the handle of his own rolling bag and instead took the woman's. He walked away and she slowly moved through the last of the screens before printing out her own boarding pass, taking hold of the bag the man left behind and heading deeper into the airport. By the time she made it through the security checkpoint, the man had walked out of a side door of the airport and onto the tarmac.

He didn't slow or show any signs of hesitation as he made his way directly to a small private plane set off to the side away from the commercial jets. A few of the luggage handlers and safety technicians dotted around the tarmac glanced his way, but most barely seemed to notice him. Private flights weren't rare from this airport. Usually they contained politicians or celebrities, but high-powered businessmen weren't unheard of. Those who had been working at the airport for more than a couple of years barely even noticed them anymore. Unless they were assigned to the actual flight and had to turn on all their charm and customer service, it was easier to just ignore them and keep focused on the next task at hand.

The man walked up to the private plane and paused for only an instant at the bottom of the steps already in place. Pressing the handle down into the suitcase, he picked it up and carried it with him through the door into the seemingly empty craft. The pilot was already shut away in the cockpit. Just as he should have been. There would be no flight attendants. No snack service. No safety spiel.

He sat down in one of the four luxurious seats and reached into the individual cooler compartment beside it for one of the tiny bottles of champagne requested to be waiting inside the plane. It opened with little fanfare and since there was no one to offer a toast to, he took a sip and stared through the window at the lights off the runways beyond.

A few minutes later, he heard the sound of footsteps on the stairs. He looked up to see another man in a similarly tailored dark suit walk through the door and down the aisle toward the seat facing him. They looked enough alike, carrying the same suitcase, their shoulders held the same way, that it was almost like watching himself board the plane. It would have been easy for anyone who had been watching through the corner of their eye and with half their attention to think they had merely seen the same person. The memory of both men crossing the tarmac and entering the plane would meld into one. Later, when questioned, very few would think they had seen two men and most wouldn't bring themselves to admit it. In a career where focus and paying attention were paramount to safety, not being able to tell if you saw one or two men would not look good for any of them.

The second man sat down and met eyes with the first.

"The skies look clear," he said.

The first man's head dipped in a barely perceptible nod. "Just stars tonight."

It was a seemingly innocuous exchange, the kind of banal small talk that strangers volley to fill uncomfortable silence and give some kind of impression of friendliness even without the intent to actually follow through. But these were not just words to these men. They weren't spontaneous or meaningless. They were doled out in a transaction, each confirming the other.

They nodded slightly at each other again.

"I'd like to see what's in your bag," the second man said to the first.

"And then you'll show me what's in yours?"

A slight smile flickered at the corners of the second man's mouth. "Of course."

The first man took hold of the bag and pulled it around in front of him. He turned it toward himself and reached down for the zipper. In a swift movement, he reached into the inner pocket of his jacket and pulled out a small gun. The silencer on it nearly lived up to its name, and by the time the steps were folded in and the plane door was locked into place, the gun was concealed again and the man was back to sipping his champagne, unbothered by the body sprawled on the floor in front of him.

There was very little blood. The small, viciously designed bullets pierced skin easily and burrowed through the body, forging a devastating path. Anyone on the receiving end of one of these bullets had only a few more heartbeats once the projectile ravaged their internal organs and sliced through veins and arteries. But at least there was little mess to deal with.

He hated leaving a mess when he didn't have to.

A slight ding from somewhere in the plane activated the Pavlovian reaction in him and he clicked his seatbelt into place. Leaned back against the plush seat, he let out a breath and relaxed into the feeling of the plane pulling back to start down the runway.

The ascent was smooth and he passed the time reading a hardback bestseller he'd picked up from one of the splashy displays at a shop in a different airport terminal. Much of his life was spent on planes and he was not one to sleep thousands of feet above the ground. So he read. He hadn't adopted the passion for electronic readers and instead always carried a book with him. He preferred the feeling of the pages on his fingers, the sound of the paper rustling against itself in the silence, and the weight gradually shifting from one hand to the other as he made his way from beginning to end. If it wasn't one of the rare days that he was home when he finished a book, he'd leave it sitting somewhere for another person to find. He liked to imagine the journeys they took.

The man had gotten through several chapters of his book by the time a glance out the window revealed they were now flying over open water. He closed the book and set it to the side, unlatching his seat belt so he could stand. The interior of the plane was designed to conceal various features, but he knew where to look for the safety harness he slipped over his shoulders and secured around his waist, then how to release the door toward the back of the plane. It opened as if he was preparing to skydive. Instead, he took hold of the dead man by the back of his collar and dragged him over. Secure in his harness that kept him held firmly to the interior of the plane, he pushed the corpse over the edge and peered down to watch until it disappeared into the darkness below.

He closed the door, engaged the lock, and stowed the harness away again before he sat back down, picked up his book, and read.

CHAPTER TWO

Now

HATE THE SMELL OF NEW CARPET.

It's one of those smells that so many people say they love and that draws them in to a new home. They step inside and take one of those deep breaths that fills up their lungs and makes their chest lift all the way up toward the ceiling like they have no thought about all the little fibers and chemical fumes that make up that smell they are now permeating their body with.

But it's not the chemicals or the fibers that I'm thinking about. I hate the smell that reminds me that the entirety of my living room carpet had to be ripped up. That it's not quite the same color it used to be because the shade was discontinued. That it doesn't feel as soft yet because it hasn't been walked on for years and it still needs to be worn in by use and the vacuum.

I hate that it's there because the carpet that had been there for years was too bloodstained to be saved.

The day I walked through the front door after getting out of the hospital, the house smelled like strong cleaner. Not in the fresh, pleasant way that makes the space welcoming and relaxing. The harsh, overpowering way that says something horrible happened and someone is trying to cover it up. I saw the stain on the carpet immediately. It was faded and the furniture had been shifted around a bit to try to cover it, but it was spread across too much space. The carpet had absorbed it too deeply in the days between the attack and when Dean and Xavier were able to go inside to clean up.

They did what they could, but the blood wouldn't come out of the carpet. It faded, but as the carpet dried, the stain came back up the fibers and darkened again. Within five minutes of seeing the stain, I was on the phone with a contractor. Two days later, all the carpet was ripped out of the living room and replaced.

It's been there for a week and the new smell is still suffocating.

It accompanies my frustration and anger as I do everything I can to go back to before the blood was on the carpet and find out what happened.

When I woke up in the hospital, disoriented and struggling to remember what happened, I found out I'd been unconscious for two weeks. I spent another week under observation, rebuilding my strength and proving to the doctors I had all my mental faculties. Sam was by my side the entire time and gave me the basic story of what happened. I remember the attack in the living room. I know I was attacked again a couple of days after and almost didn't survive.

Sam didn't want to talk about it much. He didn't want to get into any details and every time I started asking questions, he shifted the conversation to something else. They didn't know who'd committed either attack. That's all he would tell me. Both times a hooded, masked figure ran as soon as someone else arrived on the scene. That's all.

It's not enough for me. There's an official police investigation ongoing into both attacks, but I can't just sit here and wait for them to find something. I've spent the last week trying to find anything to connect the attacks to the cases I've been working. They can't be random. No FBI agent is attacked for no reason. This has to have something to do with a case I've been investigating or have in the past. I just can't figure out what.

"Babe, come on," Sam calls from the hallway outside my office. "Dinner's ready."

"Just a minute," I say, flipping back through the file I've been poring over for the last hour.

"That's what you said fifteen minutes ago. You have to eat."

"I'm not hungry."

"You haven't eaten since breakfast. You're not going to heal if you don't eat," he says.

I want to snap at him, to tell him to stop. I've already listened to the doctors lecture me for weeks. I don't need my husband doing it, too. But I force myself to bite off the words before they come out of my mouth. He's just trying to take care of me. Sam loves me and wants me to get better. I know that. He's told me so many times. I have to keep telling myself.

What happened isn't Sam's fault. I know there's a part of him that blames himself because he wasn't home when it happened. He feels guilty for being in Michigan with his aunt rather than there with me, but he shouldn't. He was exactly where he should have been and was doing exactly what he was supposed to be doing. Even if he was home that night, there's no guarantee the attack wouldn't have happened. Dean and Xavier were both there, and it still happened. If Sam had been home, he might have gotten hurt, too.

"Alright," I finally relent, setting my file aside and following him out of the office.

I can hear Xavier and Dean in the living room. They got here earlier today after being away since just a couple of days after I woke up. Dean's work as a private investigator means he is frequently on the move, going to meet clients, tracking people, doing things I will never know about and really don't want to. He's good at what he does. The best in his industry. He has saved lives and helped countless people. And with few exceptions, where he goes, Xavier goes. I miss both of them when they are away, whether it's for work or just because they are at their house in Harlan.

They both have bedrooms here. The yellow one for Xavier. The one my grandmother decorated with angels for Dean because they scare Xavier. But as much as I know they enjoy spending time here with us, it's still my house. There's always going to be that slight sense that they are guests in it. I hate them feeling that way, especially since they were Dean's grandparents, too. He should feel at home here. Beyond that, I know if they had a space that was theirs, they would be in Sherwood more often.

That thought stops me in the arched doorway between the living room and dining room. I glance to the side and watch Dean and Xavier playing an old board game Sam discovered in the attic months ago. The directions are missing, and we can't find any online, so these two have been diligently trying to figure out how the game is supposed to be played.

"Babe?"

I turn to look at Sam, who's eyeing me curiously from the kitchen. "Hmmm?"

"You okay?"

"Yeah." I glance over at the guys again. The image of them in there feels oddly nostalgic, like a memory drifting past in the back of my mind. I look at Sam again. "I just had the strangest feeling. Like I'm remembering something."

"Remembering what?" Sam asks.

"I don't know. I can't place it. I was thinking about missing Dean and Xavier when they're away and then I saw them in the living room and..."

"And?" Sam asks, still looking confused.

"And I don't know. I just got this weird feeling. Warm and cozy. Like... Christmas."

It's nowhere near Christmas right now, but seeing the guys in the living room keeps bringing to mind colorful lights and sweet smells. I can almost imagine the tree behind them. I shake my head. Maybe something is still jostled up there.

In the kitchen Sam is pulling a homemade pizza out of the oven. It's one of my favorite things he makes. He learned to make the dough a couple of years ago when I was in the field and he attempted to make cinnamon rolls to fulfill a craving. He said they ended up tasting like butter and raw cinnamon rolled up in pizza dough. After that night I've made sure there is always a batch of rolls in the freezer ready to thaw and bake, and he has vowed to only top his dough with cheese and not cinnamon. It's working out well for us.

As Sam sets this pizza on the table next to two others he has already taken out and starts to cut the first two, Xavier and Dean find their way into the kitchen. I take out plates and cups and we go through the motions of getting ready for dinner. Since the kitchen table is covered with pizza and drinks, we carry everything into the dining room and sit down.

"How are you doing, Emma?" Dean asks after a few moments.

I shake my head through a bite.

"Not good? What's wrong?" he asks.

"No. That meant don't ask me that," I explain. "We've already gone over this. I've been asked that question or some variation of it far too many times in the last couple of weeks. Including three times by you already today. I just don't want to be asked anymore. It's good. I'm good. Everything's… good."

"Well, that was certainly convincing," Dean says.

"She's trying to act like nothing happened," Sam says.

"I'm not the one trying to act like nothing happened," I point out. "Everybody around me keeps asking how I'm feeling and very specifically not asking if my brain is still working, even though I know that's in parentheses at the end there. But I seem to be the only person who will actually talk about what happened and why I was in the hospital to begin with. No one wants to even acknowledge it."

"That's not true," Sam says.

"It's not that we're not acknowledging it, Emma, or pretending it didn't happen. There's an investigation going on," Dean adds.

I scoff. "Yep. The investigation. The hospital doesn't have surveillance cameras in its elevators, stairwells, or on its treatment floors because of security risks. But apparently the risk of an attempted murderer just wandering into a comatose federal agent's room is not high enough to address in any way. But I digress. So, there's a little bit of distant footage of a shape that might be my attacker walking along the very back edge of the parking lot, out of range of the surveillance cameras that are in place. Then something that looks like his side moving just out of frame in the lobby. And… that's it."

"But it's something," Dean says.

"It's something? What is it?" I ask.

"It means whoever did it is someone who knew the hospital well enough to be able to avoid the cameras. And could move through it quickly."

I stare at him for a second, then nod. "Fantastic. So, they were able to get into my home and into a hospital without anyone knowing how or being able to determine who they are. And both times they got away after quite nearly killing me. I guess I should just kick back and let the team handle the investigation. They're doing a bang-up job."

"Emma, Eric put good agents on this. And they're working with the police. You know they're doing everything they can," Sam says.

The thing is, I do know that. Everybody told me Eric was frantic when he found out what happened and immediately created a task force to investigate my attacks. The agents on it are working directly with the local police to try to figure out who was responsible and how they managed to go undetected. He and Bellamy came to see me the night I woke up and Eric was visibly emotional talking about the situation and what little progress had been made at that point.

Not a lot has changed since then.

I stand up from the table and pick up my plate. "I'm not hungry. I'm going back to my office."

"Emma…" Sam says.

I ignore him and bring my plate into the kitchen, tipping the partially eaten pizza into the trash and putting the plate into the dishwasher. When I turn around to make my way back to my research, Xavier is standing in the doorway. He's holding what looks like one of his crochet projects.

"Let's talk," he says.

"Not now, Xavier. I need to go to my office," I say, trying to walk around him.

"And do what?" he prompts, not moving. I look at him and he lifts his eyebrows at me. "And do what? Is there something in there that you haven't read? Did you have an epiphany and need to call Eric?"

Coming from someone else, it would be offensive. From Xavier, the clarity stops any response that might have come. I've come to look for other meaning in everything he says. It's there, it just has to be found. I open my mouth and then close it, not sure of how to respond. I have read all my files. I've gone through everything. There has certainly been no epiphany.

"Five minutes and then I will come with you and we can mutter and stare at the files together. It will be fun," he says.

"Okay," I say, not really sure how else I could respond to that. It's not a bad offer.

"Good."

He turns on his heel and heads for the living room. I follow him and sit on the couch where Sam and Dean are already waiting.

"When did he send you?" I whisper to Sam as I sit.

"Right after you left."

I nod. Xavier has taken his place in front of the couch, standing on the opposite side of the coffee table. He looks at each of us.

"Life's a bitch and then you die, so we might as well burn it all down," he says.

"Well, damn, Xavier," Dean says.

"It's true, right? I mean, that's what you think," Xavier says.

"What are you talking about?" Sam asks.

"Everything in the world is dark and awful and there's nothing good or redeemable about it."

"What the hell is happening right now?" Dean asks.

I point to the bundle of pale blue yarn in his arms. "Is that your burn-it-all-down shawl?"

"It is my color, but no. And now that I have your attention, I can tell you about it. As you might have noticed, I have been dabbling in the fiber arts for a little while now. During one of the times when Dean was working, I happened on an organization I felt could be a good fit for my projects. Conveniently, it is headquartered in Mount Percy."

The small city is about half an hour away from Sherwood. I've been through there a few times while working and a couple times just to visit, but I can't place what Xavier is describing.

"What organization?" I ask.

"From Heart to Heart," he tells me.

The name doesn't sound familiar, but Sam seems to perk up a bit when he hears it.

"Those are the people who make toys and blankets, right?" he asks. He glances over at me. "They've brought some stuff up to the department. Remember when we had that drive for the shelter? They came with a whole bunch of amazing blankets and some handmade toys. They brought enough that we were able to keep some at the precinct and some of the guys have them in their trunks to give to kids who are in accidents or are around during emergency calls. Just something to make them feel better."

"I do remember that. That's really nice."

Xavier nods. "That's what they do. It's a bunch of people who make things to donate around the community. They make baby hats for maternity wards and neonatal intensive care units, blankets for senior living homes and chemo wards. Things for women's shelters and temporary housing. All kinds of things. Whoever might need some kind of help that can be made with yarn and a hook or knitting needles, they give it."

"That's amazing," I say. "And you've been doing work with them?"

"I have. I met them in person for the first time several weeks ago when I was here. They are incredible people."

"Where was I?" Dean asks.

"Sleeping. It was right after that long stakeout you had to do with the trucker smuggling goods."

"Oh, you mean the one when I was literally hit by a truck," Dean says.

"He was just backing up and bumped into you. You fell over, but you didn't even break anything."

"I was hit by a truck," Dean insists.

"Technically, yes. But back to what I was saying," Xavier says. "While Dean was sleeping off being hit by a truck, I went and met with the ladies and got a tour of their workshop. I was really inspired."

"Wait, how did you get there?" I ask. "I know I didn't bring you."

"Bruce towed me," Xavier says.

I press the thumb and middle finger of one hand into my closed eyes and take a breath. A while back, Xavier needed a decommissioned school bus to test a theory and called a junkyard to find out if they would bring one by for him. He ended up confusing the owner of the yard, who also happened to be a mechanic and have a tow truck, into coming and picking him up. As much as we've tried to convince him that he just got a ride in a tow truck, he still insists he was towed.

"You should probably stop calling him," I say.

"He doesn't mind," Xavier says.

"How did we get here?" Sam asks. "We started with life being a bitch. How did we end up here?"

"I think you need to get involved," Xavier tells him. "All of you."

"With your crochet circle?" I ask.

"From Heart to Heart was designed to help people. To bring good into the world for those who really need it. That's why the three of you got into your careers, isn't it? To do good? Sam, you became sheriff of Sherwood because you wanted to follow in your father's footsteps and take care of the town you love. Dean, you were in the military because you wanted to protect people and then when you were hurt, you went into private investigating to keep helping. And Emma, you joined the FBI for your parents and to stop as many people as possible from being victimized."

Sam, Dean, and I exchange glances. I nod.

"Yes."

"It doesn't seem like it. Not anymore. You've all become so focused on all of the bad things happening around you that you've lost perspective. You only see the world as dark and bad. Like there isn't anything good in it anymore. Just like I said. But all of you were surprised when I said that. And that's because deep down, you don't believe it. Because if you did, there would be no reason for you to do what you do. If there was no good left in this world, no possibility for redemption, nothing to fight for, none of you would have any purpose. I think being a part of this organization would help you to keep that perspective.

I blink. "Wow, that's ... quite thoughtful of you, Xavier."

He nods, as if it was expected. "It isn't always easy to see good when you are fighting the types of things the three of you fight. Especially you,

Emma. Maybe this way you could always have something to hang on to that would give you that glimmer of light when you need it. It would give you another way to preserve the good."

CHAPTER THREE

X AVIER'S INTERVENTION WORKED. I COULD ONLY SPEAK FOR MY own mindset, but I know he was right when he'd said I was start-ing to lose perspective. It's easy to slip into dark thoughts and start feeling like the world is a dark place without much in it left to redeem. I was warned about it from the moment I stepped into the FBI Academy. Grizzled men with darkened eyes and not too much faith in a female twenty-three-year-old former art student tried to intimidate me with bleak commentary about the things I would see and what I would have to contend with when I went into the field.

They told me I would lose part of my humanity out there. That nearly all of them do. Agents see too much, have to do too much. They have to let go of part of themselves and what they don't release is taken from them.

I refused to back down. I didn't let myself believe it was true and I've continued to refuse throughout the years of my career. I've been hardened. My mind has been changed. I'll admit that. There's no reason to pretend it hasn't affected me. But I always told myself I would never allow what I saw to take away my ability to care or my belief in the possibility of good. That was the entire reason I took up my shield. I suffered so much after the loss of my mother and the disappearance of my father I wanted to do something about it. I wanted to try to make sure that other people wouldn't have to feel the things I did. I joined the Bureau so I could stand between the world and the criminals hell-bent on scavenging it for their own benefit.

But that's getting harder. Little bits of me have been chipped away, and the longer I go, the more shadows I see around me. The thought of being a part of something purely good could help to buoy me. I hope it will refresh my mind and restore that sense of what I've been fighting for.

That doesn't mean I'm intending on adding a tiny pocket to my harness and carrying a hook around like I carry my gun. Xavier taught me to crochet and at one point he and I simultaneously worked on a Christmas blanket together, but my hands don't move through yarn like his do and I don't have the same ability to delegate different portions of my brain to different activities so I can do them all at the same time without losing track the way Xavier can. My grandmother always used to say she couldn't chew gum and walk at the same time. I've seen Xavier crochet, eat, read, and ride a stationary bike at the same time and still be able to answer all the questions from the episode of *Jeopardy!* playing in the next room over.

But I've also seen him hang upside down across an exercise ball for half an hour while Sam was lifting weights so they could bond over their workout. So, it balances out.

We're meeting the ladies of From Heart to Heart this morning and I'm curious to find out more about what they do and how we can be a part of it. Xavier assures us there's plenty all of us can do for the organization that doesn't involve actually making the things they donate to their long list of recipients. Though I believe deep in his heart he's hoping all of us will start spending our evenings stitching together.

I woke up telling myself I would keep thoughts about the attack out of my head today. Today is about focusing on doing good things.

That resolution didn't last too long. Partway through breakfast Eric called to tell me they've collected doorbell camera and surveillance system footage from the neighborhood to compare to the brief footage they have from the hospital. Though none of it shows the person's face, vehicle, or anything else particularly consequential, it did provide enough insight to make them confident it wasn't the same person in both sets of footage.

We've assumed from the beginning that the person who came into the house to attack me then went to the hospital to finish what they'd started. Among everything that didn't make sense, that was one detail that seemed to be logical. Two situations with masked attackers, both fleeing when someone else entered the situation, both capable of moving with little detection and escaping. It would make the most sense that it was the same person in both circumstances.

Now the situation has only gotten more complicated. With two attackers, the question hangs over me whether they were working together or if the second attacker was merely trying to take advantage of the circumstances and fulfill their own vendetta against me.

The reality is, I have no lack of people who would be happy to do away with me. Over my more than a decade in the Bureau I've collected my fair share of enemies. Criminals I've taken down, ones I'm still pursuing, corrupt leaders, twisted minds wanting to prove something or play disturbing games, friends and family of people they believe I've wronged. I'm not surprised to be a target. It no longer shocks me when I become the focus of wrath or delusion. I just need to know who.

Even with the new development, I'm trying not to let the constantly churning reel of memories, questions, and possibilities stream through my head as we pull into the parking lot of a strip mall and Xavier directs me to a spot in front of a nondescript glass door. I stop and stare through the windshield at the building. Somehow, this isn't what I was expecting when he talked about a workshop. A hand-painted sign propped on a chair set outside the door is the only thing that lets me know this is for sure the right place.

The shop space immediately to the right is empty and a hair salon takes up the corner, while a shop advertising fresh empanadas is on the left next to a chain pizza store and a dry cleaner. The strip is quiet and nearly empty.

"You coming?" Sam asks.

I realize they've all gotten out of the car and I climb out to join them.

"It doesn't look like much from the outside," Xavier says as if he's read my thoughts. "But inside is where the real magic is. Come on."

A little bell chimes over the glass door when we open it and the four of us stream in. The first room looks like the cliché vision of a classic grandma's living room. Assorted comfortable-looking furniture is clustered on a blue shag rug sitting on top of the gray industrial carpeting. A heavy wooden coffee table positioned in the middle holds a basket bearing several mismatched balls of yarn and a handful of crochet hooks and knitting needles. Printouts of patterns cover much of the rest of the surface.

On a whiteboard hanging on the wall, three different handwritings note the most pressing requests for the month. Three large plastic tubs under it seem to wait for any contributions.

"Hello?"

I look away from the tubs toward the sound of a gentle voice with a lilting Irish accent. A tiny woman with big sparkling eyes, a bright pink scarf wrapped around her neck, and a matching hat tilted on the side of her head is walking toward us from the back of the building. When I'm the stage of old and wrinkled she is, I want to be the kind of woman who can pull off a combination like that on a random Wednesday morning.

"Hi, Tricia," Xavier says cheerfully.

"Oh, Xavier," the tiny lady says with a wide smile. "You're back. It's so good to see you." She eyes us. "And you brought friends."

He nods. "These are the people I was telling you about."

"Who's there?"

The woman who comes into the room is the antithesis of Tricia. Her voice booms through the space as she towers over the smaller woman.

"Xavier," Tricia tells her. "And he's brought along his family."

"Hello!" the large woman says, reaching out a hand toward me. "I'm Pat. This is Tricia. Pat. Tricia. Patricia."

I laugh at the introduction and shake her hand. "I'm Emma. This is my husband Sam, and my cousin Dean."

Both women smile.

"We've heard a lot about you," Tricia says. "You're the FBI agent."

"I am."

"Glad you finally came to visit us. Xavier has been talking you up every time he comes in here. Do you have anything for us today? I'm just about to do some sorting," Pat says.

Xavier's eyes widen and he nods. "Oh. Right. Yes. In the trunk."

He heads back outside, then comes back for the keys. Dean follows him and they come back a few moments later each carrying a plastic tote.

"When did you make all of that?" I ask.

"Evenings mostly," Xavier says. "Come on. We'll bring them to the sorting room."

He says it with a hint of wonder and mystery in his voice like he's going to give us a tour of an ancient mystical ruin. The women lead the way and we file after them. For as small and unassuming as the shop looks from the outside, it's surprisingly large inside. A hallway leads out of the main room and into a secondary room filled floor-to-ceiling with metal racks of yarn. They are meticulously organized by color and weight, some in full skeins and others in balls seemingly compiled of leftovers overflowing from baskets.

"This is the yarn room," Tricia tells us. "Volunteers come choose whatever kind of yarn they want for their project, sign it out, and then return the project later. We have all kinds of acrylic, cotton, wool. Tiny skinny all the way to the super chunky. Everything you could think of."

"Where does it all come from?" Dean asks.

"Donations mostly. And when people are gracious enough to donate money we purchase more. Sometimes people's hearts are in the right place and they donate silk or merino. Gorgeous yarns, to be sure, but not something that's too terribly practical for the work we do. We need the workhorse fibers that can be whipped up into hats or blankets that are going to be used, dragged around, and loved, then can be tossed into the wash, dried, and used again a thousand times. Try that with one of those fancy yarns and you're in for some hurt feelings and a lot of wasted time. So, we thank them kindly for their generosity and put those yarns aside. Then once a year we have a sale and people can pay what they like, then use those for their personal projects while we use the proceeds to buy more yarn for our donation items," she explains. "It's an important part of keeping the group going. Many of our members have the talent and skill to produce the items our recipients need, but don't have the resources to purchase supplies. Others simply prefer having access to materials."

"Then there are people like Xavier who never take yarn from here and we always get surprised by what they bring back," Pat adds.

Xavier's beaming, but I can't be sure whether the comment was purely positive. Considering some of the colors I'm seeing through the side of the plastic tub Dean is carrying, I have my doubts.

The hallway continues on the other side of the yarn room and feeds into a small kitchen on one side and what looks like a conference room on the other. As we walk past, I notice a large blanket hanging on the wall of the conference room. Its cream color is simple, but even from the distance, I can tell it's made up of many different types of stitches. It draws me in, but the group has continued forward so I follow them.

At the end of the hall, double doors lead into a large open room with banquet tables set up around the perimeter with a large round table in the center. Each banquet table has a laminated piece of paper taped to the front identifying what types of items should be put into the bins sitting on top. Each of the bins is also labeled, creating a seamless system.

"This is where we do all the sorting," Tricia says. "Members come in and drop off what they've made. We bring them in here, go through them, decide if they should go into one of the basic bins or if they fill a specific request that has recently been made. We sort them and then from there, our delivery team puts together packages depending on what our clients have requested for the month."

"Sounds like quite the enterprise," Sam says.

"It can be a lot," Pat admits. "But there are always more people who need our help. The baby hats alone." She lets out a whistle. "We work with six area hospitals, and they ask for nearly two thousand hats each month. The need increases during the cold months and when there's a disaster of some kind. No matter what, the need never stops. And we're always looking for people to help us with our mission."

"Them," Xavier says, opening his hand out to the side to present us.

"But we can't make anything," Dean replies. "At least, I can't."

"I can't, either," Sam says.

"I can crochet a little, but I'm not great at it," I offer. "And, full disclosure, I tend to get distracted. I might start a hat, but I can't guarantee you I'm going to finish it any time soon."

"That's no problem at all," Tricia says with a chuckle. "We don't have quotas or any kind of expectations of our members. Every single item matters. And it doesn't matter what you want to make. We have things that are requested, but if you're suddenly inspired to make something that isn't on one of those lists, we'll still find a home for it. And if you can't make anything at all, we can still use your help."

"Absolutely," Pat says. "Making all of this happen takes far more than just the people picking up hooks and needles. We need volunteers to help sort the items, package them, sift out the occasional donation that doesn't fit our standards, identify what's needed for specific calls, make deliveries, pick up donations, seek out new recipients. There's a whole ton of things that need to be done around here to make sure everyone who needs a warm hat or blanket gets it."

"And like she said, there are plenty of them. I'd love to show you some of our scrapbooks," Tricia offers.

I can't resist and she smiles as she guides me back out of the room. As we're leaving, I notice another blanket hanging on the wall. I pause and point it out.

"That's really beautiful," I say. "What is it? There are so many stitches."

"Oh," Tricia says, coming back to stand beside me and admire the blanket. "That's called a sampler blanket. Like with cross stitching. It's a way for a fiber artist to show off their skills with different stitches or to practice different stitch patterns without it just being a scrap of fabric at the end. There are a few of them hanging around the workshop. I've always thought they were particularly lovely myself." She leans toward me like she wants to share a special secret. "But I'm the kind who likes wild colors and all kinds of stitches mixed up in a project. Keeps things interesting."

Pat shoots her a look out of the corner of her eye and I can't help but chuckle. I already know I'm going to enjoy being a part of this.

We spent far longer at the workshop than I anticipated, but I enjoyed every second of it. On the way home, Xavier can't stop talking about all the different recipients, the special projects they've been working on, and describing all of the different ladies he has met in his visits to the shop. We had the chance to meet a couple more and have plans to go back next week once they've sorted through their volunteers for the month and found a place for us. Sam is excited to be the official connection between the organization and the sheriff's department so they can always have a supply of comfort blankets and stuffed animals, and as soon as I heard that one of their recipients was in the hospital where I just spent three weeks fighting for my life, I knew I wanted to do whatever I could to get back to them.

I am even feeling like I may try to increase my stitching skills and feel a lightness and optimism I haven't felt in a long time when we get to the house. Everyone's hungry so I go to the kitchen to see what we have. Not even a second after I toss my phone on the kitchen table, though, it rings. Seeing Eric's name on the screen gives me a moment of pause. I managed not to stop and think about my case the entire time we were at the workshop. I have no doubt I'm going to end up back in my office this evening continuing to dig through my files, but I'd like to stay out of the bubble for a little bit longer.

"Hey, Eric," I say. "Can I call you back later to talk about my case? Unless you know who my attacker is."

"No. I'm still working on that. Actually, I'm not calling you because of your case. Something just came to my attention and I wanted to talk to you about it before you heard anything on the news or through the grapevine," he says.

"What is it?"

He sounds upset, but not devastated enough that I worry he might be calling to tell me something happened to Bellamy or Bebe.

"An agent has gone missing in the field. I don't think you ever worked with him. Roman Cleary."

The name's not familiar. "I don't think so. What happened? Where was he?"

"He was on a highly confidential deep undercover mission. It was through a different field office, so I don't even know all the details. But he is known to have boarded a flight just as he was supposed to, but he never met up with his contacts on the other side. No one has heard from him in more than a week. His office has reached out to others to put the word out just in case anybody knows anything."

"Thank you for letting me know," I say. "If I hear or think of anything, I'll call you."

"Thanks. If I hear any more or they give me other details, I'll tell you."

I have a heavier feeling in my heart when I hang up the phone. Being an agent brings with it certain inherent risks. It's just a basic reality of the career and no one goes into it without knowing and acknowledging those risks. That doesn't change the fact that every time one of us hears of another agent going missing or being killed in the line of duty it cuts deep. Even if we don't know them, it's like losing a friend.

CHAPTER FOUR

THE DAY AFTER I WENT TO THE FROM HEART TO HEART WORK-
shop for the first time, I could feel the weight of my case along
with the news of Roman Cleary's disappearance pulling down on
me again. I decided to push back on it by venturing to the craft store,
where I bought a massive supply of yarn and five different sets of crochet hooks because I couldn't decide which one is going to be the best
for me. It was without a doubt going overboard, but it hearkens back
to my art days when the stack of canvases in the corner was never tall
enough and my supply of paints tumbled out of every nook and cranny
in my studio, bedroom, and frequently the living room.

That afternoon, I started what I intended to be a scarf. Now nearly
two weeks later, it is officially reaching super scarf territory. The nine-
ty-inch behemoth is coiled in my lap like an anaconda and trailing
down into the plastic bucket at my feet as I review a newly enhanced set
of surveillance images I've just received. I hear the front door open and
footsteps pound through the living room.

"Emma?" Sam shouts the second the door's open.

"In here."

He rushes down the hall and into the office.

"Why didn't you answer your phone?" he demands, his face red from worry.

"It didn't ring," I say. I reach over to where my phone is always sitting at the corner of my desk and realize the sound is off. "Oh, damn. I put it on silent when I was having a video call earlier and didn't turn it back on. I'm sorry. Look at this." I hold up the scarf. "It's a lot narrower than I intended it to be. And really long. Maybe I'll just keep going and then wrap it around myself at Halloween. I'll be an avant-garde mummy. What do you think?"

I smile lightly, but Sam is clearly not in the mood for jokes right now. He takes a breath and tries to calm himself. "Emma, I've been calling you for the last half an hour," he says.

"I'm sorry. I didn't realize the sound was off. Chance at Headquarters sent me some new stills and some enhanced footage from the surveillance cameras. I've been trying to pull out more details. Look at this one." I click through some images on my computer screen. "Do you see this? I think that's a logo on the cuff of a hooded sweatshirt."

"You haven't spoken to Xavier."

That stops me. I turn to look at him, heat prickling the back of my neck at the look in his eyes.

"What's wrong with Xavier?"

Forty minutes later Sam and I park behind a black sedan that is one of several vehicles parked haphazardly in a craft store lot. Vibrant yellow tape has already been stretched from a column on the sidewalk at the corner of the building across the entrance to the smaller side lot to the tree on the opposite side. The gray sky and continuous sheet of fine rain make the scene even more ominous. We get out and I pull the collar of my jacket up over my neck as I stalk toward the uniformed officer standing at the tape.

"Agent Emma Griffin, FBI," I announce, holding my shield out toward him as I approach.

Without hesitation, he lifts the tape and I duck under it, heading directly for the large blue tarp structure that's been set up around several marking spots in the center of the row. Off to the side a detective in a long camel jacket and wide-brimmed hat stands between the structure and Pat, who's huddled beneath the building overhang. Her arms wrapped tightly around herself and her back hunched, the woman who seemed to have no issue taking up as much space as she could both literally and figuratively when I first met her looks diminished and fragile.

"Pat," I call out to her.

She looks up and immediately comes toward me. I embrace her and feel her shaking against me. When we step back from the hug, tears are streaming down her cheeks, leaving trails in her makeup and reddening the whites of her dark eyes.

"Thank you so much for coming. I'm sorry I didn't call you directly. I couldn't think straight. When I... the only thing that could come to mind was Xavier. I knew he would be able to get in touch with you and so I called him. I feel horrible. I know he must be so upset. She was..."

Pat's voice cracks and she looks down, taking in a shuddering breath as she tries to pull herself together. There's no need for her to do that. If there is any situation when it is acceptable to fall apart, she's in it.

"Don't worry about it. I'm glad you called him. He actually called my husband first. You remember Sam."

I step to the side slightly to gesture to Sam behind me.

"Of course. Hi, Sheriff Johnson. Thank you so much for coming."

"Absolutely," he replies with the measured empathy that everyone understands means that he can't exactly say he's glad to be here. "When Xavier called, he said he wanted to make sure they knew we were coming. I already reached out to the Mount Percy department."

The detective who was talking to Pat when I came up comes toward us. He reaches his hand toward Sam.

"Sheriff Johnson, I'm Detective McGraw. Call me Gene. I got your message."

Sam shakes his hand. "Good to meet you. Sam. This is my wife Emma."

Gene tips his hat and shakes my hand. "Agent Griffin. Of course. Mrs. Ledger told me she'd reached out to you. Glad to formally meet you. You worked as a consultant on a drug case I investigated out of North Carolina a few years ago before I relocated here."

I shake my head slightly. "I'm sorry, I..."

He gives a forgiving smile. "You have no reason to remember. We never actually spoke. But you were very valuable in the case, so I'm glad I get the chance to thank you in person."

"Thank you." I look over at Pat. Her shoulders are hunched and her eyes keep darting over to the blue tarps. "Pat, let's get you out of the rain."

"I'm going to call Xavier and let him know we're here," Sam says when we get back under the overhang. "He's with Dean at the workshop. I told him he couldn't come here, but he insisted on being close."

"That's actually a really good idea. Ask him if there are others there with him and see how many of the volunteers he can get there. They'll need to be questioned." Sam nods and walks away as I look over at Gene. "I'm sorry. I don't mean to step on your toes right out of the gate."

He shakes his head. "No. That will save a lot of time and effort. I appreciate it. I know there's a personal element to this for you, so I'm happy to have you involved as much as you want to be."

"I absolutely want to be. I'd like to be brought current on the situation. I'm sure you can appreciate how difficult this is for Mrs. Ledger. I'd like for Sam to bring her home."

Gene hums in the affirmative. "You've been very helpful. I'm sorry that you went through this and for your loss."

"Thank you," Pat says.

"I'll be in touch if I need to speak with you again," Gene says.

Pat looks down and I wrap an arm around her shoulders.

"I'm going to bring her to Sam. I'll be right back."

Sam is just getting out of the car again when I get Pat under the yellow tape and into the lot.

"Xavier says there are several of the volunteers and members at the workshop and he's started a phone tree to get more there," he says.

"Good. We'll go over there shortly. For right now, can you please bring Pat home? I don't think she's in any condition to be driving herself," I say.

"Of course."

I turn to Pat. "We'll arrange to get your car home. Is there anything you need? Anything we can do for you tonight?"

She shakes her head. "No. I can't thank you enough. I just don't know what I'm going to do next."

"You don't have to think about that right now. Just go home and try to get some rest."

When Sam's car disappears out of the parking lot, I duck back under the tape and walk over to Gene. Without a word he leads me to the tarp structure. One side is mostly open, revealing the back of a car. We step into the structure and as we come around the side of the car, I see the spray of blood across the white paint.

A crime scene photographer is crouched on the pavement, taking careful pictures of the body sprawled beside the car. Two canvas tote bags sag on the pavement beside her, skeins of yarn in several shades of blue tumbling out.

"She was buying materials for the Hat Not Hate project," I say.

"What's that?" Gene asks.

"It's an initiative in schools across the country. Students and even teachers wear blue hats to protest against bullying. From Heart to Heart recently committed to donating five hundred hats to the local schools. They must have received a donation and she came to buy the yarn to have at the workshop for it."

"Did you know her well?" he asks.

I look down into the bloodied face on the ground in front of me. Sherry Talley.

"No. I only met her a couple of weeks ago when Xavier brought us to the workshop for the first time."

"Xavier," Gene says. "That's who Mrs. Ledger called after discovering the body?"

"Yes. He's been a member of the organization for a few months, I guess. But when Xavier gets involved in something, he's all in. And he's been very active with them. Pat knows we are very close, and Xavier can get in touch with me, and with Sam, very easily. Like she said, she was so shocked by what was happening, she couldn't think of how to get in touch with me directly, so she called Xavier for help."

"And why did he bring you to the workshop?"

I look at him through narrowed eyes. "Am I being questioned, Detective McGraw?"

Spots of color appear on his cheeks. "I just thought you might have some information that would be helpful."

"I'm working on a scarf."

A slight chuckle bursts out of his mouth before he can stop it, then he clears his throat. "Sorry."

I ignore it. "I have been to the workshop four times. Sherry was there three of those times. We exchanged a few words the first two times and had a longer conversation the third. It was about crochet and her preference for corner-to-corner stitches when making blankets."

He shakes his head slightly. "I'm not familiar with any of that."

"Well, that's all I have to tell you about her. Now, why don't we get back to you filling me in on what happened here?"

He sighs. "The call came into emergency dispatch about two hours before you arrived. Mrs. Ledger said she came to the shop and noticed Mrs. Talley's vehicle parked over here. She searched around the shop for her, but didn't run into her. She called her cell phone a couple of times, but there was no answer. Feeling concerned, she walked over to the vehicle and discovered the body. Initial investigation shows three gunshot wounds. Her cell phone is missing, but her wallet is still intact and in her pocket."

I think about my own venture to the craft shop in Sherwood. Roaming down the aisles of yarn, standing in front of the displays. The sea of colors and textures. I've never really paid much attention to it before, but stopping to really notice it all was almost dizzying. I know from the conversations I had with Pat how much she adores yarn. I have to admit, it sounded silly when I first heard her talking about it. But as she described learning how to knit from her aunt when she was a little girl and how they used to unravel old, damaged blankets and sweaters to turn into new things, I could see how precious it really was to her. Her eyes misted when she told me that to this day, every time she picks up knitting needles and works on a project, she feels like she's spending time with her aunt.

That thought brings a tightness to my throat now. The simplicity of the pleasure she got from shopping for new yarn or churning out another of the cheerful lap blankets she favors won't ever be the same. Never again will she be able to just browse the aisles or dream up new ways to complement the balls of remnants she likes to use up. This will mar every one of those trips for her. She will forever remember the confusion and concern taking over the excitement she felt when she thought she was running into a friend at the shop, and then the horror of discovering Sherry's body.

"Three bullet wounds," I say. "This was intentional. She wasn't a bystander who happened to be caught in crossfire. This was a targeted killing. You say her wallet was still in her pocket."

"Yes, and it doesn't appear to have been disturbed. It still had cash and credit cards inside."

I nod in acknowledgment. "And she's wearing a fairly large diamond engagement ring, a wedding ring, and gold earrings. That suggests theft wasn't the motive. It's unlikely someone would attempt to rob an older woman in a store parking lot, fail to take anything, and shoot her three times in retaliation."

"But that leaves the question of what kind of motive anyone would have to kill Sherry."

I let out a soft grunt. "Seems like we need to get to work."

CHAPTER FIVE

NTERVIEWING THE VOLUNTEERS AND MEMBERS WHO HAD COME TO the workshop after hearing the news of Sherry Talley's murder yesterday was long and difficult. With the rain lashing at the windows and everyone sitting by themselves, staring as if into some not-so-distant memory, there was a sense of unsettling quiet, a distinct feeling of something missing from the space. Sherry wasn't as bold and dynamic as Pat, but she had a strong presence at the workshop. Kind and welcoming, she was also a firm keeper of the volunteer schedule and a stickler for organization.

The first day I came to the shop I watched her sift through some of the donations that had already been sorted and remove several items, relocating most into different categories and taking two away altogether. Out of curiosity, I asked why she'd taken them and she told me without hesitation that they didn't suit her standards. There wasn't any cruelty in the evaluation but also no apology. It simply was the way it was.

There's a hollowness at the thought of her being gone. I barely even knew her and I could feel it. Around me, those who had Sherry in their lives for years tried to grapple with not just her loss, but the horrific way she was torn away from them.

I sat in as Gene spoke with each of them, collecting every detail about her life that he could, hoping one of them would lead him somewhere. Their answers made my sleep fitful and this morning I can still see the worry etched across Gene's face when we walk out of the shop and watch Tricia lock the door.

"This isn't going to be easy," he says quietly. "Sherry Talley was a retired woman who devoted her life to charity. She was recently widowed after a forty-year marriage. No one had any reason to dislike her. Yet someone put three bullets in her. I don't know where to go from here."

I call Gene just before Sam and I leave the house. Sam still insists I shouldn't be alone after my head injury even though the doctors have cleared me for all but the most intensive of physical activity. Sam worries something is going to happen and I'll go unconscious again or my memory will be impacted. I know that fear stems from his experiences with Dean and the terrifying blackouts my cousin has suffered since he was a young teenager. Though the chances of that having any kind of genetic origin that would expand to me without there being any indications of it all the way into my mid-thirties are extremely small, this whole experience has made Sam jumpy and overly cautious.

Gene tells me he is heading back to the crime scene. I agree to meet him there so I can get a better look at the area. The rain has stopped and the sun is trying to come out from behind the cloud cover. More light and the area being clear of the investigators and cars will help provide a better view of how the murder might have unfolded.

He's coming out of the store when Sam and I drive into the parking lot. He gestures toward where his car is parked in the front lot and Sam pulls into the spot beside him. We went through a coffee shop drive-thru in town before arriving and offer one of the cups out to him as I climb out of the car.

"Oh, lord, thank you," he says, accepting the cup with a relieved, grateful look that makes me wonder if his own night of sleep was broken by the voices of the women trying to get through talking about Sherry's death.

"I have cream and sugar," I say.

"Some of each, please," he says.

I hand him several tiny containers of creamer and packets of sugar and watch as he augments his coffee in much the same heavy-handed way as Sam. I've often teased my husband that his occasional morning cup is essentially just drinking hot melted coffee ice cream.

"Babe, I'm going to work. Call me if you need anything and let me know when you want me to be back to pick you up," Sam calls through the window.

"I'll be fine," I say. "Thanks, babe."

"I love you."

"Love you."

He drives away and Gene eyes me with a raised eyebrow.

"Bonding?" he asks.

I chuckle. "Not exactly. I had an injury recently and he's worried about me being by myself. I feel a little like a kid getting dropped off for school by my parents."

"I think it's sweet," Gene says. "It's nice to have someone worry about you."

That tilts my lips up into a hint of a smile. I guess it is.

He swirls a bamboo swizzle stick around in his cup for a few seconds, then takes a sip. His shoulders relax.

"Good?" I ask.

"It's delicious. But even if it wasn't, it's caffeine," he says. "And I'm going to need it."

"Were you able to talk to the manager?" I ask, indicating the shop with a bob of my head.

I bring my cup to my lips and enjoy the hot, bitter sip that washes over my tongue.

"Yes. She is going to get me surveillance footage, but she did warn me that there isn't a lot of coverage around here," he says.

"That sounds familiar," I mutter.

"What's that?" Gene asks.

"Oh, no," I say, shaking my head. "Sorry. Nothing. When will she be able to get it to you?"

"Since this is a privately owned store, she needs to contact the owner and get his permission to release the footage. But she was already on the phone with him when I left the store. Hopefully he'll get here shortly and we will have access."

"Why didn't he come yesterday when all this was happening?" I ask.

"Apparently he was out of town on a business trip and just got back late last night. I asked the manager to make sure he knew I'll need to speak with him."

"I know you spoke with the manager and the other employees working yesterday, were they able to tell you anything else today?" I ask.

He shakes his head. "Same story. According to them, they were familiar with Mrs. Talley, so they all noticed when she came in. Several of them spoke with her while she was shopping. They all say she was in perfectly good spirits. A few of them mentioned she was especially looking forward to trying a new type of yarn that was just released. Something about"—he looks down to his notes—"really good stitch definition. I don't mind admitting to you that I'm out of my element when it comes to this. I'm not sure what that means."

I smile. "It means it would have been good for more complex patterns. But it sounds like she was enjoying her shopping. She comes in here a lot to buy yarn and they were happy to see that she picked out something new she was excited about. It's something for them to hold on to. Something good they can set as her final moments so they don't have to think about what she went through in the actual final ones. It's something I've encountered in nearly every murder case I've worked on during my career. Especially in the earliest stages of the case when the friends and families are still processing the death, people place happy moments in the victims' heads. Sometimes it seems like they believe if they keep thinking about these good things, they can somehow retroactively make things better for the victim. The Tinker Bell Phenomenon."

That makes Gene frown in confusion. "The what?"

"Xavier," I say. "The man who got me involved in the organization. That's what he calls it."

"I don't follow."

"In the original story, the fairy is injured and dying and can only survive if the magic in the world is revived by people clapping their hands and declaring their belief in fairies. It's as if the friends and family of the victims believe they can somehow take away some of the horror and pain if they keep focusing on the good, the magic of that individual person," I explain. "And somehow that magical belief will make things alright, even though it's not alright."

"Xavier has an interesting perspective on things," Gene remarks.

I take another sip of my coffee and nod. "That's an understatement." We get to the parking spot where Sherry's car was parked yesterday. It was towed away this morning, but there's still blood on the pavement.

"What else? Other than them talking about yarn, what else did they say about yesterday? Did any of them see anything, hear anything, notice anyone with her?"

"Nope," Gene says. "She was shopping alone, looked perfectly comfortable, and left like it was a normal day. None of them even noticed her on her phone."

"And none of them heard anything after she left the store or went outside before the first responders arrived?" I ask.

"Right."

I step over to the spot where Sherry was likely standing when she was shot and turn to look in the direction of the store's entrance. The angle makes it so that this area is concealed from the entrance, so no one inside would have been able to see her once she went around to the side of the building.

"It was raining yesterday, so she probably stayed on the sidewalk as she was walking out to the car," I say. "Which means they wouldn't have been able to see her anymore after just a few seconds. But that begs the question; why did she park over here rather than in the lot directly in front of the store? When Sam and I got here, there were plenty of spots available," I say.

Gene shrugs. "Maybe this was just where she preferred to park. A lot of people get into habits when it comes to their parking. Especially if she came here frequently, she might have just had a routine."

"I can see that. Pat did mention she noticed Sherry's car sitting there. She drove a really common make and model. There isn't anything immediately identifiable about it. No stickers or decorations. Not even a vanity plate. It would be difficult to be completely confident it was Sherry's car from the distance she would be at when parking her own car. If this was always where Sherry parked, however, that would make sense.

We need to find out how long it was between her leaving the store and Pat arriving. I would assume there were other people in the store during this time and it's possible some of them left before Sherry's body was discovered. We'll need to track them down."

I walk back over to the sidewalk and look at the parking spot, imagining the car parked there.

"What are you doing?" Gene asks.

"Do you have access to any of the crime scene photos?"

"Yeah," he says, pulling a small tablet out of his pocket. He goes through a few screens as he comes toward me, then holds it out to me. "Here. What are you looking for?"

I glance at the image of the car parked and then scroll through until I get to one that shows Sherry's body as it was when the first officers arrived on the scene. Using the photo as reference, I walk out to the parking space, glance left and right, and turn back to Gene.

"This is approximately where Sherry was standing when she was shot," I say.

"Yes."

"But she pulled directly into the spot. She didn't back into it. Which means the driver's seat was on the opposite side of where she was standing," I say.

"She was probably putting her bags in," Gene offers. "They were found right there on the ground. She came out of the store and walked around the car to put the bags in the back or possibly in the passenger seat."

"In the rain?" I ask. "She wouldn't have wanted those bags exposed to moisture any longer than was absolutely necessary. I'm surprised she wasn't using a plastic bag to protect the yarn, but she definitely wouldn't have come all the way out here and taken the extra time to go around the side of the car just to put the bags in. She could have put them in through the back door on the driver's side or just gotten in and put them on the passenger seat."

"So, what does that mean?" he asks.

"I don't know yet. It's just something to note." I glance around. "The medical examiner should be able to gauge the probable trajectory of the shots. That will give us a better idea of where the shooter was when they pulled the trigger. It won't be completely conclusive. She didn't drop where she was standing. If you look at the blood splatter, it suggests she moved between the first and second shots, then the third occurred while she was lying on the ground. This wasn't a frantic shooting. The shooter wanted to ensure she was dead. That all but guarantees a silencer on the gun and someone familiar with the area."

"No one noticed anyone running away from this area of the parking lot either. Shooter must've either fled into the wooded area or behind the store," Gene supplies.

I follow his pointing finger to the two areas he indicates. "I would venture to say the wooded area is the best bet, considering the loading area of the store would be far more likely to have surveillance cameras. Let's find out what's on the other side of the woods."

Gene and I spend another hour going over the crime scene and exploring the wooded area that separates the parking lot of the craft store from an apartment complex. We take pictures of a few things we notice that might be connected to the shooting and might mean absolutely nothing considering the scattered trash and debris among the thick undergrowth and downed branches. That will be another job for the forensic team. Gene called them while we were still in the woods and asked them to come back out and process more of the area while we went down to the apartment complex to talk to the manager about getting their surveillance footage and doing a canvas of the area.

As we are chatting with a young couple out for a walk with their newborn, Gene gets a call from the owner of the craft store letting him know the footage is available.

"I'll go talk to them," he says.

"I'll meet you back up there."

He leaves and I turn my attention back to the wife. Her alabaster skin and inky black hair cut in a blunt bob at her chin enhances her young features and makes her seem even more vulnerable than the trembling of her lip already had.

"We didn't even know what was going on. We took Hudson up to get his one-month portraits done, so we weren't even home when it happened. When we got back, a neighbor told us what was going on. A few people were gathered around the wood line trying to watch what was going on, but you can't really see it from here. I just can't believe something like that would happen to a woman who did such good things," she says.

"Did you know her?" I ask, surprised by the sentiment.

She shakes her head and wipes a tear from under her eye. "Not her personally, no. But as soon as I heard she was involved in that organization, it hit me really hard. Hudson was a preemie and when he was in the NICU he got hats, a blanket, and a little octopus toy that they'd made. I remember the little tag that was on the blanket. It was so sweet. Neither of us have family in the area, so it was really nice to feel like we weren't alone. That there were people out there who cared about what we were going through and wanted to make us feel better. Not for personal recognition or money. Just to do good."

"To make the world better," I say.

She sighs. "I don't understand how anybody could hurt somebody like that."

"I don't, either. Thank you for talking with me. I'm going to leave you with my card. If you think of anything, if you hear anything, please don't hesitate to reach out to me. I'll probably be back over the next few days to talk to more people. Hopefully someone saw somebody suspicious or a car they didn't recognize. Anything to give us a jump in the investigation."

"If we can help in any way, we'll call," the man says, wrapping a comforting arm around his wife's waist and pulling her in against him as if trying to protect her from the threat that has already passed through their neighborhood.

CHAPTER SIX

WITH THE SURVEILLANCE FOOTAGE IN HAND READY TO PASS over to the cyber forensics team for analysis, Gene and I make our way back to the police station. He brings me to the small conference room he has set up as a war room and shows me several files spread out across one of the tables.

"I had the team pull everything we have on the most recent murders in the area. We've been tracking a couple of potential serial killers who may have been working around here. I thought it might be valuable to compare the details of Mrs. Talley's murder with these to see if there could be any connection."

"That's a good idea. Let me reach out to the Bureau and find out if there are any active cases that share any of the details. Since right now it seems we don't have anything to go on, we can't overlook any possibility. All I can say with certainty right now is that this was not an accident. These were not stray bullets. For one reason or another, she was targeted. And until we can rule out the possibility that it was a random targeting, we have to try every avenue."

I take off my jacket and hang it on the back of one of the chairs. A coffee maker off to the side beckons me and I make myself a cup. Setting it down on the table, I wind my hair up onto the back of my head and clamp it in place with a large black plastic clip. Ready to settle into the investigation, I sit down and take out my phone. I make a quick call to Eric explaining the situation and ask for any information he can give me on cases that resemble this one. It isn't much to go on. Shootings aren't uncommon among serial or spree killers. If anything, they're a preferred method of execution. What we have to look at is the demographic of the victims, the location of the murder, and any identifying features such as the location of the bullet wounds.

For the rest of the morning and into the afternoon, Gene and I go over each of the cases, noting similarities, but also finding contradictory factors in each. By the time we are both ready for lunch, I'm certain Sherry was not the victim of any of these killers.

We both need a break from the inside of the police station, so we decide to take a quick drive to grab a bite to eat. As we are walking out, I see a familiar face crossing the parking lot toward the door.

"Tricia?" I call out.

She looks up and seems relieved to see me. I move quickly toward her and she reaches out a hand to grasp mine like she's trying to close the space between us as soon as possible.

"Emma," she says. "I didn't know you were going to be here."

"Detective McGraw is letting me stay close to the investigation," I tell her. I tilt my head to him.

"Hello," she says.

"This is Tricia Donovan. She's the founder of From Heart to Heart," I tell him.

Gene shakes her hand. "Nice to meet you, Mrs. Donovan. I'm so sorry for your loss."

Tricia gives a shaky nod. "I'm so sorry I wasn't able to be at the workshop with everyone last night. My neighbor had surgery two days ago and I was at the hospital with him so his wife could get a break. I left my phone in the car." Her head drops to her hand and her shoulders shake with a wave of sobs that comes over her. "I didn't even know. Pat called me a dozen times. I must have gotten fifty text messages and voicemails. I should have been there."

I squeeze her hand. "Don't think that way. You had no reason to think anything was going to happen. You were helping your friend, which was where you needed to be. I'm glad you're here now. I'm so sorry."

I hug her, feeling how tiny and frail her body seems in my arms. When it comes to her personality and how she interacts with the world around her, I would never say she's delicate, but it's hard not to use that word to describe her slight frame.

"I want to help. Any way that I can." Tricia tugs a fuchsia scarf closer around her neck to ward off cold I'm not feeling. "Or are you going somewhere?"

"We were actually just going to get lunch. You're welcome to join us," Gene says.

She agrees to follow us to the restaurant. When we arrive, we request a table toward the back of the diner so we can talk without feeling like we're the lunchtime entertainment for those around us. Though larger and clearly newer, this place reminds me a lot of Pearl's back in Sherwood. It has much of the same cozy neighborhood vibe that makes me think it's probably a frequent spot for the officers. Large red letters across the front of the menu advertising that it's open 24 hours a day offering a full breakfast menu makes it seem even more likely.

We take a few moments to browse the menu and order, waiting for our drinks to get to the table before diving back into the conversation.

"What can you tell us about Sherry?" Gene asks. "How long did you know her?"

"Five years," Tricia says. "Almost six. It doesn't sound like long, but she was a dear friend. We spent so much time together at the workshop it seemed like we'd known each other much longer. I met her through a former volunteer who noticed her sitting in a coffee shop knitting up what she described as a pile of baby booties and approached her. It turns out at the time she was expecting her first great-grandchild and was very eager to fill the entire nursery with as many handmade gifts as she possibly could. She wanted to create heirlooms that could be passed through the generations of the family like the ones she'd grown up with."

I nod. "My grandmother made a blanket for me when I was born."

"It's a beautiful tradition. There's nothing like holding something someone has made for you with their own hands. Sherry fit right in from the very beginning. She started off just making items and donating them, then she started volunteering at the workshop. Very quickly she became indispensable. There are so many things … I don't know how we're going to do it without her."

She looks down at her lap, pressing a handkerchief to her cheek to try to stem new tears.

"I know this is really hard for you, Tricia, but there are some things that we need to ask you about Sherry. Things that might help us figure out what could have happened to her."

She draws in a breath like she is steeling herself against the experience to come. "Go on."

"What do you know about her family life? Her husband, her children, siblings?" Gene asks.

"Sherry was a widow. Her husband died before she joined. It was one of the reasons why she was so happy to get involved. She was still very much grieving and wanted something, anything, to distract her from that empty place in her life. She always said she was so grateful that she found us. That it almost was just as much for her as it was for the families we helped. I don't think I have to tell either one of you that we don't live in a society that shows much favor towards women once they reach a certain age."

I can certainly see her point there.

"Things are getting a bit better in that regard, but it's still easy to feel invisible when you aren't young and beautiful and vital anymore. The world looks through you and pretty soon you can start feeling like you don't have much substance, like you aren't good for anything. I've refused to let anyone make me feel that way. After all, I'm only 75. I still have a good while before I'll let myself even consider myself old. But it's good to feel useful. To do what we do without being seen."

"I can understand that," I say.

"How about anyone else?" Gene asks. "Did she have conflicts with anyone?"

"Sherry had two children, both live across the country, but she is very close with them and her grandchildren—and now three great-grandchildren, I think. She traveled to visit them all the time and they all came here to her during the holidays for big family celebrations. I can't pretend I know everything that went on in her family. There are always closed doors. But there was never anything that hinted to me there was anything wrong. Certainly not anything that would make one of them want to shoot her in a parking lot."

The waitress arrives with the food—chicken fried steak for Gene, an omelet for Pat, and a club sandwich for me—and we wait while she distributes it, checks in with us, and walks away before we continue.

"Is there anything else?" I ask. "Anyone you can think of who might have something against Sherry?"

"How about projects she was working on with the organization?" Gene asks. "Could she have crossed someone with the work she was doing?"

Tricia stares across the table at him and I watch her eyes narrow slightly. They drop to her hands set on the table beside her plate, then lift to me.

"Come to think of it, she did have a confrontation with a man just last week. I didn't even think of it before because it didn't seem to bother her all that much. But after this…"

"What kind of confrontation?" I ask. "With who?"

"About a year ago, Sherry reached out to a local home for battered women. Porchlight House. It's a place they can go to escape their abusive partners and be safe with their children. Somewhere safe and secret where families can live temporarily, and they offer services like childcare, job support, help with medical needs and legal representation."

"It sounds like a very valuable place," I say.

"To be sure. Sherry spoke with them and built our relationship with the director. As you can imagine, she is quite wary of bringing people into the circle with these people who are so vulnerable. Above all, she wants the women and children to feel safe when they are with her. Sherry was able to establish trust and has been the liaison to provide shawls, blankets, winter items, and toys for the little ones. We will probably all say we can't pick favorites when it comes to our recipients because they are all deserving. But I know that particular project held a very special place in Sherry's heart."

"So what happened with the confrontation?" I ask gently. I'm grateful to have the background on the place, but sometimes when interviewing the friends or family of victims, they have a tendency to ramble on about the ancillary details instead of wanting to discuss the tragedy directly. It's slightly different from the Tinker Bell Effect, and an impulse I understand—but I still need to make sure things don't get too off the rails.

Pat takes a breath to steel herself. "Unfortunately, her last delivery to them did not go smoothly. When she arrived, she found that the husband of one of the women staying there had somehow found out where she was. He was outside the house shouting and trying to get his wife's attention. It was a pretty fraught situation. Sherry—against her better judgement I dare say, though she would never have thought of it that way—decided to try to defuse the situation herself.

"The police had already been called but she wanted to try to calm him down, so she went up to talk to him. He lashed out at her and started yelling about how they were destroying families, breaking up homes. He said they'd kidnapped his children without his permission and that they had all brainwashed his wife into thinking she could leave him. He didn't threaten or touch Sherry exactly, but he was very forceful and aggressive, according to what she told me."

"I can see why his wife wanted to leave," I remark.

She shrugs. "Thank the heavens police arrived shortly after and took him into custody. Sherry was a little shaken up, but it didn't affect her severely. By the next day, she was barely even thinking about it," Tricia says.

"But what if that man was still hanging on to a grudge," Gene suggests. "Do you remember his name?"

"No. I didn't ever catch it."

"I'll look it up. There'll be a record of his arrest and I can find out what happened to him. It's possible he was so angry at his wife leaving him and taking the children that he decided to retaliate against the people he blamed for it. And since Sherry came in direct contact with him, she might have been his target."

"What do you think?" Sam asks later as he's driving me back to Sherwood.

I lean back against the headrest and stare out the window for a few moments. "I don't know. It doesn't feel right. I mean, yes, it makes sense to think a man who is being accused by his wife of being abusive and then had a confrontation with a complete stranger has the capability of violence. In fact, if you were to tell me he had shot the director of the shelter, or his wife, or even one of the volunteers who comes into the home to do job counseling or child care, I wouldn't blink. It would fall right in line with the expected behavior. But it doesn't make sense when you look at Sherry's murder."

"Why?" Sam asks.

"Because it's so disconnected. Sherry had that interaction with him more than a week before she was shot. Gene found out he was booked into the jail that night, and essentially released immediately. He didn't even spend the night. Why would he have waited so long to seek out his revenge? And why would he do it in the parking lot of a craft shop? I might be completely off base here, but I'm going to take the leap to say that man probably isn't a prolific fiber artist. There's nothing else in that area that points to a logical reason that he was there, happened to see Sherry in her car and was able to recognize her, followed her, and shot her three times in vengeance for being connected to an organization helping his wife. It just doesn't make sense.

"Gene is trying to track him down to find out if he might be living in those apartments or if there's any other reason he could have just happened to be in that parking lot at the time Sherry was. Like I always say, we can't eliminate anything just because it doesn't sound right, so we need to follow it to its end. Men with a history of abuse are capable of horrific things and tend to be unpredictable. They work on a set of thoughts, justifications, and logic that don't make sense to other people, so their behavior doesn't line up with what's expected from other people. It could be the answer. But I just..." I go back to looking through the window at the stars overhead. "I'm not convinced."

CHAPTER SEVEN

S OMETHING SMASHES INTO MY HEAD AND THE SOUND OF THE crunch reverberates through my body. Sticky heat pours down my face and I fight to get up.

For a moment, I don't know where I am. Everything around me is dark and blood is stinging in my eyes. I realize I'm in the living room. The masked figure is hovering over me, a piece of pipe held up over their head.

I duck away from the next blow and an instant later I find myself standing in the middle of the coffee table. I don't know how I got here. I look down and see my bare feet covered in remnants of the snacks and drinks I kicked out of the way.

In the next second, my body crashes into the figure and we hit the ground. Pain radiates through me. I dig my knee into my attacker and another blow forces my eyes closed.

When they open, the living room is gone. I'm outside, standing in damp grass with the smell of dirt and blood in my nose. Around me I hear screaming. I reach up to touch my head and realize it doesn't hurt. There's no blood on my hand when I pull it back. My feet are no longer bare and thick rubber soles on ankle-high boots protect them as I take off running in the direction of the screams. Something glitters in the distance. The smell of heat and ash takes over and I see it's a campfire. Whipping around, I see the outline of cabins against the dark blue night sky. Another scream gets me running again.

A man comes out of the shadows clutching an ax. Blood glistens on the blade but goes dull where it has soaked into his clothes. I lunge toward him, but he doesn't acknowledge me. He doesn't even seem to know I'm here. I try to tackle him, but rather than hitting him, I seem to fall straight through his body into an abyss. A hard landing takes the breath out of my lungs and I blink against the lights bursting in front of my eyes. It takes a second for me to process that the colors I see aren't from the impact of the landing, but instead are the flashing of bright lights reflecting on a highly polished marble floor.

Rolling over, I hit the stone side of a large fountain. In front of me an escalator leads up toward a mezzanine of stores. The mall. The realization hits an instant before the sound of the first shot slices through the air. Chaos. I get up and slip in blood pooled at my feet. All around me, I see bodies scattered on the floor.

I look up toward the escalator again, but it has shifted. I'm no longer looking at the interior of stores glowing from above me, but Christmas lights glistening on a Ferris wheel. Music filters into my thoughts and a shiver rushes down my skin. The smell of pine and sugar makes my throat sting. I hear another scream behind me. My heart pounds in my chest as I turn to run toward it. But instead of running deeper into the theme park, I sprint across dark, overgrown school grounds. Ahead of me a rusted swing set stands out against the storm glow on the horizon. A figure glides back and forth on one of the swings, a hood concealing their face.

I run toward the swings, struggling for breath, fear and fury nearly blinding me. Everything goes dark before my hands can tighten around the neck of the figure now walking slowly toward me. When my eyes open again, everything is bright and quiet. I'm sitting in a cream armchair with gold accents, my hand rested on the head of a shimmering peacock statue beside me.

I start to stand up and flowers tumble from my lap. I didn't even realize they were there. They cascade across the carpet, ending at the toe of a black shoe. I look up and take in a sharp breath as the knife clutched in the hand of a young man covered with blood comes down toward my chest.

Stumbling back toward the chair, I land with my head on my knees and Sam's arms wrapped around me.

"Hey," he murmurs softly. "Babe, what's going on?"

I shake free of the sheets and blankets tangling my legs and arm, not wanting anything but Sam touching me. My fingers digging back into my hair, I rest my elbows on my knees and draw in deep breaths to try to calm my shaking. A rush of rage makes my skin hot.

I know it was a dream. I knew it was while it was happening. That doesn't take away the comfort and reassurance of Sam close beside me, his breath on my neck and his heartbeat against my side.

"Just a bad dream," I finally tell him.

"What was it about?"

I lift my head. "I don't even know. But it felt... familiar. Like it had all happened before, but none of it could have."

Sam kisses me on the side of the head and gently guides me back down onto the pillow.

"Try to get back to sleep. I'm right here. Everything's alright."

He cuddles close beside me, his thumb gently stroking my arm as he drifts back to sleep. I lay looking through the bedroom window at the lamppost across the street. A faint memory of fog coiling around it crosses my vision before my eyes close and I sink back to sleep.

The rest doesn't last long. The sun is only just beginning to bring a tinge of pink to the sky when I decide I can't lie in bed any longer. Sam has another hour before his alarm goes off and I don't want to take it from him. Fortunately over the years I've been well-versed in the skill of sliding out of the bed while barely disturbing the covers. I get coffee brewing and start a pot of oatmeal. Moments from the dream keep flashing through my head, leaving me confused.

It was so obviously a dream, and yet it felt incredibly real. I could smell it. I could feel it. Even more intense than that was the feeling of anticipation. In each those environments, a sick feeling in my stomach told me to be afraid not of what I was already seeing and experiencing, but of what was going to come *next*. It wasn't the kind of fear that came from not knowing, from wondering what I was going to face. Instead, a part of me knew. I just couldn't access it.

The frustration at not being able to understand that feeling or pull any of the memories forward just makes me more determined to find my attacker and know what happened that night and why. Carrying my coffee into the living room, I stand on the new carpet where the old was once soaked with my blood. I stare at the door.

If there is one thing Sam is completely intent on, it is making sure the house is securely locked. The entire suite of locks on every door and window of the house were changed and updated a few years ago when a rash of break-ins left him feeling uneasy. They go far beyond just the basic thumb turns and doorknob keys that were in place when I moved back to Sherwood. A few of them are even operable through an app each of us has on our phone that allows us to activate and deactivate the locks from any location.

I consider those a safety measure above any of the others. When we are out of the house, those are the only locks that are engaged. It ensures that even if one of us loses our keys or otherwise needs immediate access to the house, we have the ability to get inside. Though Dean and Xavier also have keys to the house, it's comforting to know that either one of them could call us and in an instant would be able to get inside if they needed to. When we are home, there are other locks in place to keep us secure.

Those were fully engaged the night I was attacked. It's a habit to lock everything up as soon as we are inside. I don't leave the doors unlocked if I'm home. Even if I have the front door standing open during nice weather to allow air in, the storm door has three locks including one set into the top of the door frame.

Yet that night there was no indication of someone breaking into the house. Something woke me up, but it couldn't have been the amount of noise that would have happened if someone broke through the locks to get in. That would have not only woken up Xavier and Dean, but it would have most likely jarred my neighbors out of their sleep and my attacker never would have had the chance to do what they did. It would have been only a matter of moments before the yard would have been swarmed with people clutching cell phones and possibly the types of weapons the people of Sherwood favor. Primarily baseball bats and kitchen knives.

But that didn't happen. Somehow this person got through the locks and into the house without waking anybody up. It's a disruptive question, but not the one that is most disturbing. As I look around the living room, envisioning myself on the couch and the movie on the TV screen, I can't help but wonder what the person was after. Just me? Or something else?

CHAPTER EIGHT

IT SEEMS APPROPRIATE THAT THE SKIES ARE GRAY AND CLOUDY THE morning of Sherry's funeral. In the week since she died, I've learned so much more about her and all the incredible work she's done. But we've gotten no closer to finding out who murdered her or why. Gene tracked down Cody Hayes, the man who aggressively confronted Sherry in front of the Porchlight House days before she was killed.

As it turns out, he was released pretty much immediately after being arrested that day, but he didn't make it on the streets for long. He was arrested two days before Sherry's murder in another county for being belligerently drunk in public and then getting behind the wheel of his car. He only managed to drive a few blocks before veering off into a ditch so no one else was hurt, but he was sitting in jail with a few bandaged injuries at the time someone was lurking in that parking lot to shoot Sherry Talley to death.

When questioned about the confrontation with Sherry, he couldn't even remember her. He remembered having an argument outside of what he described as the house where his children were being held hostage, but he seemed to have no awareness that Sherry was associated with the shelter. As far as Hayes was aware, she was just a meddling old woman who didn't like his screaming.

Of course, he could have been lying. He could be playing dumb to discourage suspicion. But Gene is confident that's not what's going on. He has years of experience dealing with criminals and doing interviews. Anyone with this kind of career knows that during these kinds of interviews, it isn't really the words that the person says that matter. The answers can be useful, but most investigators go into them intending to put more attention into how they say things and telltale physical signs of dishonesty than the answers themselves. He had absolute certainty Hayes is nothing more than a pissed-off jackass who doesn't know how to deal with the fact that for once in his existence he isn't getting what he wants.

Not pissed off enough to do something like hire a hitman to hunt Sherry down and kill her. But certainly enough that people are going to want to keep their eye on him and his ex and children when he gets out.

Though I hadn't been convinced of the possibility that Hayes was actually involved because of his anger toward the shelter, there's still a sense of disappointment when what amounted to the only lead in the case came to an abrupt and conclusive end. It means having to start all over again, facing that same sense of not even knowing where to look next.

I haven't been able to be an active part of every day of the investigation because of other cases I'm handling, but Gene sends me regular updates and asks questions so I can stay involved. Yesterday he finished interviewing Sherry's family members and left with no new information and only more of the frustration and anger that comes when a murder seems so senseless.

Those family members are standing along one side of the steps leading into the old church as I approach the funeral. I start to go toward them to introduce myself, but a man I'm assuming is the funeral director appears at the doorway and beckons them inside. Sam holds my hand tightly as we walk into the sanctuary and slide into one of the pews toward the back. I didn't know Sherry well enough to feel like I should take up space close to the front, but I can see Xavier among several of the volunteers and members of the organization just behind the family. He mentioned they'd asked him to sit with them and it lifts my heart to see that he's willing to do it.

This isn't easy for him. Funerals aren't easy for anyone, but they are particularly challenging for Xavier. He has a different perspective on death and a difficult time processing how he is supposed to feel and behave. Adding to that internal struggle, the strong emotions of the people around him make the experience overwhelming. But he's here. He is among people who I know he hasn't strongly bonded to, but who he has enough of a rapport with that he wants to support them.

It's one of the moments of incredible strength I admire so much in Xavier and that could be so easily missed. He has told me many times before that being afraid doesn't mean you aren't brave, and strength doesn't mean not feeling like you're going to break. It means you still feel those things, still know you feel them, and still do what everything inside you tells you not to do. It is being willing to be afraid and willing to break if that's what it takes to do what needs to be done.

The service is short but sincere and touching. We file out of the church and make our way to the cemetery. I feel like I'm walking a very fine line being here. Trisha asked me to come. Xavier wants me here. But I can't pretend that even while I am one of the mourners marking the loss of someone I knew, I am also an investigator trying to solve a murder.

Whether it's that feeling of not fully fitting in or the impulse to constantly observe everything around me, I find myself on the periphery of the gathering at the graveside, watching the others. I catch sight of three men on the opposite side of the gathering. They are also on the edge of the group, standing with their hands clasped in front of them just like most of the other men, but there's something about them. I can't stop bringing my attention back to the three of them. They don't seem to fit in with the rest of the mourners. I don't recognize them, but then, I don't recognize almost anyone here, so it isn't that. There is just something off about their presence.

As the service ends and everyone drifts apart, I guide Sam's attention over to the men.

"Does anything strike you as odd about them?" I ask.

He shakes his head. "Not especially. They look like just about everybody else here. Sad and in black."

"I guess." I look over at them again, watching them walk away without speaking to anybody. It occurs to me that Sam used the word 'sad' to describe them. Their faces were certainly drawn and hard, but I wouldn't jump immediately to describing their emotion as sad. "I'll be right back."

I cross quickly to Tricia and accept the hug she offers me.

"Please say you'll come to the reception we're hosting," she says.

"I will. Can you tell me something?"

"What is that?"

I gesture toward the three men who have nearly crested a hill in the cemetery. The small area could only accommodate so many vehicles close to the gravesite, so I can only assume they had to park elsewhere. I'm glad to have been able to point them out before they got out of sight.

"Do you know who those men are?" I ask.

She cranes her neck to catch a last glimpse of them. "I don't know them personally. They're distant relatives of Sherry's. Apparently, they've come to represent those extended branches of the family tree."

I nod and turn back toward the hill, but the men have disappeared.

The reception carries through the late morning and by the early afternoon Sam and I have said goodbye to Dean and Xavier, who are heading to Tennessee for a few days to investigate a missing persons case, and are home in Sherwood. It's a disorienting feeling to have already accomplished something as heavy as a funeral and still have most of the day stretched ahead. It's the far more saturated and intense version of walking out of a movie theater into the afternoon sunlight.

I walk into the kitchen and open the refrigerator. There isn't much inside. I move on to the cabinets and the pantry and realize there's not a lot anywhere.

"Hey, babe," I call.

"Yep?" Sam says coming into the kitchen.

I close the pantry door and look over at him. He's already out of most of his funeral clothes.

"We've been home less than ten minutes," I say.

"Which is far too long to remain in a suit. I'm home."

"Yes, you are. In a home with no food," I say.

"What?"

"We're not at freeze-dried rations level yet, but it's not looking good. When was the last time you went to the grocery store for a whole shopping trip? It hasn't been since I was home," I say.

He grins sheepishly. It hasn't escaped my notice that he has stocked up on frozen dinners and microwave meals instead of the staples needed to keep the kitchen full.

"Um...."

"Okay, well that's not a great answer. I think I'm going to run up and do some shopping," I tell him.

"Alright, I'll get dressed," he says.

"No. You don't need to. Just stay here. I'll go."

I can see the hesitation on his face, but he doesn't want to argue. "You don't have to do that."

"I know. But I want to. It's been long enough. The doctor didn't say I needed someone guiding me around everywhere and that I wasn't able to drive. I haven't had any problems. No passing out. No blackouts. Nothing."

"But it's only been—"

"Babe," I cut him off, walking over to Sam and cupping his face with both hands, "listen to me. I know you're worried about me and I appreciate that so much. I love you. But I can't keep being treated like I'm not capable of anything on my own anymore. I'm starting to feel trapped just staying at home all the time and having other people do things for me or having people always with me. I need to just do something on my own. It's just the grocery store."

He doesn't look convinced, but it doesn't really matter. I don't want to upset him, but I can't just keep going like this. I know he wants to protect me and that the time I spent comatose gave him reason to worry. But I've always cherished my independence and held onto it almost aggressively, and he's always known that. It could have gone a very different way. My mother's murder when I was only eleven and my father disappearing from my life the day after I turned eighteen could have left me with a terror of abandonment and a desperate need for other people around me.

It didn't. Instead, it left me with a desire to take care of myself. To prove to the world that I could be what my father saw in me. I was worth his trust and the belief he had in my ability, in my strength.

That drive isn't as intense as it used to be. My father's return into my life and building my family has allowed me to trust more, to be more willing to accept others around me. But not so much that I'm okay with being told I can't do anything on my own or have any time to myself.

He finally smiles and kisses me. "Be careful."

"I will. See you in a bit. Anything you want me to get while I'm there?" I ask.

"How about some of those freezer corn dogs?"

I roll my eyes. "Actual food, I mean."

Almost as soon as I turn out of the neighborhood, my phone rings. I glance over to where my phone is secured on the dash and see Bellamy's name on the screen.

"Hey, B," I answer on the speakerphone.

"Eyeballs don't just explode, right?" she asks.

I blink. "What?"

"Just as a matter of principle. Eyeballs don't just explode. That takes some fairly specific conditions to happen, right?" she asks.

"Um. Is this a personal question?" I ask. "Are you currently experiencing one or more eyeballs that have exploded?"

"Not me. Remember that cult sacrifice case out of Maine I've been consulting on?" she asks.

"Not an easy one to forget," I say.

"Two more bodies have been found in the general area as the original victims and there's some question as to whether they are linked. They were found in a cave and have some of the same types of markings as the other victims but are also missing some of the telltale signs. But both of them experienced traumatic injuries to their eyes and there's some question as to whether that's a sign of torture or could indicate the sequence of death. I was wondering if there's a possibility that the eyes could have just… you know," she says. "On account of them being underground."

The visual makes me shudder, but I recover soon enough. "Well, as far as I know, the pressure that would be required in order to cause that kind of damage would not happen in just a normal cave. If they were discovered by another person and that person's eyeballs are still intact and functioning, I think it's safe to assume that there are some other factors at play here. Hasn't anyone thought to ask the medical examiner? That is kind of the point of their job."

Bellamy starts to respond, but a glance into my rearview mirror takes my attention from what she's saying. A car is driving close behind me. There's no one else on the road and we aren't traveling on a busy highway. I'm still on the quiet streets of the residential area of town. Not that any area of Sherwood really necessitates any kind of close following, but it is especially strange here.

"…don't you think?" Bellamy asks.

I have completely missed everything that she said. I turn my attention back to driving rather than watching the maroon van behind me.

"Sorry. I didn't hear you. What did you say?" I ask.

"I was pointing out that it's an important distinction because we've already established that the cult murders don't involve any kind of prolonged suffering of the victims. They are sacrificial in nature and it looks like the victims are held in certain, almost divine regard before they're brought to be killed."

"Nothing like that roller coaster of emotions," I remark.

"Yes. But it means if those people in the cave were put through something meant to inflict pain or hardship on them, it would make it less likely that they are linked to the cult. This could be a copycat killer or someone who just happens to use some of the same imagery."

Her voice has shifted during this part of the conversation. Bellamy has been my best friend for a long, long time now and I've gotten very familiar with the way she talks about her thoughts as she's working through something. Her career as a consultant for the FBI means I frequently get phone calls that allow me to listen in as she starts by telling me something, then her voice lowers and sounds slightly distant as she moves into simply thinking out loud rather than actually intending for me to give any input.

Eventually she'll loop her way back around and I'll be expected to engage in the conversation, but for now, I'll let her work on untangling her thoughts while I look back through the mirror at the van. It fell back slightly but is now gliding up close again. The windshield is slightly tinted and the visor is pulled down, making it difficult to discern any identifying features for the driver. I can't even tell if it's a man or a woman.

I don't want to overreact. There doesn't seem to be any malice in the way they are driving and it's entirely possible this is just someone who has a shaky grasp on the basic tenets of physics and how they apply to sudden vehicular movement. I don't mention the car and instead decide to change routes. Rather than heading directly to the grocery store, I instead decide to detour through a side neighborhood to go to a little gas station tucked in the back corner. It's known for terrible gas prices and exceptional fried chicken. Right now what I care about is the open and public parking lot.

I take the next turn down a street that leads into the next neighborhood and the van follows right behind me. It continues as I weave through, backtracking and turning a couple of times to try to dissuade them. The van continues to get closer, nearly brushing against my back bumper. Bellamy is still talking, but I interrupt her.

"There's someone following me."

"Following you? Where are you?" she asks.

"I'm in the car. I'm driving to the grocery store and I noticed a van following behind me. They've been there since just a couple minutes after I left the house."

"You're sure they're following you?" she asks.

"I've been driving around this neighborhood taking all the turns and backtracking and they're still right behind me," I say.

"Can you see who it is?"

"No. I can't see the driver."

I notice the person behind the wheel make a movement and every muscle in my body tightens. My hand instinctively moves toward the gun on my hip. I'm anticipating rounds smashing through my back window when I realize their hand is up beside their head like they're holding a phone. It looks like they're wearing a hat and large sunglasses, which wouldn't be unusual.

As the van slows, so do I. As much as I don't like the idea of being followed, I want to figure out what they are up to.

"Get off the phone and call the police."

"Wait. It looks like they're talking on the phone. They're looking around and slowing down."

I watch as the van slows almost to a stop in the middle of the street, then backs up and turns to pull into a driveway.

"Emma? What's going on? Are you okay?"

The car stops and I hesitate at the end of the block in front of the stop sign. The driver's side door of the van opens and I see movement as if the driver is reaching for something in the back before getting out. I let out a breath.

"Yeah, I'm fine. I feel completely ridiculous, but I'm fine."

"What do you mean? What happened?" Bellamy asks.

"Apparently, they weren't actually following me. Or, they were following me, but maybe they thought they were following somebody else. They were on the phone and then just pulled into a driveway and are getting out of their car. I'm sorry. I'm getting myself all worked up about something so minor," I say.

"You don't need to apologize. You've been violently attacked twice in the last couple months. You have every right to react however you want to react to anything. Especially considering your attacker is still unaccounted for, I think feeling a little nervous when you notice a car right behind you is perfectly understandable."

"Attackers," I correct, emphasizing the 's' sound at the end of the word. "Didn't Eric mention the new surveillance footage that shows it was two different people who attacked me?"

"No. He and I have agreed that we're not bringing our work home with us anymore. We both spend so much time wrapped up in what's going on with the Bureau that we realized we were essentially working twenty-four-seven rather than spending any time just together. So we've put the kibosh on that for the foreseeable future. Of course, now I'm regretting that a little bit since I'm just finding out that there isn't one potential psychopath after my best friend, but two," she says with a heavy sigh.

"To be fair, it's not the first time," I say, trying to bring some levity to the conversation and let the adrenaline buildup settle.

We chat until I reach the grocery store, then hang up so I can shop. Though we'd started talking about her and Eric's wedding plans by the time I got to the store, I can't ever be sure of how the conversation is going to shift again and I don't need my neighbors overhearing more of the talk about the cult murders.

I take my time wandering up and down the aisles, fulfilling the list Sam texted to me and gathering up the things that look good to me along with ingredients to have on hand for meals we don't have to put a lot of thought into. The cart is overflowing by the time I finish and the bags fill nearly all of the available space inside the car. The bag I chose to ride shotgun beside me just so happens to be the one with a bag of my favorite chips at the top and I've just pried it open to fuel myself the rest of the way through the drive when movement in the rearview mirror catches my eye.

I glance up and see a green sports car come up close behind me. I speed up just slightly and it matches me. Turning in the opposite direction of my house does nothing to create separation between the cars. But what it does is keep them away from my house. Because this time, I'm positive I'm being followed.

CHAPTER NINE

THE CAR COMES CLOSER, THEN DROPS BACK A FEW FEET BEFORE rushing forward again. I need to maintain control of the car and not put anyone else at risk as much as I can, so I don't want to increase my speed excessively. The green car repeats the move of sliding backward, then surging forward again, this time tapping my bumper. It's not enough to cause damage, but enough to jolt my body and send me a clear message.

I maintain control of the car, but this is getting intense. There's no way I'm going to guide whomever this is back to the house, so I make the decision to head for the sheriff's department. Calling emergency services wouldn't do any good. If anything, seeing them coming would only cause more erratic behavior as they tried to escape. I'm better off getting there as fast as I can and giving a report of what I saw.

Wanting to give Sam notice that I'm on my way and ask him to have a deputy in a vehicle ready to pursue the green car when I get closer, I reach for my phone. Another bump makes my hand jump forward and hit my phone. It falls out of the cradle holding it to the dash and falls into the floorboard of the passenger side. I glance over and see it wedged near the edge of the door. It's too far for me to reach.

I have to forget about it. I need to keep my attention on driving the car and getting any information about the driver of the green car that I can get. Veering off the smaller road onto a larger two-lane road that leads to the sheriff's department, I look in the mirror again to try to see more of the driver.

Just like with the driver of the van, this person is the epitome of non-descript. Also wearing dark sunglasses and a hat, they're showing few details about themselves other than general size. The estimated height and width of the person compared to the seat gives me the impression it's a man, but that's all I can get.

Anger rushes through me, making me grip the steering wheel even harder, but there's also fear in the frustration and rage as the pursuit continues. There are more cars around us now that we're on the larger street, making me worry that other drivers could get involved. We're close to the station. If I can just stay in control until then, I can keep anyone from getting hurt.

Focusing on that takes over trying to see the driver. This person could be responsible for trying to kill me. I'm not going to let them kill someone else.

The time of day means the road is getting increasingly busier as people slip out of work early or start their rounds of afterschool activities with their children. I'm extremely aware of them on the road with me, trying to pay attention to the distance between my car and the one in front of me so I don't get too close even as the green car stays mere inches from mine.

I'm only blocks from the turn to the station when the green car suddenly veers to the right, coming up alongside me in a sweep that forces me into the opposing lane of traffic. Horns blare and tires scream as I fight to maneuver away from the truck coming directly at me. Quick action by the driver of the truck and me—combined with a massive load of luck—prevents a head-on collision, but the vehicles still scrape and crunch against each other. Another bounces into the corner of my bumper and a fourth crushes the back of the truck, but the other drivers on the road are able to divert their paths and avoid any other wreckage.

The green car shoots away as I rip my seatbelt off and scramble out of the car.

"Did anyone get the license plate from that green car?" I shout. "Did anyone see it?"

"Are you alright?" asks a woman I recognize as working at one of the clothing stores on Main Street as she gets out of her car.

She'd pulled off the side of the road to render aid and is now looking at me with widened eyes that make me wonder if I'm injured in some way I haven't yet realized. I look down and brush pieces of broken glass from the window off my shirt, but don't notice any blood or other serious issues.

"Did you see that green car?" I ask, walking toward her.

"Green car?"

"What happened? Are you okay?" a man from the car that hit me asks.

"I'm fine. The green car. Did you see it?"

"Yeah. Driving away from here like a bat out of hell. What was he doing?" he asks.

"Following me. He hit me twice and tried to run me off the road. Did anyone get his license plate? Or a description of him?" I ask. They all shake their heads. "Shit."

I look over at the truck and realize the driver hasn't gotten out. Sirens cut through the chaos as I climb over the car that hit me, which is now stopped at an angle across the road, to get to the driver's door. The windshield is broken and I can see blood on some of the glass. My stomach sinks. I didn't think the collision was too severe, but now I worry this driver might have been more seriously injured when the other car hit him.

Horns are still honking and I whip around to face the impatient, red-faced driver of a sleek luxury car in a similar crimson shade. He's leaning out the window craning around as if trying to find somewhere he can wedge himself to continue on his way. "I said out of the way," he snaps, his voice dripping with condescension. "Can't anyone—"

"Shut up!" I scream. "I don't know what the fuck you think any of us can do right now, but no one is moving out of your way. In case you didn't notice, there are four cars smashed together in the middle of the road so I'm sorry for the *inconvenience* of you not being able to get to your golf game or home to your dinner or to the seedy motel to meet your mistress or whatever the hell you *think* is the most important thing on this planet right now, but you're just going to have to deal with it. So I suggest you get your head out of your ass long enough to get it back in the car, roll up your window, and sit there."

"Emma."

My head snaps back the other way. Sam is jogging up from behind the truck, his face etched with worry. His car, lights flashing, is down the road wedged in the stopped traffic coming the other direction. Two other cars from the department are right behind his and the lights from the fire truck and EMS sweep around them. Sam gets to me and grabs me in a tight hug.

"The driver," I say, pushing back away from the hug to gesture at the truck. "The driver hasn't gotten out. He's not responding."

We get to the door and see the man sagged over the steering wheel. He's slightly out of his seat, more hanging from the dashboard than slumped over it.

"He's not wearing his seatbelt," Sam says. "He must have been thrown out of his seat and hit his head."

He shouts back to the EMTs and then opens the door. His fingers go to the man's neck and I see the relief relax his shoulders.

"I've got a pulse. It's steady."

We step back and let two of the paramedics extract the man from the truck and lay him on a backboard. As they start toward the ambulance, the man's eyes flutter slightly.

"Another bus will be here in two minutes," Seth reports.

"You're getting on that one," Sam tells me.

No offer. No question of whether I'm feeling any pain. Just the announcement that I'll be getting on the next ambulance that arrives at the scene.

"I don't need to go to the hospital," I tell him. "I'm fine."

"Emma, you're going. You just suffered a severe head injury less than two months ago and now you were involved in a car crash. Doctors need to check you out to make sure you are actually alright. I'm not going to argue with you about this," he says.

"Sam, this was not just an accident."

The second ambulance arrives and Sam takes my hand to guide me toward it.

"Over here, guys."

"Sam, stop," I say.

"Emma, no. You're going to hospital whether you get in that ambulance or you get in my car and I take you. But you're going to get checked over by the doctors."

There's a rumble in his voice I'm not used to hearing. I meet his eyes for an instant before stalking toward his car. Climbing in the front seat, I slam the door and latch the seatbelt. Sam stares at me through the windshield for a beat before coming to get in with me.

"I don't understand why you have to be so stubborn all the–"

"Someone did this," I snap. "Someone was following me."

"What?" he asks, his eyes snapping over to me briefly as he tries to navigate his way backward away from the scene.

"Someone was following me and then ran me off the road. That's what caused the wreck."

"Why were you over here? I thought you said you were going to the grocery store," he says.

"I did. But when I was on the way there, I noticed someone behind me."

I tell him about the maroon van and the strange way it behaved as I was making my way through the neighborhood, then how the green car forced me off the road. A standalone emergency department is less than a mile away from the sheriff's department. The driver of the truck will likely be brought to the large hospital where I was treated after my attack, but I'm grateful that Sam is only making me go to the smaller center. It means a lot less of a chance of sitting in the waiting room for hours or being ushered back to the emergency room only to wait there. It will be a faster process and I can get to the department to file my report and start investigating the crash.

Sam doesn't say anything about what I told him until we've been quickly processed through signing in and then brought to the back. Once the nurse has given me a preliminary check and seems as convinced as I am that I don't have any kind of pressing injuries, Sam sits in a chair beside the bed and leans close.

"I need you to tell me everything that happened after you saw the van pull into that driveway. If you noticed anything strange at the store. If you saw someone there in the parking lot."

"Sam, I'm not one of your 911 calls. Clearly there was nothing strange happening at the store or I would have noticed. I spent more than an hour in there shopping. I didn't even see the same person in more than two aisles, much less felt like someone was staking me out. And the green car that was following me wasn't exactly subtle. It's not like it was a champagne-colored family sedan. There aren't ten thousand of them everywhere you look. If that green car had been parked in the lot at the grocery store waiting for me, I would have noticed it. This wasn't a coincidence, Sam. They were waiting for me. Both of them."

"Both of them?" he asks. "I thought you said the maroon van pulled into a driveway and someone got out. That they were on the phone right before that. Did the driver of the green car do the same thing?"

"No," I tell him. "Because the driver of the van had to. It was a distraction. They knew I'd seen them and had figured out that they were following me. They had to do something to make me not suspicious of them, so they pretended to be talking to somebody, like maybe they thought they were following someone somewhere and then realized I wasn't that person, or they were lost and trying to find a place and just happened to need to weave all over the place, too. Then they pulled into a driveway and acted like they were going to get out.

"But I didn't actually see them get out," I explain. "The door opened and I saw a glimpse of them leaning into the backseat, but that's it. They never fully got out of the car. And there were no other cars in the driveway. It wasn't like someone was there waiting for them. I think they chose the first random empty driveway they saw and pulled into it because there wouldn't be anyone to pay attention. And if a neighbor happened to see them stopped there and question it, they could always say they were lost and were trying to find their way. Anything to seem like it wasn't anything to give a second thought."

"You think both of them were intentional?"

"I think it's possible. If two different people can be behind my attacks, then two people could have been following me," I point out. "They planned to follow me and to either send me off the road or into the path of another car. They managed to do both. Too bad for them I'm a fucking good driver."

The doctor comes in and by the look on his face I have a feeling he's already been briefed on the accident. He has a tablet in his hand and his eyes sweep over my medical record. He asks me a few questions about my hospitalization and coma, and then how I'm feeling after the accident.

"I am fine. I'm only here because my husband insisted," I say.

"That was a good move on his part," the doctor says. "I want to run some tests to make sure everything is as fine as you say it is and then we're going to keep you overnight for observation."

I shake my head. "No. Absolutely not. I don't need to stay here. I'm not bleeding. I didn't hit my head on anything. Like I said, I'm completely fine. The impact jostled me pretty good, so I'll probably be sore as all hell for a few days, but honestly, that's not exactly something I'm unfamiliar with. Let's just compromise on a couple of pain pills, an hour nap, and we'll call it good."

"As impressed as I am with your persuasive skills, Agent Griffin, I really make it a point in my career not to compromise when it comes to patient health and well-being. If you want me to, I'll give the doctors who treated you up at Cloverfield Memorial a call to let them know you're here so they can have input in the treatment plan. They might even want to come up here and check you over themselves. But you need the tests," he insists.

"I'm fine."

"It's very easy to think that everything is fine and you didn't sustain any injuries because immediately after traumatic incidents like these the body can respond by shutting down pain signals and causing swelling that masks signs of serious issues. Those can get far worse without proper treatment. But if we detect them through the proper tests, we can make sure that they're addressed and don't lead to more difficulties. This is especially true for someone like you who has already put their body through so much recently."

"I didn't put my body through anything," I point out. "It's not like I did it intentionally. Spending a couple weeks in a coma isn't exactly what I would consider a relaxing vacation choice."

The doctor smiles and lets out a sigh. "Well, this is going to be just a quick getaway. Settle in. Get comfortable. And I can certainly get you some of those pain pills to help you deal with the soreness because you are absolutely right, that's going to be a bitch tomorrow."

He walks out of the room and I drop back against the pillows with an exasperated groan.

"I can't believe I'm being held hostage in another hospital bed," I say.

"You don't need to be so dramatic," Sam says. "This is exactly where you should be."

I sit up and narrow my eyes at him. "Where I should be is out there trying to figure out who decided to find out if third attempted murder is a charm."

"That's not going to happen," Sam says.

"Excuse me?"

"You shouldn't have gone out alone today. I knew I shouldn't have let you," he says.

I scoff incredulously. "You shouldn't have *let* me? You can't be serious right now. Hospitalization or not, head injury, attack, car pursuit, whatever, it doesn't matter. You're not going to tell me what I can and can't do," I snap.

"If you hadn't gone out alone today, this wouldn't have happened," he counters.

"Because you have some sort of magical powers that prevent people from wanting to hurt me? You think that they would have seen that I had a man in the car with me and decided there was no point in them continuing with their plan because clearly it wasn't going to work?" I ask.

"It isn't about that," he says. "It's that –"

"That you think I can't be trusted by myself anymore. Or that somehow I don't have the ability to handle anything. Maybe it would have made a difference if you were in the car with me. Maybe they would have seen that there was another person with me and decided that made it too risky. Or maybe they would have just seen you as another step in whatever mission they're on right now and you would have ended up smashed into that truck, too."

He opens his mouth and then wisely closes it.

"The point is, I chose this life. I chose to be in the FBI. I didn't want to sit behind a desk. I didn't want to answer phones and take notes. When I left art school it was because I was going to become a special agent in the Bureau and that meant I was going out in the field. I made the decision to put myself in dangerous situations, and I've been doing it for a long time. I know what I get myself into. *You* know what I get myself into. And it's not going to change. You can't keep me wrapped in bubble wrap at the house forever. I'm going to have to go back to normal life eventually. I'm going to run errands on my own. I'm going to work. You have to accept that."

Sam's jaw twitches and he bites down to try to stop it. His eyes belie a clash of emotion he's trying not to express on the rest of his face.

"I don't want you in danger. Every day I hate thinking about what you might be doing or what might happen to you. It scares the living hell out of me, Emma," he says. "I already came so close to losing you." A single tear drips down his face and he wipes it away quickly.

"I know. And I love that you worry so much about me. But I need you to trust me. Can you please trust me?"

He nods. "I'm sorry. I shouldn't be … I shouldn't treat you like you can't take care of yourself. You're right, and I'm sorry. I do trust you."

My lips finally curl up into a slight smile. "If it's any consolation, I can't say I wouldn't do the same if you got hurt," I admit. "I would rip this town in two to find who did that to you."

That makes him finally bark out a laugh. "That's my girl."

He looks up at me with those blue eyes, now rimmed with red, and the sheer weight of his love washing over me is so powerful that I almost have to look away. But I don't. I'm lucky to have someone who loves me this much. I hope to never forget it.

Sam clears his throat and blinks away the emotion, putting his sheriff mask back on. "Right now, I want to put everything in my power into finding out who did this to you. What can you tell me about the driver? Either of them."

"Nothing," I tell him, aggravated I can't come up with any sort of identifying feature or personal tick that might help to narrow down the potential suspects. "Both of them had on hats and big sunglasses. Nothing that looked out of the ordinary. I saw at least three other drivers out there wearing essentially the same thing. By the size of the person in the green car, I would say it was a man, but that's not a positive identification. I wish there was something else I could give you. But this wasn't random, Sam. I'm not overreacting to normal aggressive drivers or even road rage. This wasn't random or coincidental."

Sam recites his most steadfast philosophy. "There are no such things as coincidences."

"Which is why I know I was targeted. I'm getting close to something, but I have to wonder."

"What?" Sam asks.

"Which investigation I'm getting close on. My own, or Sherry Talley's?"

CHAPTER TEN

M Y TIME IN THE HOSPITAL IS UNEVENTFUL. JUST LIKE I TRIED TO
tell the doctor and Sam, I got out of the accident relatively
unscathed. I was absolutely right about being sore, but I didn't suf-
fer any kind of serious injuries and my brain is showing the same level
of healing and recovery it did before leaving the hospital after I woke
up. I never contemplated the idea of having a life quota of the number
of brain scans I was willing to have, but I have officially reached it at
this point.

With a clean bill of health but a stern warning to pay attention to
how I'm feeling and alert my doctors to any changes in my state of mind,
vision, memories, sleep patterns, and any number of other indicators, I
am out of the hospital within twenty-four hours. I appeased Sam with
a day of hanging out on the couch with my work spread out on the coffee table rather than going anywhere, but this morning I'm headed to
Pearl's to meet up with Jeffrey Newsom, an investigator I've been working with on another case.

This is a meeting I was supposed to have weeks ago. I had an appointment with him the morning after I got attacked, which I obviously wasn't able to keep. He's been handling the bulk of the case since then with occasional calls and emails to consult with me, but I'm ready to get back into the midst of it. This is one of those cases that sticks with me and I'm determined to not only bring the person responsible to justice, but do everything I can to help prevent anyone else from falling victim to his rampage.

If I'm completely honest, there is also a personal element to it. I don't particularly enjoy working with Jeffrey. He is stubborn and self-righteous, and makes no secret that he doesn't appreciate being partnered up with me. He's the type who takes any sort of suggestion that working alongside someone else who has proven themselves skilled and effective is a personal slight. I haven't had to work with him much, but even in the brief time we have, he manages to make investigations feel like trying to Slip-N-Slide on sandpaper.

From what I hear from other agents, he's been alternating complaining that I dare go into a coma and leave him with all the work for the investigation when we were supposed to be doing it together, and crowing about all his own accomplishments and the fact that I didn't get replaced on the task force because obviously he is more than capable of managing it all on his own. He fails to mention to anyone that Eric has put three new agents under him to help with the details of the investigation and has also assigned Bellamy to consult on the case. All that along with the stack of my own notes and research, he's sitting in a pretty cushy situation.

Diving back into this case will ensure all that work doesn't go to waste and will hopefully hasten getting this finished so that my partnership with Jeffrey is behind me.

He's already waiting at a table when I walk in. Pearl looks my way and lifts the coffee pot in her hand. I nod and she starts over, grabbing a fresh cup from the stack on the corner of the counter as she comes. I slide into the booth and Jeffrey doesn't even look up from his phone. Rather than holding it, he has it flat on the table, leaning over it as he reads the news.

Pearl puts down the mug with a bit more zest than she might need to, making him jump slightly with the sound. She smiles when he looks up with his eyebrows knitted together. Pearl doesn't appreciate rudeness.

"Morning," she says sweetly, filling my mug. "Your usual, Emma?"

I smile back at her. "Thanks, Pearl."

Her smile goes from sugar to saccharine when she looks at Jeffrey. "And for you?"

There's a subtle hidden message in that, a reminder that even though he gives off the air of thinking he's the most important person who has walked in a room, in some places, no one knows him. He's just another face. The tinge of red that appears on his cheekbones says he got the message and is not enjoying it. He orders breakfast and Pearl walks away.

"Nice place," Jeffrey says with a grunt.

"I enjoy it," I say. "Along with everyone else in this town. Have for generations."

"Yeah. Well, I should probably start getting you caught up. There's been a lot of developments in the case since you were unfortunately detained and we don't want to waste a bunch of time."

I try to prevent my irritation from showing, but I'm sure it's in my eyes. Not that I care. "Oh, I don't need a full update. I've been following along with all of the notes and reports submitted to Eric. I've also been doing my own research and investigation. Like you said, I was unfortunately detained in the hospital for a couple of weeks, but I've had quite a bit of time since then to continue looking into the case."

His jaw tightens slightly. He obviously didn't anticipate me coming to this meeting not only prepared but ready to surge ahead rather than taking the time to get myself on the same level. I reach into the satchel I sat on the booth beside me and take out my notes on the case. I'll admit that looking into my own attacks and Sherry's case has taken up some of the time I would have otherwise devoted to this case, but I've still done a considerable amount of research and digging into details of the individual incidents in the case. I have a feeling Jeffrey forgot that the agents assigned to help out were also at my disposal, meaning when I wasn't able to actually go to a location to look into something or test a theory that came to mind, I had people who could do it for me.

This equipped me with hundreds of pictures and pages of documents I can add to the overall pile of evidence we've been gathering. We've only just scratched the surface when Delilah comes to the table with our food. The young waitress always looks chipper and full of energy, as if working here at the diner is the fulfillment of all her life's dreams. And it may be. At least for now. I happen to know she has a degree hanging on the wall in her mother's living room and there's a cute pear-shaped diamond sparkling on her left hand. She is the picture of one of those young women who have the entire world laid out in front of them and can do anything with it, but are happy right where they are, taking in every second.

I admire her for that. I've always been hungry and driven to keep chasing that next thing. The next case, that next takedown. There's a lot to be said for, as Xavier once put it, enjoying the raindrops on your face now rather than looking at the forecast for tomorrow.

My first bite of the biscuits and gravy on my plate remind me of how long it's been since I've been here and indulged in one of my favorite foods. Sometimes I try to recreate it at home, but I've never been able to quite get the same indulgence that Pearl manages. I let myself enjoy a couple more bites before going back to my case notes. I haven't gotten far when out of the corner of my eye I notice something strange outside the window.

"Excuse me for a second," I say.

I hurry outside and meet Eric just before he comes through the door. I give him a quizzical look. He hasn't been in Sherwood since just after I got out of the hospital and he hadn't told me he was planning a visit.

"Hey," he says.

"Hey? What are you doing here? Did Sam call you? Honestly, I'm fine. And I don't need whatever kind of intervention the two of you are planning."

He raises a hand to stop me. "I'm not here to plan an intervention. Promise. I came because I knew you were here meeting with Jeffrey. I need to speak with you."

His voice is grave, low enough to not be heard by people passing by on the sidewalk but with enough intensity for me to know this is not a casual visit.

"Come sit."

Jeffrey looks confused when we approach the table. He dabs his sausage-greased lips with a napkin and stands partway, reaching out to shake Eric's hand.

"Supervisor Martinez."

Eric gives him a polite smile. "Hello. I'm sorry to interrupt your meeting."

"It's fine. We just got our food. Call Pearl over and order something," I say.

Eric shakes his head. "I'm not hungry. But I'll take some coffee."

I offer my cup to him and look around to make eye contact with Delilah. I gesture toward Eric and she nods, heading for the cups on the counter. He has drained my coffee by the time she gets there, so the waitress fills both cups.

"Thank you," he says gratefully. He sounds exhausted, like he didn't get much sleep last night after an already difficult day. "Emma, I know you've been working on this case with Jeffrey. I've seen the work that's been done and I know good progress is being made. It's a difficult case, but I have all the confidence it will be resolved."

"What's going on?" I ask.

"Sir, if I may," Jeffrey starts. "I really appreciate the faith you have in me and the recognition of all the hard work that has gone into this case. I can assure you I will continue putting as much diligence and determination into it as I have since you first assigned it to us and there will be a resolution soon."

It sounds like a self-serving acceptance speech. I look at Eric.

"Are you taking me off the case?" I ask.

Eric's eyes slide to Jeffrey. "I appreciate the sentiment, Agent. I know you and the rest of the team supporting you have given this case a tremendous amount of attention and it has been noticed. And, as I said, I am confident it will be brought to an end soon. With Agent Griffin's help." Jeffrey's smile melts. He looks over at me. "But I'm going to need you to head up a new case."

"What case? What happened?"

Eric looks pained. "A police department out of Willow Bridge, Maryland reached out to me this morning. A body was found late last night. They believe it might be connected to a Virginia case and because it crossed state lines, they contacted me. I recognized the information they gave me about the victim and went to confirm them."

"Who was it?" I ask.

Eric takes a breath. "Tricia Donovan."

It's only a few hours to get to the police department just over the state line into Maryland, but it feels like the drive will never end. My head is spinning as I go, trying to process the handful of details I've been given. The rest of the information will come from the officers handling the initial investigation into Tricia's murder. The murders of the two women are undeniably connected. Like Sam says, there's no such thing as a coincidence. And even if there was, this would be too much.

Even without any leads or anything beyond their personal connections to conclusively link them, I can't believe the murders of these two women, stalwarts of From Heart to Heart both, have nothing to do with each other. This means the case is now mine. Rather than both police departments working individually to investigate the cases, I'll work with both to handle this as one case. But before I can start, I have to wrap my head around it. I have to deal with the idea that the sweet, welcoming woman with the bright pink hat and glistening eyes has been brutally killed far from home.

I'll be in Willow Bridge at least until tomorrow, but I don't bother to stop by my hotel before heading to the police station. Instead, I go straight there and introduce myself to the lead detective.

"Kevin Coolidge," he says as he approaches me in the lobby area of the department. "We spoke on the phone."

"Detective," I say in greeting, shaking his hand. "Emma Griffin. Tell me what you know."

I don't have the time to engage in small talk and pleasantries. Tricia's body was found last night and according to the information I got from Eric, they aren't positive how long she had been dead before an anonymous passerby called the police to report her. That puts me hours behind on the chase and I have no intention of losing any more time.

Detective Coolidge nods and leads me into the back of the building to a conference room. Pictures have already been set up and there are several folders stacked on the table. I go to the first of two easels displaying crime scene pictures. I grit my teeth to steel myself against the image of Tricia's body on wet, dirty pavement.

"Where was she found?" I ask.

"The Golden Iris. It's a motel right outside of town. The 911 call came in just after one this morning. The caller didn't leave a name or any personal details, but said they were passing through the parking lot and thought they saw a dead white woman on the ground."

"Charming," I mutter.

"At least they called," he says.

"At least they called?" I ask incredulously.

"It is what it is. You know as well as I do that it isn't always guaranteed. I might work in a fairly nowhere place in Maryland now, but I didn't always. And I've seen some brutal shit. People get killed and their bodies just lie there because nobody wants to get involved. They act like they didn't see anything because if they didn't see it, they can't be blamed for it."

All I can say in response is, "ugh."

"So, yeah. At least they called. And considering who this victim was, I'm going to be very appreciative because I wouldn't have been surprised in the least if I found out fifty people strolled right by her and didn't say a single word."

"Considering who she was?" I ask, feeling defensive and angry. "What do you know about who she was?"

"She was an old white woman with a nice car and a bunch of knitting in her backseat. That's not what people see around that area. And if they do, they're suspicious of it. They're going to want to know why she was there and what she was doing. In fact, if I'm going to be completely honest with you right now, I would say that there was no real reason for you to get involved. No disrespect to you and I know you've done some amazing things in your career, but getting the FBI involved was not my decision. The head of the department made that call after I'd already been assigned as the lead detective for the case.

"He said she's linked to a murder in Virginia and that warrants FBI involvement, like this is a serial killer or some shit. But I'm telling you it's far more likely this woman wandered into a place where she didn't belong, saw something she wasn't supposed to see or said something she wasn't supposed to say, and she ended up paying for it. It's unfortunate and I'm sure it makes no difference one way or the other for the people who knew her, but it isn't anything I haven't seen before. Things like this happen. It's the kind of world we live in. The stark, unfiltered reality of it is most likely we're never going to find out who killed her. It was some anonymous gang member or drug dealer—and, remember, nobody ever sees anything. So as interesting a part of the story it makes to work with you, I think I could speak for both of us when I say this is probably a waste of the Bureau's time and resources."

He's looking at me like he expects commiseration. He wants me to tell him he's right or to be impressed by his blunt perspective of the world around him, to approve of him not still being green and soft, too optimistic or rose-eyed.

Every word he said is crawling along the bones of my spine and twisting my stomach into angry, burning knots. I draw in a breath and try to count my way through the surge of heat that goes through me, but it won't dissipate. It sets every nerve alight and settles on my skin like an acid film. I turn my head to face him. The expression on his face twists until it almost turns into a smile. I don't want to scream at him. The burn is too deep for that. I take a step toward him.

"There is nothing more significant than human life. Ever. You might have seen things, but *nothing* compared to what I have. I have seen people get dumped, bloody and broken, out of cars onto the side of the road. I've encountered bodies that have no face anymore, nothing to even find out who they were much less what happened to them. And I've seen people who were murdered for walking too far out of the lines someone else drew for them or not falling into the behavior that was expected of them. I know people can be vicious and cruel and far closer to animals than anyone would want to admit. But do you know what else I know?"

I step up closer to the easel of pictures and press a fingertip hard onto the image of Tricia's body. "I know her. And while you might see just a person who doesn't fit the demographic of what you think should have been in that area of town, I see a human being. I see an incredible person who devoted her life to helping other people. And I see somebody who lost an extremely dear friend less than two weeks ago. So while you might want to think that this is just another example of how this entire world is just a twisted, fucked-up place where people are getting picked off for walking on the wrong sidewalk, the reason I'm here is because there's more to it. You might want to just toss this into your pile of cold cases and forget about it, but the reality of it is you toss in one more murder over the next couple of weeks and you have a serial killer.

"I, for one, want to make sure that third one doesn't happen. Whoever made that 911 call might not have left their name or any identifying information, but they did the right thing. That makes them a good person, not a moment of contrast to give you proof that everyone else around them is bad. I don't need you to be a part of this. I'm not here as your partner. I don't need your cooperation or for you to even want me here. I'm here as a federal agent leading an investigation into the murder of two people who are without a single doubt in my mind linked.

"I'd be more than happy to hold the door open for you so you can leave. But you're not going to get camaraderie from me. Not about this. You said it doesn't make a difference one way or the other for the people who knew Tricia how she was killed. That might be true. The manner of her death doesn't really matter. In the end, she's gone and nothing is going to bring her back. What does matter is the way she's treated now and how her murder is managed. Because it absolutely does make a difference to us whether she's treated like a victim who deserves recognition and justice, or like a number that's pushed into a file and forgotten. Thank you for the information, but you can be on your way now."

He stares at me for a second, then starts for the door.

"Oh, and Detective Coolidge?"

He pauses and looks at me over his shoulder. "What?"

"Don't *ever* take it upon yourself to speak for me."

His jaw twitches and he walks out of the room, closing the door behind him.

Almost an hour later, the door opens again and he walks back in.

"Did you forget something?" I ask, standing bent over one of the files, not bothering to lift my head or move my eyes toward him.

"You know, I walked out of here earlier thinking you were a bitch with an over-inflated sense of ego and importance who wanted to find something dramatic in every situation because it makes you look good," he says.

That catches my attention and I straighten slowly, turning to look at him.

"Oh?"

He nods and I notice he doesn't look angry. Instead, his expression is something between resigned and sheepish.

"But I went out, took a break, and thought about what you said. Now that I'm done being embarrassed because you essentially handed me my balls, I know you were right. I didn't realize you knew her. Nobody mentioned that to me. I'm sorry."

"That I knew her or that you acted like everything that's wrong with city homicide detectives?" I ask.

He chuckles slightly. "Both."

"Alright."

I go back to reviewing the information in the file, jotting thoughts that come to mind on a yellow legal pad. Coolidge stands in silence for a few seconds until the feeling of him standing behind me starts to make my skin crawl. I look over my shoulder at him and he takes a slight step back.

"So, are we cool?" he asks.

I stare at him for a beat, then gesture toward one of the files with the end of my pen.

"We're looking for descriptions of cars that any of the witnesses might have seen. Any mentions of vehicles." I go back to my own notes for a second. "Just don't ever ask somebody if you're cool again."

He snorts. "Okay."

We carry on in silence for a few seconds before I lean slightly toward him.

"And just so you know… I am kind of a bitch. But I earned every bit of my ego."

He smiles and bounces his head in a single nod. "Okay."

CHAPTER ELEVEN

I HAVE DETECTIVE COOLIDGE BRING ME TO THE CRIME SCENE AFTER
I've gone over all the information available. It has a harsher impact on
me then when I went to the parking lot where Sherry died. That scene
was softened by the area around it. She died near her favorite craft store,
just on the other side of a strip of trees from a lovely apartment complex. Yes, the trees weren't perfectly kept and there was litter and debris
scattered around the parking lot. But it was paradise compared to where
I'm standing now.

The Golden Iris sounded shady as soon as I heard the name, but
I wasn't prepared for what Coolidge led me into. If I didn't have proof
to the contrary, I would think the motel had been shuttered and abandoned years ago. The parking lot is a stretch of aged pavement broken
into pieces and marked with veins of dried grass and weeds coming up
in the fissures. Refuse fills the gutters and piles up in corners like strange
collections. There are bits of yellow crime scene tape frayed and faded
among the fast food containers, paper, and discarded clothes. Some of

the tape is still tied tightly around a nearby light pole and cement barrier. They aren't from Tricia's murder, but rather grim souvenirs from all the other times this parking lot has seen violence and crime.

"I don't understand it," I say, kind of looking around to take in the surroundings. "Why the hell was she here?"

"You said she was a part of an outreach organization, right?" Coolidge asks. "For homeless folks and such?"

"Yes. She founded a charity organization that provides handmade items to people in need. Not exactly a threat to society."

"No, but it could explain why she was here. We found a bunch of blankets and handmade items in the back seat. Maybe she was bringing them to somebody."

"That still doesn't make sense. This isn't how they do it. First, this is far outside of the service area for the organization. I'm sure she would help anyone who needed it, but it's a really small organization. They pretty much stick to the Mount Percy area. It doesn't make sense to stretch out all the way here."

"Maybe they were expanding," he offers.

"Maybe. But even if she did start wanting to work this far away from home, she wouldn't do it this way. She wouldn't have just shown up to a seedy rundown motel in the middle of the night and started handing things out. She would have already made connections with local organizations and coordinated resources to figure out what's best needed here," I say.

"What about the other murder? The one you think is connected to this one?" he asks.

"Sherry Talley. She was also shot three times getting into her car in a parking lot. And she was very actively involved in the same charity organization. She had just purchased a bunch of yarn to use for one of their projects and was bringing it back to the workshop. She was also found on the passenger side of the car and there was an apparent time lapse between the actual shooting and when the body was noticed or reported to police. Surveillance from the craft store shows that she left half an hour before the emergency called was made."

He furrows his brow. "We don't know how much time passed after Tricia was shot, but our 911 caller didn't mention seeing it happen and we didn't get any reports of gunshots that night from this area," he tells me. "But those are definitely some distinct similarities."

"Yes. But there are also stark differences. Sherry was somewhere she had been literally hundreds of times before. People expected her to be there. Maybe not in that exact moment, but people knew she would be going to the store to get yarn for that project. Her body was found by another member of the organization, someone she knew. Two of the shots were from a further distance and one was point blank. With Tricia, this isn't a place she frequents—at least, I can't imagine why it would be. She was found by someone she doesn't know and it was reported anonymously. All three shots were from a distance and it looks like they were done from the opposite side of the car according to the crime scene photos.

"This whole situation is very strange. It seems extraordinarily unlikely they were killed by two different people in unrelated incidents. And that means it could be a budding serial killer. But why would a serial killer target older women in a charity organization that helps people with handmade blankets and hats?"

Coolidge shakes his head. "I don't know. Makes no sense."

"No, it doesn't. Have you heard from the medical examiner yet?"

He briefly checks his phone and then shakes his head. "No update. But they'll probably at least have gotten through their initial exam of the body by now. Probably not the full autopsy, but it could be valuable. We could head down there and see."

I grunt my agreement and begin walking. Despite our initially disastrous first impression, Kevin Coolidge has impressed me, and seems willing to springboard off of me so we can push each other higher. I appreciate that in a local detective.

"I'm also going to want to see her car and everything that was in it," I say. "I'm not extremely familiar with everything the organization does and all the groups they help, but maybe if I see the donation items she had in her car, it can help guide us toward who she might have been meeting or why. It might not give us everything, but it's a step."

I often think there's a lot that can be learned about a person from their office. How they decorate it. How they furnish it. The types of items they decide to keep around so they can see them—and display them to others. Sometimes what you learn is that they are easily led and can be molded into someone else's vision. And sometimes it's that they don't have the energy or impulse to put a tremendous amount of thought into putting together their office so they have someone do it for them and end up with the same generic office as everyone else.

But the really interesting ones are those who give you a glimpse of who they are beyond their career or even beyond what they realize they are telling you. As I'm waiting for the medical examiner to come speak with me, I look around his office and take in all the little details.

There is a common misconception that medical examiners are inherently dark or gloomy people and their surroundings well reflect that. This has never been my experience and for the most part, their offices look essentially like any other doctor's office. A desk. A filing cabinet in the corner even though nearly everything is on the computer now. Pictures of family on the desk and sometimes cute silly little knick-knacks or decorations to add a bit of whimsy.

This office feels more like I took a wrong turn somewhere and walked into the office of a high-powered attorney. Every piece of furniture is heavy, dark-stained wood, including the desk that takes up a considerable portion of the space. Bookshelves take up one entire wall from floor to ceiling and are stuffed with cloth-bound volumes and gilded collections. But it's the framed picture hanging on the wall between two windows that catches my attention the most. I walk over to it to get a closer look.

The simple frame is a relief of contrast with the intense furniture. The basic wood surrounds cream-colored matting holding a photograph of a Ferris wheel. It was taken at night and some of the bottom of the wheel is shrouded in shadows, but at the top, the silhouette of the gondolas is eerily beautiful against the moonlit sky.

The sound of the door opening makes me turn. The man who walks in is younger than I would have anticipated when gauging the feeling of the office. I eye him at possibly his late forties, though the lines around his eyes might mean a few extra years.

"Agent Griffin," he says.

"Yes," I say.

He smiles and comes toward me with an extended hand for me to shake.

"Good to meet you. I'm Caleb Portier. Please call me Caleb." He gives a slight point toward the photograph of the Ferris wheel. "You like the picture?"

"I do. It's really interesting. Is it by a local artist?" I ask.

Caleb laughs and shakes his head as he walks around his desk to sit down, gesturing at the chair across from him in invitation for me to sit.

"I've been called a lot of things in my life, but an artist isn't one of them. No. I took it. A really long time ago," he says.

"It really is beautiful. Is that Ferris wheel around here?"

"No. It was in a tiny, old amusement park near where I grew up. A place called Trinity Pointe," he tells me.

I feel my eyes widen slightly. "Really? I'm from Sherwood."

He smiles. "I know. This is certainly a small world." He looks at me for a few seconds with a motion in the back of his eyes I can't quite place. They move away from me and back to the photograph. "Anyway, I took it before I left for college. The park had been closed for a while, but I felt like I needed a picture of the wheel. I keep it there as a reminder. It helps me keep going on hard days."

"It's always valuable to have something like that around."

"I think so. But you are here to talk about Tricia Donovan, correct?" he asks, directing us back to the reason I came to his office.

"Yes. I'm leading the investigation into her murder and the murder of a woman close to her a couple of weeks ago."

"I haven't performed the full autopsy yet, but I am happy to share my initial findings with you. I can confirm that she did sustain three gunshot wounds. One of them also had an exit wound, but the other two bullets are still embedded in her body. There are no signs of a physical struggle. No scrapes or cuts or bruises, or anything like that."

"So, it doesn't seem like she got into a physical altercation with anybody and they ended up shooting her in the midst of it," I say.

He tilts his head slightly. "That's a fairly good assessment of it. Obviously, I can't tell you exactly what happened, but if I had to take a guess I would say she was surprised by her killer. She didn't run from them or try to fight back. From the angle of the shots, it seems the killer was at a distance and on the opposite side of the vehicle from where she was found. She was likely standing outside of the car, possibly waiting for somebody, and was shot without realizing what was happening."

I hang my head low. "At least that's a blessing. She didn't have to see and be afraid. Not that much would have scared her."

His eyebrows twitch. "You knew her?"

"Briefly, but in that short time I learned that what she lacked in size, she more than made up for in spirit. She was an incredibly sweet and kind woman, but she also pushed through some immense adversity of her own and never shield away from facing the hardships and difficulties of other people. If she thought she could make a difference to them, she would do anything she could to make it happen."

"I heard one of the officers mentioned some sort of organization she was a part of. What was that all about?" Caleb asks.

I describe From Heart to Heart to him and he gets a thoughtful expression on his face.

"What is it?" I ask.

"You talking about the organization reminded me of something I noticed when she was first brought in. She was very clearly beyond any sort of resuscitation or lifesaving measures when first responders arrived, so they didn't cut her out of her clothes or anything like that. Everything was fully intact when she entered my exam room. As I was removing her clothes and documenting each piece, I found a scarf."

I frown. "A scarf?"

"She was wearing a long scarf. It wasn't visible immediately. It was tucked under the neckline of her shirt. Not just a little to keep it out of the way, but all the way in so it was barely even touching her neck anymore. I found that pretty odd. It was a cold night, so you would think that she would want to pull her scarf up around her neck and maybe even over her mouth to keep herself comfortable. The officers told me they checked her car when they responded to the emergency call and it was cold. That engine hadn't been running for a long time. Which means she could have been standing out there for quite a while. Yet, her scarf was pushed so it was over her shoulders and then down the middle of her torso, but underneath a shirt."

"That is strange," I say. "Can I get a look at the scarf?"

"There was blood on it, so it's being kept with the evidence. It's been chronicled, tagged, and bagged."

"Perfect. Thank you. If you come upon anything else, please let me know," I say.

I return to the police station and go to the evidence locker where I'm able to access everything that has been collected from Tricia's crime scene, including the scarf she was wearing when she died. Wearing gloves and spreading it out painstakingly across a crisp white sheet to ensure any hairs or other small bits of evidence are collected effectively, I look over the length of the long, somewhat overdone scarf. I can see and appreciate the fine, well-controlled nature of all the stitches, but it's just a little chaotic to me.

It takes a few seconds of looking over it to realize it reminds me of the sampler blankets hanging in the workshop. Those are far more manageable, likely owing to their much larger size. It's easier to visually take in that many different stitches and patterns on a bigger scale than when it's all packed together like in this scarf. I remember the way Tricia looked at the sampler blankets and wonder if her admiration of those made her experiment in creating the scarf.

A hard lump forms in my throat when I touch the stitches stained deep rusty red. I didn't get the chance to know her for long, but I was already becoming fond of her. Murder is always tragic, but having a reason behind it can make it easier to face. Not better. Not more palatable. But having some sort of explanation gives it context. This kind of brutality towards women who only do good is hard to take.

"Did you come up with anything?" Coolidge asks when I go back to the investigation room.

I shake my head, dropping down into one of the chairs at the table. I only sit for a second before getting right back up and walking over to the easel of pictures.

"No. The medical examiner pretty much confirmed everything I thought. He was bothered by the way she was wearing her scarf, but I looked over it and it was really long and thick. I'm guessing it just got too hot or she didn't like the way it felt pressing in around her neck and so she moved it out of the way right before she was killed.

"I just can't stop wondering why she was there in the first place. I know how committed she was to the mission of the organization. It meant everything to her to be able to help people. Even when the requests for items were overflowing, she would still try her best to accept new recipients or at least put something special together. She just wanted to be able to help. I admired her so much for her dedication. And it's not that I doubt she would go out of her way to help people who might not be recognized, but I just can't make it make sense. I'm still confused about her being at that place, at that time. It doesn't line up with any of the service areas of the organization, any of the normal dropoffs, any organization, any recipient. The people in that neighborhood certainly fit the demographic, but, again, Tricia didn't just walk out into random neighborhoods and start handing out blankets. Groups who already had working relationships with those in need let her know items that they could use most, members and volunteers made them, then they turned them in to that group in order to be distributed. But what's bothering me more than that is the items that were in the backseat of her car."

I grab a handful of photos from the board and pass them over to Kevin.

It wasn't unusual for her to have donation items in her car at any given time, but if you look at these pictures, what she had is a really strange assortment. There are some of the expected things that people would need during cold weather: hats, scarves, gloves, blankets. Things I would expect for her to want to get out into the community. But then, look." I point to one of the pictures of the items spread out on sheets like when I examined the scarf. "There are baby blankets."

"People have babies," he points out. "And it's important to keep them warm during the cold months."

"Sure. But these are pretty elaborate, lacy patterns. They're warm weather blankets or blankets for the NICU. These aren't the kind of blankets that people in this neighborhood, at this time of year, would need."

"But if they are going through desperate times, they would probably accept anything."

"Okay, yes, but what about these?" I ask.

He looks a little more closely at the picture. "What are those?"

"Squares. Members stitch them individually and then they are sewn together into blankets. When I first saw them, I thought they might be washcloths. That would almost make sense. They're usually made and put into bags with toiletries to be handed out to the homeless, people in shelters, or people who have been displaced for one reason or another. It would seem a little strange for her to just hand washcloths out individually by themselves rather than with soap or shampoo or anything, but I suppose it could happen."

"And that's not what they are?"

"No. The dimensions are wrong. And if you look at them compared to the other pieces, you can see that they're made from the same type of fiber. I didn't notice it at first, but look. Compare one of these squares to a blanket. You see how they're both a little fuzzy-looking? That's because they're made out of acrylic yarn. There are some acrylic yarns that are very slick, but for the most part they have that kind of haze around them. That's called a halo."

I flip over to find one more picture and point closely at the side.

"Now, look here. This is what I didn't notice. In this picture, there's a bag sitting on the center console. I remember seeing Tricia carrying that bag a couple of times at the workshop. Look how much smoother the stitches look. That's because it's made out of cotton. Cotton yarn has a completely different texture and it's what's used for things like market bags, like that one in the picture, and washcloths."

"So, those squares aren't made out of cotton yarn, which means that they aren't washcloths," Coolidge says.

He sounds unconvinced, and I can't really blame him. Observation and noticing tiny details are skills I bring into every investigation. They're critical to unraveling even the most complex cases. But this isn't anything like any of the evidence I've ever used. Nitpicking the fiber content of items found in the back seat of a charity worker's vehicle seems minute and ridiculous when her body was found just outside, shot three times for seemingly no reason. At this point, though, there's nothing else for us to go on. Minutia is all we have when things aren't deeper. Smaller. So, that's where I am.

"Yes. They aren't washcloths. Now look at the colors and the patterns," I say.

He tries, but gives up after just a minute. "I don't know what I'm looking at. None of it goes together."

"Exactly. That's what you're looking at. Remember, these squares are made to be stitched together into larger blankets. Which means that they should at least have something in common. A color palette. A general type of stitch. Some of the blankets that are put together are a variety of different stitches and patterns. But there's always something cohesive about it. If there wasn't, it would just look like a mess, which isn't something that these women would do. Let's say Tricia was going to bring a bunch of the squares with her to maybe meet with an outreach group and teach them how to sew the pieces together into larger blankets. It wouldn't be out of the scope of activities that the organization does. But, she would bring pieces that go together. Not just a random assortment," I say.

"So, what do you think that means?" Coolidge asks.

I shake my head. "I don't know yet. But it's something."

CHAPTER TWELVE

HEAD BACK TO SHERWOOD THE NEXT DAY WITH ALL THE FILES AND information about Tricia's murder. It makes more sense to centralize the investigation in one place rather than attempting to straddle locations just because of the spot where she died. Other members of the team I'm leading will be in Maryland, handling elements of the investigation such as interviews and canvassing of the surrounding area. My time is better spent focusing on the larger picture, investigating both deaths as linked events rather than individual, isolated incidents.

Though I have no concrete proof that the same person killed both Sherry and Tricia, the evidence makes that the strongest theory. Focusing on each death separately could obscure connections and shared details that may be key to finding out who is responsible. And the most effective way to find those connections and dig deeper into the story that exists behind these murders is to go back to the beginning. Back to the foundation of not only my link to them, but theirs to each other.

Sam is at work when I get back to our house so I drop off my luggage and head right for the From Heart to Heart workshop. Xavier let me know they have been continuing on with business as usual, continuing the mission Tricia began and Sherry so wholeheartedly picked up and carried. It's what the two of them would want. They wouldn't want people in need of something to warm their bodies and their hearts to have to do without because the volunteers and members are caught up in mourning them.

That sentiment seems to have invigorated the workshop. When I arrive, it's busier and more active than I've ever seen it. There seems to be a heightened energy, an almost staticky feeling in the air as everyone strives to honor Tricia and Sherry in the way we all know would mean the most to them. Part of me wishes I was only here to participate. I know none of them want to be a part of why I've actually come. But I need to talk to them about some of the details of the murders and try to get more insight into who these women were as people.

The participants in this organization are the people who knew them best beyond their families. Maybe even including their families. And if I can get to know both of them better through their friendships and the memories that continue to live on in those friends, it might help guide my investigation.

"Emma, it's so good to see you," Pat says, coming out of the back room as I walk down the long hallway.

"It's good to see you, too. How are you doing?" I ask as she pulls me in for a hug.

She shrugs and manages a smile, but it doesn't extend to her eyes. "It helps to be here."

"I can imagine it does." I glance around trying to gauge how many people are actually in the workshop right now. "Is there a way we can gather everyone here into the front room?"

Suspicion draws lines at the corners of her eyes. "Does that mean you're not here as Emma, but as Agent Griffin?"

It seems like it should mean the same thing, but I know it doesn't. "I'm here as both," I tell her.

She sighs. "I'll get everybody in there. Should I make some coffee?"

"It wouldn't hurt. Thank you, Pat."

She nods and walks away. I let out a puff of breath as I head back to the front room. I look at the whiteboard on the wall. Tricia's handwriting is still in the corner, encouraging anyone visiting to whip up a few extra hats to fill the holiday bins. In the last couple of weeks she'd been talking about her hopes for the next holiday season, wanting to provide at least two thousand warm hats for the community. The number seems dizzying even with the large group working on it, but I have no doubt they'll achieve it. It makes my heart ache to think that the time will come when the dry-erase marker on the board will chip away and need to be erased.

Turning away from the board, I see the furniture clustered in the room filling with women coming out of the different areas of the workshop. I can't bring all their names to mind right off the bat, but I recognize most of their faces from the night Sherry was murdered. When Pat comes into the room pushing what looks like an old, gray, plastic library cart holding a pot of coffee and an assortment of mismatched mugs, I take it as the signal that everyone is here.

"Hello," I start, waving one hand to get the attention of the ones leaned in toward each other talking low under their breath. "For those of you who don't know me, I'm Agent Emma Griffin. I'm with the FBI. I talked with a lot of you right after Sherry Talley's death. As I'm sure you know by now, Tricia Donovan was also murdered a couple of days ago. The similarities and some of the details of these murders have caused the Bureau to get involved. I will be leading the investigation," I say.

"Investigation?" one of the women asks, sounding shaky and suspicious. "Does that mean you think someone here killed them? Are you here to interrogate us?"

Muttering voices ripple across the room and I hold my hands up to stop them.

"This is not an interrogation," I clarify. "I'm here because these two women spent most of their lives in this workshop. They probably interacted with many of you several times a week, if not nearly every day. I didn't have the opportunity to be as involved as you are and didn't know either of them especially well. I'm here to talk to you about them. I need your help to find out as much about them as I can so I can hopefully find a direction to head in this case."

"You don't have any idea what happened?" someone else asks.

"Unfortunately, right now there aren't any answers. There isn't a lot to go on in either case. We have officers continuing to canvass the neighborhoods and other surroundings areas around both crime scenes, talking to witnesses, and reviewing some initial evidence. The case is developing right now, but in order to get anywhere with it, we need as much information as we can possibly get."

"What do you need to know?" Pat asks.

"Everything. Anything," I say. "I'm not asking about their deaths. I'm asking about their lives. I apologize for my bluntness, but I'm going to speak frankly here. These deaths were not accidental. And they didn't just both happen to be killed days apart. They were targeted, and I want to know why. That's where you're going to help. I just want you to talk to me about them. Share your memories about how you met, the things you've done together, anything in particular about either one of them that comes to mind when you think of them. I'm looking for anything that stands out. Anything that might give some clues as to why anyone would want to kill either of these women. If we can trace a why, it might lead us to a who."

"It has to be random," Lois Keegan, one of the first people I met here, says from where she's squeezed into an armchair with a woman whose first name I remember as Diane but whose last name I can't bring to mind. "It just has to."

"Random?" Macy Garth says incredulously. "You can't be serious."

"Of course, I am. Think about who they were," Lois says.

"They were both shot," Macy tells her. "Two weeks apart. Less than that. Three times, in parking lots, with no witnesses. That's not random."

"There were no witnesses," Diane says. "I heard somebody at the craft store saw somebody running away. And where they found Tricia was in a really bad part of town. The news report I heard said there's been a string of crimes there in the last few months."

"And that makes a difference?" Macy asks. "Because one person who was shopping at the same time maybe saw the person who shot Sherry, and Tricia went to some cheap motel in a rough neighborhood that means it has to be just… what? Bad luck? Oh, no, we just both happened to walk into the path of a crazed shooter?"

"Macy," Pat says.

"No, this is ridiculous. Two women who spent as much time together as the two of them did getting killed within two weeks of each other is not random," Macy insists. "That doesn't happen. Whoever shot them did it on purpose because it was them."

"I just can't believe that," Diane says.

"Neither can I," Lois argues. "Who would ever want to hurt Tricia or Sherry? They were lovely people. They worked for charity, for God's sake! Nobody would have any reason to hurt them."

"That's not necessarily true," I interject before the argument can escalate. "I know it's not something that any of you want to think about and it goes against what most of us feel about the world, but none of those factors make a difference to whether someone could be a victim of violent crime. Both of these women *were* lovely, but that doesn't make them immune to hatred or anger. In fact, sometimes volunteers, social workers—people who devote their lives to helping others—can often become the focus of ire of those who are against that kind of help. Or against the people who are receiving that help."

Lois's eyes bulge wide. "People do that?"

I nod grimly. "Unfortunately, yes. Not everyone believes helping each other through dark times is good. Some people would much rather believe that people who are going through difficult things have somehow earned their way into that. That they did something along the way or are simply a type of person who was born deserving of less in this world—and, of course, that they deserve their own success. They think that bad things happening to others is warranted, celestial justice of some kind. And anyone who helps them is rewarding whatever personal brand of evil those misguided people have assigned to them. My point is, attacks on volunteer workers, outreach programs, religious figures, essentially anyone you can think of who might be trying to reach out a hand to help someone up, aren't uncommon. That's why one of the first things we investigated was the types of projects Sherry was working on before her death. Now that we're also investigating Tricia's murder, a possible explanation we have to keep in mind is that someone objects to whatever organization or recipient they may be working with."

Gasps flutter through the room and I notice some of the women reach for each other, their eyes flashing around the space as if they are looking for threats among the familiar faces and in the corners of their beloved workshop.

"Do you really think that might be what's going on?" Pat asks. She sounds calm and in control, keeping herself together for the good of everyone else. "You think they might have been targeted because they help people?"

"At this point, it's our primary link," I say. "Are there any particular projects they worked on together?"

"The women's shelter and the halfway house," Lois offers.

"The drug rehabilitation center," Macy adds. "The prison outreach."

"Two months ago they did that big push for the LGBTQIA+ youth center," another woman says. "Putting together kits for teenagers who have been kicked out of their homes. And stuffed hearts to hold onto when they feel alone."

Her voice cracks slightly as she seems to be overcome with emotion thinking about the kindness and love Sherry and Tricia poured out to so many people throughout the community. Unfortunately, though, that means the list of possibilities seems about as long as my arm.

"They both worked with a lot of people who would unfortunately be considered undeserving by some facets of society. And those kinds of beliefs can certainly contribute to violent backlash. But right now, there's nothing to clearly point to that being the reason behind this. It's why we can't focus in only on that possibility and have to keep looking for and following any other leads that come up," I say.

Diane frowns. "I don't understand. You say it can't be random, but then you say you can't link it to anything, either."

"We just don't have clear indications. The thing is, when there's an attack based on belief or bias, it's not done subtly or quietly. When that's the case, it's generally done as a demonstration. The people who commit the act of violence make sure it's known why that person was a target. They might not identify themselves as the ones who did it, but they make sure that they send a message through their violence. They are making a statement about their own beliefs and how they feel about the victim or something the victim was standing up for. It isn't meant just as a punishment to that person, but as an example to anyone else who might try to do the same things they were doing. It just wouldn't have the same resonance without that kind of advertising.

"Neither one of these crime scenes had any evidence that pointed to that kind of motivation. And there has been no communication, no statements made, no videos posted on social media. Nothing taking responsibility or handing out a warning linked to these deaths. Until there is, we have to keep looking for other explanations. And that's why I need to know more about these women. I'm not here to speculate or go over theories with you. I'm here to ask anything or everything you know about their lives. I wish I could stand here and tell you why this happened to them and who did it. But I can't. Not yet. What I can tell you is that I'm going to do everything in my power to make sure that whoever did this is held accountable. I'm asking for your help," I say.

"And we're going to give it to you," Pat says. "Right, ladies? I've made coffee and there's plenty more to last a good long while. We can call Sebastian at the Empanada Market to deliver us a spread." She looks at me. "We're here for as long as you need us, Emma. Thank you for doing what you can to be their voice."

I can't help but smile. She seamlessly stepped in to control the situation, finding the strength that was stolen from her when she found Sherry's body.

"Maybe you'd like to look through these," a woman named Shawna offers, coming toward me with photo albums cradled in her arms. "We can tell you about the pictures."

I've already looked through some of the albums, but these two don't look like the same ones. Some of the other women move off a couch to one side of the room so I can sit. Shawna sits down beside me and places one of the books in my lap. I love the look of the green leather cover and the plastic sheets inside holding pictures and little notes. It's old-fashioned and sweet, something more tangible and meaningful than just online photo storage. A caption typed into a web form will never compare to preserved handwriting.

As we flip through the pages of the book, I take in all the details I can about each of the women. Something occurs to me as we move on to the next book. I take back the first and look through the last couple of pages, then flip quickly through the first pages of the second book. I point at a picture of Tricia with an emerald green scarf looped around her neck.

"Did Tricia always wear a scarf?" I ask.

"Not always, but most of the time. Even in the summer she would wear cotton ones. It was the first wearable thing she learned to make, so she really enjoyed making them. Whenever she tried to learn a new stitch or pattern for something bigger, she would make a scarf with it first. Sometimes we would tease her that she was only wearing them to cover up her neck so people would think she was younger." Shawna laughs softly. "She would say if her scarves were distracting people from her face enough to not realize how old she was, she was either doing something really right or really wrong."

I look over a few more pictures, paying attention to Tricia's scarves. She obviously had a vast array of them, but it's not the colors and patterns I'm paying attention to. I'm looking at the way she wore them. In every picture, the scarf is tied at the front of her neck like the way the bright pink one was the day I met her. Knotted and displayed on the front of her shirt more like a silk version of a scarf, they were always very visible no matter what she was wearing.

"And she wore them like this? Not around her shoulders or out of the way?" I ask.

The corners of Shawna's mouth tug down and she shakes her head. "Nope. Like that. To show off the pattern. When it was hot she would pull it further away from her neck and tie it more loosely, but she was really sensitive to the cold, even air conditioning, so she usually had them fairly close. Does that mean something?"

"Maybe. I don't know yet," I admit.

"Emma?"

I look up from the album to see Macy standing in front of me. Her hands are wrapped tightly around a mug of coffee and her eyebrows are pulled tightly together in a thoughtful, concerned expression.

"Hi, Macy," I say. "Did you think of something you wanted to tell me?"

"Not exactly," she says. "I…" she glances over her shoulder at two other women I'd seen her chatting with right after I sat down with Shawna. "Are we in danger?"

Shawna's head snaps up from her focus on the pages of the photo album and her eyes dart to me. "Danger? Do you mean here at the workshop?"

"What about the workshop?" Diane asks.

"Is something wrong?" Lois asks. "Do you know something we should?"

"No," I say firmly. I put down the photo album and stand up so I can make sure everyone in the room can hear me. "Everybody, listen to me. This situation is difficult enough without falling into conjecture and rumors. I need you to trust that I will tell you anything that I can, when I can. I'm not going to keep things from you just because. That wouldn't do anyone any good. But you're also going to have to understand that there will be elements of the investigation that I won't be able to discuss. Macy asked me if I think you are in danger. That does not mean that I know anything or that anything has come to light that might suggest a threat," I say.

"But you do agree that their murders are connected," Macy points out. "And the biggest thing they had in common was this organization. Which means if there's someone out there who has a problem with what they were doing here, any of the rest of us could be targeted."

"I'm not going to give you false reassurances," I say. "Because I don't know the motivation behind these murders, I can't stand here and tell you with absolute certainty that there's no risk. That would be irresponsible of me. I believe all of you should be exercising caution and paying close attention to your surroundings."

"We should close the workshop," Diane says.

"No," Shawna argues. "We can't just stop."

"She just said she can't guarantee we're safe," Diane points out, waving a hand in my direction.

"Don't blame Emma," Macy says. "She didn't do this. She's here trying to help."

"By letting us be here without any warning that we could be sitting ducks?" Diane asks.

"That's not what she said," Macy says.

"I'm not allowing you to do anything," I point out. "And I'm not giving you instructions, either. I assure you if there is a significant enough threat at any point, I will tell you to close down the workshop and pause activities. But for now, that's not up to me. It's up to all of you."

"No one is forcing you to be a part of anything," Pat finally pipes up over the din. "If you don't feel safe and don't want to be here, then leave. But I'm not going anywhere. The good we do here is important. The people we help depend on us. We shouldn't let them down because of fear. Especially fear that isn't grounded in any specific threat. All of you are welcome to make the decision that you want to make. Continue on with what we have been doing because it's what we do and to honor Sherry and Tricia, or leave and wait until you feel safe to come back. The decision is yours. But I know mine."

"I do, too," Coraline Mathews says. "I'm not going to let this person take this, too."

"Neither am I," Shawna agrees.

A few others voice their agreement, but Diane steps back toward the door.

"I can't. None of us know what's going on and I'm not going to just pretend everything is normal. I just can't."

She snatches a coat off the rack by the door and storms out. Lois chases after her. I look back at the others.

"What you do is your choice. I understand being afraid. But I also believe in continuing forward. And if you decide to keep the workshop open during the investigation, I support you. But I suggest you implement a few new protocols to help keep you safe. Never fewer than two people in the workshop at a time. Make sure you arrive and leave during daylight hours. Only use the front door. Don't park around back. For now, I recommend a pause on any new members or new recipients. Keep the list that you have and do what you can, but try not to make new connections.

"I would also recommend not publicizing when or where you'll be making drop-offs to your recipients, but keeping extremely careful records of who you contacted, where you're going to make the drop-off, and what time you'll be checking back in. Make sure everyone you speak to at all your groups know about this new policy. And if you see anything unusual, even if you don't know why you think it's unusual, but it doesn't sit right with you, don't hesitate to reach out to me. Please don't worry about feeling like it's too small or that you're wasting my time. Sometimes it's the gut feelings that turn out to be the most valuable piece of an investigation."

CHAPTER THIRTEEN

THE MEMORIAL SERVICES HELD FOR TRICIA ARE A STARK CONTRAST to Sherry's funeral. Sam, Xavier, Dean, and I walk into a warmly decorated funeral home to the sound of music playing and the smell of food. We're directed to a room with wide open doors and an enlarged portrait of Tricia with her eyes glittering and her mouth open in a wide laugh. She looks so happy.

Her laugh is silent, but voices from inside the room are providing the sound. I can't help but smile when I walk in the room and see everyone in the vibrant colors requested on the memorial notice. No black. No gray. Wear something bright and add some sparkle if you can. That was the only guideline. A long table filled with food ends with another displaying an elaborate assortment of bottles of liquor. I watch several people make themselves drinks, then turn and hold their glasses up toward the urn presented on a pedestal at the far end of the room.

I go to the table and Pat steps up beside me.

"This certainly is different than Sherry's funeral," I note.

THE GIRL AND THE DEADLY SECRETS

"Yes, it is. But it's what she wanted. Trisha was never afraid of her mortality. She recognized that she was, as she said, getting on toward elderly. She wanted to make sure things were sorted, so a few years ago, she sat down with an attorney and drew up her last wishes. She made sure everything was written out clear and concise. No mopey funeral service. No graveside. No sad songs. She wanted people to eat, drink, laugh. That was her. Don't be sad when you could be living just because I'm not anymore, she told me.

"I remember her telling me she had come up with the plans and it gave me the shivers. I just didn't even want to think about it. It seemed morbid. I thought maybe she was feeling depressed or like she had gotten some sort of bad news from the doctor and didn't want to tell any of us. But I realized that that wasn't it at all. It wasn't sad to her. She said she wanted to make the plans so that she knew her friends wouldn't be stressed or worried when she left. Don't you love that? When she left. That's how she put it. She was just planning that last big trip. And now she's on it and I'm doing the best I can to be happy for her the way she would want me to be."

"That's beautiful," I say.

Pat finishes making her drink and holds up her glass. "Cheers."

I smile and mirror her gesture. "Cheers."

We both turn and hold our glasses out toward the urn, then take sips. As the liquid warms my throat and hits my belly, I notice four people standing off to the side. Each of them is holding a glass, but I don't see any of them lift one to their lips.

"Have you eaten?" Pam asks.

"No," I say, touching her arm to stop her as she makes her way toward the food. "Who are those people?"

They're behaving the same way as the strange group who was at the graveside service for Sherry. I don't mention that, wanting an explanation without coloring it. Pat glances over in the direction I'm looking.

"I'm not really sure. Some sort of relatives. I introduced myself, but they weren't particularly chatty. I think one of them said his name is Finley. He's the only one who spoke. He just said his name and that they're extended family."

She steps up to the food and starts filling a small plate without another word, but the explanation doesn't sit well with me. I try not to think about it too much, concentrating on immersing myself in the final farewell Tricia wanted, but they keep coming to mind and I bring it up to Sam as we're getting ready for bed.

"They were acting just like the people at the cemetery. Standing off away from everybody, just kind of watching. Acting like they were a part of it, but not really looking like they fit in," I say as we pull back the covers and climb into bed. "And then Pat said she introduced herself to them and only one gave his name, then told her they were relatives."

"So?" Sam asks. "It wasn't a conventional funeral the way that Sherry's was, but it was her memorial. It would make sense that her family would attend it."

"But that's the thing. Tricia didn't have any family. She didn't have any children. She was widowed thirty years ago. One person there even specifically mentioned Tricia always talked about the organization as her only family. That's part of the reason it meant so much to her. I mentioned that to Pat and she said maybe she misunderstood what they said. That seems like kind of a leap, don't you think? How do you misunderstand someone saying they are relatives of someone at that person's memorial service?"

Sam reaches onto the nightstand for his book and looks over at me with a gentle smile. "Babe, I think you might be overthinking the comment. She might have just meant the organization is the family she's chosen. Like the way we see Eric, Bellamy, and Xavier as our family. Some people don't talk about their extended family. There could be drama. There could have been divisions a long time ago. Bad blood we don't know about. But a funeral or a memorial service tends to overshadow things like that. People come out for them because it's their last chance. Maybe that's all this is. Did they look like the same people? Or just like they were acting the same way?"

"Just acting the same way. Except for one of them. One looked exactly like one of the people from the cemetery. There was something about the way he was holding himself. It really stood out to me. The others didn't look familiar as people, but it was the way they were acting. I don't know how else to explain it."

"So, maybe it's just that both women have members of their families who don't know anybody else. Or who aren't the most social. It's a trope for a reason when strange family members come out of the woodwork at weddings or funerals. Everybody seems to have that weird offshoot of the family that doesn't really fit in."

I give him a look and laugh. "You realize who you're talking to?"

He grins. "I didn't think I had to say it out loud."

"Yeah, yeah."

He leans over to kiss me. "I don't know. Not everybody's secrets are twisted and dark. But everybody has them."

That's what I've been worried about this whole time. Tricia and Sherry were such lovely people who dedicated their lives to an amazing cause. But what secrets could they have possibly held that led to such a horrific fate?

The next day I go back to Mount Percy to talk to Pat.

"There was a guest book at the memorial service last night," I say. "Do you know who has it?"

"I do," she tells me. "I wanted to have somewhere for people to leave their names and any little notes about Tricia. But she didn't have a husband or children to take it, so I have it. I thought I'd keep it here. Not on display or anything, but for a memory of her."

"And Sherry had one, too. At the reception, right?"

"Yes. But her children have that one," Pat says.

"Could you get in touch with them and ask for them to send you scans of the pages?"

"I could. Why?" she asks.

"I want to look over the people who attended both. See how much of an overlap there is. A lot of the investigation has been focused wide, looking for people outside of their personal circles who had a reason to want both of them dead. But that might not be the case. It could be someone closer."

"You think it was someone they knew?" she asks, sounding horrified at the idea.

"It's possible. Not necessarily someone close, but someone in their orbit, someone who might have been able to integrate themselves into something like their funeral without looking out of place. Often people go to memorials, vigil, memorials, things like that to be a part of the whole process of death. They want to watch the emotions and reactions of the people there, see how it's impacting them," I say. "It also lets them gauge how much people know about what really happened, see if they overhear anything about the investigation, and even ask direct questions about if there are any suspects or what the police are doing."

"But if the person who killed them went to their memorials, wouldn't they want to stay as unnoticed as possible? Why would they write their name down?" Pat asks.

"They might be trying to hide in plain sight and throw off suspicion. After all, if it was someone who knew her personally, and that person just up and left town immediately without attending the funeral, that could be suspicious in itself. But people wouldn't suspect someone who seemed to be experiencing the pain of the loss along with the others. I'm not looking for any specific name and there might not be anything to be found in the books. But it's worth looking. Everything is worth following up on."

"Let me get Tricia's book for you. I'll call Sherry's son."

"Thank you."

She's back in a few moments and I sit down to look over the list of names while she is making the call.

"Anything stand out to you?" she asks when she comes back in the room.

I shake my head, flipping the next page. "Nothing so far. Did you get in touch with Sherry's son?"

"Yes. He's going to take pictures of the pages and send them to me. Should all be done in a few minutes."

"Great. Thank you. How about pictures? Do you have any pictures of the funeral, graveside service, or memorial?" I ask. "I know it's not something that's generally photographed, but if would be helpful if there are any."

"I have a few on my phone. But what might help you even more is the remembrance recording from the funeral home. There are cameras set up in the room of the memorial service and it's recorded. Usually they're recording a whole funeral service, but since Tricia didn't want a formal service, that was the alternative. I think it was all uploaded online as well. I can send you the link for it."

"That would be amazing," I say. "Thank you for your help."

For the second night in a row, I sit in bed thinking about the strange people at the funeral. I printed copies of the pictures Pat sent me along with scans of all the guest names written down at the services for both women. They're spread over my legs as I watch the video made of the event, scanning through to speed up the hours of footage.

I've managed to connect people to most of the names in the books, but there are still some guests I don't recognize and some names that I haven't linked. Several times, the odd group of men appear in the recording. The camera was programmed to move slowly back and forth, pausing and zooming in occasionally, which means they're caught in the same place each time, barely moving, not even speaking among themselves. But toward the end of the event, something catches my eye.

I go backward and watch the footage again. I'm on my third watch-through when Sam gets into bed beside me.

"Did you have to bring the funerals to bed with you?" he asks, eyeing the pictures on my lap.

"Yes," I say, then hold the tablet over toward him. "Look at this. These are those guys. I don't recognize those three, but this one is the one I said looked like it may be the same person as from Sherry's graveside service."

"He looks fairly generic to me," Sam says.

"I know. He is. But watch." The footage plays for a few seconds, then the group starts to walk toward the door of the room. "There. Look. He's limping. Watch the way he's walking. There's a very distinct dip in his step when he's on his left leg. I noticed that when he was at Sherry's funeral. I thought it looked like he was in pain. But seeing it now, it's probably a lingering injury of some kind. Either way, that's him. That's the same man. Somehow he's both a distant relative of Sherry and of Tricia."

"Okay, there's absolutely no way that's a coincidence."

"Right? And he showed up with two separate groups. That's just too bizarre to discount. Besides, one of them said his name was Finley. And there's no name by that in the guest book."

"Curiouser and curiouser…" he muses. "Hey, I just thought of something. Do you know who else was at both services?"

"Who?" I ask.

"You."

"I'm gonna smack you with this pillow," I grouse as he tosses his head back in laughter. But even as he starts winding down for the night, I scan the footage back so I can watch it again. I'm convinced now this is the same man who was at Sherry's funeral. Both groups are clearly linked and I believe they have something to do with the murders. Now I just need to find out who they are.

CHAPTER FOURTEEN

ERIC LOOKS EXHAUSTED ON OUR BIWEEKLY DINNER VIDEO CALL. He, Bellamy, and I used to spend every day together. We met before any of us had officially joined the Bureau and have been extremely close ever since. Well, it was more like both of them were close with me individually. They got along well enough, but I was the mutual friend between them—or so I thought. Turns out that when I moved away from Quantico back to Sherwood they'd started hanging out behind my back, and before I could even blink they'd shacked up, had a baby who's now a toddler, and now they're planning their wedding. It blew my mind with how sudden it happened, but I truly couldn't be happier for them. My two best friends could not have found better partners for each other than each other.

We spend holidays together and make an effort to visit as much as possible, but these dinners ensure we stay connected even when those visits fall fewer and farther between because of the pressures of our jobs. Sometimes Sam or even Xavier and Dean all join in, but tonight it's just me. Xavier and Dean are coming into town later and Sam is working a community event, so I'm alone at the house. Sam is less than pleased about this. For all his rumblings about not wanting me to go out alone and how often I stayed at home alone all day during the first few days of my recovery, Sam is jumpy about me being by myself at the house at night.

I can't really say I blame him for this one. We still haven't figured out how my first attacker got into the house that night, which means we don't have a way of preventing it from happening again. Having the video call with Eric and Bellamy makes Sam feel like I'm less alone and ensures if something does happen, at least they will know about it. Perhaps not the height of personal safety, but it's better than sitting on the couch and waiting.

"Long week?" I ask Eric. He groans and I laugh, twirling my fork in the plate of pasta we've all made so it's more like we're eating together. "Have you heard anything more about Roman Cleary's disappearance?" As soon as the question is out, I stop myself and put a hand over my mouth. "Oh. I'm sorry. Is that against the B and Eric Summit Agreement of not talking about work?"

"It's fine," Eric says.

"Don't worry about it," Bellamy adds from the side of the screen. "That's about the two of us not giving each other a blow-by-blow of all the horrific nonsense we encounter on a daily basis while cooking dinner or giving the baby a bath. Don't exactly want to chat lightly about international sex trafficking rings and drug pushers while browsing the farmer's market. That kind of thing."

"It's a good system," I tell her. "But if it's fair game for me to talk about it, I'm really curious about Roman."

Eric takes a bite of garlic bread and sets the rest down on the edge of his plate. He wipes his hand on a dark green linen napkin. There was a time when Bellamy's entire house was decorated in white. Everything was pure, sparkling white, right down to the blankets draped across the back of her pristine couch. It was like burying yourself in a snowball. But that has gone by the wayside a bit with Eric and baby Bebe in her life.

"It's still very much an active investigation," Eric says. "He's listed as missing, but we're extremely worried about his safety, and also the integrity of the work."

"Are you any closer to figuring out what happened? There hasn't been a ransom call or any demands or anything? And no indication of where he might have gone or what he might have been doing between getting on the plane and not showing up where he was supposed to?" I ask.

"We've been able to confirm that the correct flight was in place and he did get on the plane. According to the pilot, the flight went smoothly, perfectly according to plan. But then Roman was set to have a meeting with his contact at an appointed time the day after landing. He never got there, and he never reached out to that contact, his handler, or any of the go-betweens to note anything that would keep him from getting there at the right time. And nothing to indicate he was in any kind of danger," Eric tells me.

"And there's been no sign of him of any kind since," I say.

"None. The team has found a few small pieces of evidence, but I'm not convinced they're completely authentic. One of them is a note that was supposedly found in the airport close to the door he used to go out onto the tarmac. It says 'Team' on the front and the note inside is 'you'll never find me,' signed with 'R.C.' at the bottom."

"Roman Cleary," I say.

"Yeah. I understand it's his initials. But don't you think it's a bit convenient that it was found? The news has picked up the story of the missing agent. People are crawling around the airport and taking over pages of social media to talk about this case. But he left a note just sitting in some random spot in the airport? With just 'Team' written on the front?" He shakes his head, a dismissive look on his face. "No. That's just not something he would do. It's not something any agent would do. It's ridiculous to think he would believe his team would come to the airport looking for him and that he would decide the best way to communicate with them is with a note he jotted down on a piece of paper and just kind of stuck somewhere with the hopes they'd run across it."

"It does sound kind of ridiculous," I note. "But does that mean that the note has absolutely nothing to do with it? Was it maybe just some kid playing an admittedly pretty dark game of hide and seek on a layover? Or did someone write that note with the intention of people linking it to Roman Cleary and believing he wrote it to make people think he defected?"

"Or maybe whoever wrote it knew damn well if it was found, no one would actually think it was authentic."

"What would be the point of that?" I ask.

"To cause confusion?" he suggests. "I don't know. It's a really shitty situation. There's no doubt he's in serious danger. But we also have to think about the integrity of his work. His mission was compromised by him going missing. The information he had could have already ended up in the wrong hands. That could have very serious consequences."

"I know."

With dinner over, I go back into the living room and sit on the floor with the crime scene pictures from Sherry and Tricia's deaths spread across the coffee table. The inconsistencies with the scarf are still bothering me. I'm comparing the pictures of the scarf and of her body when Dean and Xavier come in.

"Hey," I say without looking up.

"Hi. What are you up to?" Dean asks.

"Sherry Talley and Tricia Donovan," I say, letting out a breath.

"Any leads?" Xavier asks.

"Nothing concrete. There are a couple things that are sticking with me, but I don't know what they mean or what to do with them."

I tell them about the men at both of the services and about the scarf.

"What's this?" Xavier asks, picking up a picture at the corner of the table.

I glance over at it. "The crime scene investigators found those in the backseat of Tricia's car. They look like donation items."

"They don't look right," he says.

"I know. I told Detective Coolidge that. I'm not convinced Tricia was at that hotel to donate things to anybody. It doesn't make sense considering the location. There aren't any hospitals, schools, or shelters anywhere around there, and I've never heard of her just showing up somewhere in the middle of the night to hand things out. But even if that was the case and she did sometimes just go offer things to people who were in need, those items don't make sense. Especially the squares. Those aren't washcloths. They're acrylic squares. That's not something she would be handing out to people," I tell him.

"Yeah, but it's more than that," he says. "There's something wrong with them. I can't place it. Is there any way I could see the actual ones? Do you have them?"

"I don't have them here, but I think they're at the police department. Her car is still impounded there. I could get in touch with the detective there. They weren't considered evidence, so they weren't transferred with the items I requested be sent here."

Early the next morning, Xavier and I make the drive to Willow Bridge where Detective Coolidge is waiting for us. He brings us into a property locker and pulls a cardboard crate off a shelf.

"These items aren't being considered evidence in the case. They're just personal property. But in order for them to be claimed, it has to be next of kin or at least a family member. We haven't been able to locate anyone to fit that yet. But you're welcome to look at them, obviously."

My mind immediately goes to the strangers at the memorial service. If they really were members of Tricia's extended family, they should have been contacted to come claim her personal property. Along with not having anything to do with the arrangements for her service or claiming the guestbook, the story of them being relatives is getting thinner and thinner.

We bring the crate into the conference room so we can take each of them out and look them over. I stand back while Xavier examines them.

"You were right. These squares aren't cotton," he says. "They aren't washcloths." He looks closer to one of the baby blankets and frowns. "These stitches..."

His voice trails off. He doesn't elaborate on what about them has caught his attention, but I can tell something is wrong with them.

"What do you think?" I ask.

"I need to go back to the workshop," he tells me. "I need to show you something."

Feeling like I'm more than making up for lost time in terms of being out and about, I get back in the car and start the long drive back to Mount Percy. A couple of hours later, we arrive at the workshop and Xavier leads me directly to the distribution room. He goes to a large container in a corner and reaches inside. He pulls out a few items, checks tags attached to them, then selects one and brings it over to me.

"Tricia made this. It's a design she was working on just before her death. I can tell the items that were in her car were made by somebody else. She did not stitch any of those."

"But that really isn't all that strange, is it? The donations aren't always delivered by the individuals who made them," I point out.

"That's when it comes to normal donations. It wouldn't make sense for her to have this kind of rogue delivery for things she didn't make. Everyone here stitches things with particular recipients in mind. Maybe not an exact group or an exact individual, but they know the recipient groups that have been identified and receive donations. Trisha takes... took... integrity extremely seriously. She would never donate something to someone she knew the stitcher wouldn't want to receive it."

"I thought the whole point was to help anyone who needed it."

"At its core, it is. But the truth is, even people who do work like this can have biases in their soul. It's why sometimes you'll see on the back of the tags a little note about who the maker wanted to receive it. It might be that they specifically want it to go to a chemo ward in a hospital because they battled cancer and want to help others. Or they might specify that because they don't want it to go to a religious organization that they disagree with. Trisha was very serious about respecting that. She would never take pieces that were made by other people and donate them to unauthorized recipients," he explains.

"What's going on?"

Lois and Pat come into the room carrying stacks of items to distribute into the plastic bins. Lois has a concerned, almost suspicious look on her face. She takes several hats from Pat and puts them in their bin, then adds a stack of baby blankets to the next.

"If I showed you some pictures of items, do you think you could identify who made them?" I ask.

"Not necessarily," Pat says. "I can usually identify telltale things, certain signature techniques of certain members, but I wouldn't be able to tell you right off the bat who made every single item."

"Why do you ask?" Lois asks.

"Some items were found in the back of Tricia's car and Xavier doesn't think she made them. I would like to try to identify who did," I say.

"I'll look at them," Pat offers. "I might remember who turned some things in."

"Sure," Lois nods. "Some of the other ladies are here, too. I can ask them to look."

"That would be great."

I'm feeling a bit of optimism as the women pass around pictures of the items that were in the back of Tricia's car, but one by one they shake their heads and tell me they don't know who made them.

"And none of you knew she was going there that night? Or that she had been there before? She didn't mention a new recipient group, or maybe a sister organization in Maryland that she could have been working with?" I ask.

More denials take away every shred of optimism I might have felt.

"I told you," Xavier says. "She wouldn't have done that. You don't paint with another artist's paintbrush, and you don't take another man's knife to a street fight."

"What does this mean?" Pat asks.

"It means there's more to this situation than we've unraveled and there are still questions to be answered," I say.

"I can't deal with this," Lois says.

She walks out of the room and I notice a couple of other visibly upset women follow her. I know this isn't easy for them. This is still raw for them. I can understand them feeling sensitive to it, but the reaction still stands out to me.

"We're going to go," I say.

"You don't have to," Pat says. "This has all just been a lot."

"I know," I say. "And the longer it takes to resolve it, the harder it's going to be. I want to find who is responsible and end this. For all of us." I gesture at the piece Xavier took out of the container. "Is it alright if we bring this with us?"

"Of course," Pat says, sounding confused at the request but not wanting to deny me something that might help. I start toward the door, but her voice stops me. "What scarf was she wearing?"

I turn back to look at her. "Tricia?"

Pat nods. "Yes. That night. You were asking Shawna if she always wore them and how she wore them. It just made me wonder," her fingertips touch the side of her neck and run down over her collarbones and along the sides of her chest. "Which one was the last one she wore?"

She meets my eyes. There's no hesitation in them. No wavering. But there's also no welling of emotion. I know the sadness is there. I've seen it in her since the night I was called to Sherry's murder scene. But in this moment, any hint of it is far in the back of her eyes. Somehow it makes her unflinching gaze more unsettling.

"It was periwinkle," I say.

"Oh. That was one of her favorite colors."

CHAPTER FIFTEEN

"Can I see the scarf?" Xavier asks when we drive away from the workshop. "You said it's here?"

"It's being held as evidence, but you can look at it. I had it transferred here to have it with the evidence from Sherry's case. We won't be able to take it with us."

Xavier looks displeased but dips his head in acknowledgement and we head for the police station. He stands over the scarf, looking down at the discolored stitches. He leans close to examine it and stretches it out so he can look over the entire thing. I can see the gears turning in his head and know he's on his way to figuring something out, but there's no use asking him right now. He's not going to say anything about it until he's ready. It's just as well. The way his mind works it's unlikely he'd be able to fully explain it to me at this point anyway. He needs the time as much for figuring out how to lay it all out for other people to understand as he does unraveling it for himself.

"I'll be right back. I need to make a call," I tell him. "Don't try to steal the scarf, they'll know."

Outside, I call Coolidge.

"Emma," he says. "I feel like I just saw you."

I manage a half-laugh at his attempt at either humor or being charming. "You mentioned you're looking for a next of kin to give Tricia's personal affects to. I have an alternative for you. Pat Ledger. She worked closely with Tricia at the organization for many years and they were very dear friends. Pat actually arranged her memorial service. She would be an appropriate choice for handling the belongings."

"Thanks for looking out, but that's not going to be necessary," Coolidge says.

"Oh?"

"A family member already came and claimed the items," he says.

I grip my phone tighter in my hand. "A family member? Who?"

I know that isn't true. Despite what was said at the memorial service, I know Tricia had no family. But I keep my suspicions to myself. I have a strong sense that elements of this investigation need to be kept close to my chest. The difficulty with a case with no strong leads isn't just that it's harder to find footing and get to the resolution. It also means not knowing who can be trusted and who is looking over my shoulder for their own benefit. I feel like I'm walking on a very thin wire right now and can't risk even the slightest misstep.

"I'll have to check the sign-out sheet. I'll give you a call back," he says.

"Thanks." I hang up and immediately call Pat. "Do you know if anyone went and picked up Tricia's belongings?"

I try not to put any kind of emotion in my voice. I want it to sound like I'm just wondering if they've been picked up, not that I'm concerned about who might have done it.

"Tricia's things? From Maryland?" she asks.

"Yes. The things from her car," I say.

"No. Not that I know of. I know I certainly didn't. I can't imagine who would want to go all that way to get them. Would they just turn them over to an acquaintance?" she asks.

I find the choice of words interesting. She didn't ask if they would turn them over to a friend but specifically an acquaintance.

"Well, without family to transfer belongings to, it can be more difficult to determine the chain of custody for those items," I explain. "And Tricia didn't have a family."

It's not exactly accurate, but that isn't the point. I want to hear Pat's response.

"That's true. I hope there wasn't anything significant in there," she says. "I wouldn't want to think it could end up in the wrong hands."

I go back to the conference room. Xavier is leaning down close to the scarf again.

"It reminds me of the sampler blanket hanging in the workshop," I tell him.

His eyes shift to me then back to the scarf. "Me, too. It's not like any of the scarves I've seen her wear."

"It's not like any of the ones in the picture albums, either," I tell him. "And the way she was wearing it has been bothering me."

"The way she was wearing it?" he asks.

"The medical examiner told me she had it tucked under her shirt, coming down over her shoulders rather than around her neck," I tell him. "It wasn't visible at all until she was undressed for the post-mortem. It looked like she had gotten hot and wanted it out of the way."

"No," Xavier says. "She didn't wear them like that. Ever. If she was hot, she would have just taken it off. The whole point of wearing them was so that they would be seen. There wouldn't be any reason to have it out of the way like that."

My phone rings and I answer.

"Hey, Coolidge."

"Hey. I got that name for you. Dennis Wicks."

"Dennis Wicks," I repeat.

"Yep. Mean anything to you?" he asks.

"No. But thanks. I'll keep looking."

Xavier is silent on the drive back to my house. He goes right to the table of crime scene pictures, pushing past Dean who has his feet propped on the corner as he eats a bowl of pasta on the couch.

"What's going on?" he asks, lowering his feet. "What is he looking at?"

"Pictures of the scarf Tricia Donovan was wearing when she was murdered. There's something about it that's bothering him. It hasn't sat well with me since I first saw it, but I can't figure out what it is," I say. I drop down beside my cousin and snitch one of the noodles from his bowl. "What are you eating?"

"I made some pesto. It's in the kitchen."

"Which means I have to stand up again. And I'm recovering from a head injury." I look over at him and he gives me a look. "No? Can't pull that card?"

"Not when you're out investigating all day."

"Alright. Well, fair enough." I launch myself off the couch. "Anybody want some?" Dean hands me his nearly empty bowl. "X?"

Xavier doesn't respond. He's too engrossed in the pictures, lining up several images of the scarf alongside the partially finished project we'd taken from the workshop. I go to the kitchen and refill Dean's bowl then fill one for my own to carry into the living room. There are pictures I haven't shown Xavier and I hesitate to take them out. I feel like he needs to see them, but I don't want to upset him. Setting my bowl down on the end table, I pull a folder out from under the coffee table.

"Xavier," I say and wait until he looks up at me so I know he's paying attention. "I have pictures of Tricia. Would you want to see how she was wearing the scarf?"

He doesn't hesitate before nodding. "Yes."

He takes the folder and opens it, adding the pictures to the collection he's looking at. No emotion crosses his face. He's relegated the reality of Tricia's death to a place in his mind where it doesn't bother him. As long as he leaves it there, he won't be sad. He may have already used up the sadness he would expend on these deaths. This isn't like when Millie died or the way I see his face change when he talks about the death of his friend Andrew, the murder that wrongly sent him to prison for nearly a decade. It sounds harsh to anyone who doesn't know Xavier, but I understand it. He cares. Very much. But in the way that he can. It's not like other people. He mourns through finding out what happened.

While Xavier pores over the pictures of the scarf and of Tricia, lamenting not having the physical item with him, I eat and watch TV with Dean. He's still immersed when I finish, so I go over the guest books again, trying to find the name Dennis Wicks. It doesn't sound familiar and I don't find it among the mourners.

Xavier gets up at one point and goes to my office, coming back with paper and a pen. I've detoured back to the case I'm investigating with Jeffrey when my phone ringing breaks my concentration. Thinking it might be Sam letting me know he's wrapping things up and will be heading home, I pick it up without looking at it.

"Hey, Babe," I say.

"Emma?"

The shaky voice coming through the phone isn't Sam.

"Lois?"

"I—I need to speak with you," she says.

"Alright," I say.

"No. It can't be over the phone. I need to see you in person. It's urgent. Can you meet me at the workshop?" she asks.

"Of course. I'm in Sherwood, but I can meet you there in an hour."

I changed into my pajamas thinking I was just going to be at home and wanted to be comfortable, so I rush up the steps to my room to change. I come back down the steps securing my gun to my hip.

"I have to go to Mount Percy. I don't know how long I'll be there," I tell him.

"Do you want me to go with you?" Dean asks.

I shake my head. "No. It's fine. I'm just going to meet with Lois. I'll call you when I know what's going on."

"Emma, hold on," Xavier says before I get to the door. "I might have found something."

He sets two pictures of the scarf in front of me, then the partially finished piece from the workshop. He runs his finger along rows of stitches in the pictures and then the piece he's been holding. He then shows me the screen of his computer where he's pulled up images on the organization website and zoomed in on them.

"I don't know what I'm looking at," I say.

"I think there's a code in the stitches."

CHAPTER SIXTEEN

'M TAKEN ABACK BY THE REVELATION AND I SHAKE MY HEAD, CONfused. "A code? What do you mean?"

"Look. These patterns repeat consistently throughout the pieces, but they don't make sense given the full context of each item. They don't flow correctly and there are changes that aren't something a skilled, experienced fiber artist like Tricia would do."

"You said she sometimes used her scarves as a way to experiment with different stitches and patterns," I say.

"She did. But she wouldn't put together odd patterns like this in several different pieces. These patterns of stitches just show up randomly among established patterns. But they aren't in every piece with those stitches or of that style."

"Xavier, everybody who stitches for them changes up what they make and how they look. It keeps things interesting."

I can feel the time slipping and am getting impatient.

"Right. But look." He changes the image on the screen. "These are already divided up by recipient. The unusual patterns of stitches are consistent by recipient. They always show up in items made for specific groups, but not in others."

I'm stunned, but still not sure what to think of what he's showing me. "So this was some sort of message or code to a specific group?"

He tilts his head. "That's what it looks like."

"Have you made out any of the words?" I ask.

"I think I might have, but I'm not sure yet. I'm still working on it."

"Keep going. I have to get to the workshop. Call me if you figure anything out," I say.

He agrees, and I run out to the car. With this new information in mind, I'm even more curious to know what Lois has to say. When I arrive at the workshop Lois and Shawna are standing outside in the parking lot. Considering the tension between the two of them during my meeting with the women, I'm surprised to see them together. They don't look particularly close or friendly, standing slightly apart and each seemingly lost in her own thoughts.

Both look extremely upset. Shawna stands with her arms wrapped around herself, rocking slightly back and forth while Lois occasionally goes over to the door and peeks inside the darkened workshop. She comes toward me first when I climb out of my car.

"What's going on?" I ask.

"The workshop has been broken into," Lois tells me.

"While you were here?" I ask, heightened concern rising up in me.

"No," Shawna says. "We were here working late with a couple of the others. Several of them left and I was in the back doing a couple of last-minute things. Maude came back in and said Lois was having trouble with her car, so I went out to see if there was anything I could do to help."

"Why did they come for you?" I ask.

"My dad was a mechanic," she says. "I picked up a few things watching him while I was growing up. I wouldn't say I'm an expert or anything, but I know enough that I can fix little things or sometimes pinpoint what's going wrong."

"My car has been giving me trouble for a couple of weeks," Lois adds. "I keep meaning to bring it in to get looked at, but with everything..."

"I'm sure it hasn't exactly been at the top of your priority list," I say.

"Anyway, I couldn't get it started, so Lois called the tow truck," Shawna says.

"They said it was going to take a few hours and none of the others could stay that late, but Shawna offered to bring me home so I could wait there and then I could have my neighbor bring me to the mechanic's shop tomorrow morning. We got to talking on the way and I invited her in to have a cup of tea. With everything that happened the other night I was feeling like I might need to make amends a bit. It was a little while later when we realized the door to the workshop hadn't been locked."

"It's my fault," Shawna says. "I came outside to help and didn't go back in. Everybody else already had all of their things with them and I'd grabbed my bag so I'd have the little flashlight I carry with me. I didn't even think about it."

She looks devastated and Lois finally steps up beside her to wrap an arm around her.

"You didn't do it on purpose. You were trying to help. I should have thought to ask if it was locked," Lois says.

This is a lovely demonstration of support and camaraderie, but I'm very aware of standing in the parking lot and not having any details about why they called me.

"What happened after that? Why am I here?" I ask.

Both women look up at me with stung expressions in their eyes, but Shawna wipes her tears and points toward the side of the building like she's indicating the alley behind it.

"We came back and went to the back door. It was unlocked, like I thought. Then we realized someone had gone inside," she says.

"What made you think that? Was there a car here? Did you see someone?" I ask.

She shakes her head. "No. Even Lois's car had already been taken."

"Show me what you saw," I say.

They lead me inside and when Lois turns on the lights nothing looks any different than it has every other time I've been here. The front room is neat and organized. The white board still has Tricia's handwriting in the corner. We continue through to the yarn room and I notice the first signs of something being off. It's nothing dramatic. A few skeins of yarn seem to have fallen from the shelves and are on the floor. A couple of the baskets of remnants have been tipped over, the balls of leftover yarn tumbling across the floor. It's not chaos, but definitely noticeable in the usually organized space.

Even so, I don't feel comfortable with them going further into the workshop without me going through it first. They mentioned it was the back door that was left unlocked, yet we went through the front door, meaning if someone did come into the shop, they could still be inside.

"Alright, ladies, I need you to wait in here for me. Don't touch anything or clean anything up. Just stand here while I check everything out really fast," I order them.

They both gasp, stepping into the middle of the yarn room so they are in the brightest part of the room with their backs toward a wall rather than the hallway on either side. I notice the bathroom door is closed and walk over to it. I tap on it, my hand resting on my gun.

"Hello?" I call. "FBI. If anyone is in there, make yourself known."

There's no response and I open the door. The room is empty, so I leave the door open and continue down the hallway. Following basic protocol, I have my gun in my hand as I go through each room, sweeping the interior to make sure that no one is hiding inside. The conference room and kitchen both seem to be at the same level of disruption as the yarn room. A few things are out of place and the surfaces look a bit messy, but it's not extreme. Nothing is broken or seriously damaged.

The distribution room at the far back of the building is the most disheveled area by far. Rather than neatly placed in the bins, items are piled up beside them, some on the floor. The table in the middle is spread with a few dozen hats, blankets, and scarves. The container that held the partially finished item Xavier told me Tricia was working on for a new project is laying on its side. It's empty, but I notice a couple of the things that had been in there are now draped across the chairs on that side of the room.

Someone has definitely been inside and caused some mischief, but I don't see anything blatantly threatening or dangerous. I make sure the back door is secure and then go back to the yarn room. Lois and Shawna are whispering to each other, still looking very distressed.

"No one is here," I report. "I saw what you were talking about. If everything was like it usually is when you left, something definitely happened. It doesn't look like anything too severe. Why did you call me? Why didn't you call the police as soon as you suspected someone had broken into the workshop?"

"We didn't think they would take it seriously," Lois says. "Like you said, it doesn't look like much, but we know what it's supposed to look like. We know someone came in here and did all this. We thought since you are an FBI agent and the one in charge of investigating the murders of two people who spent all their time here at the workshop you would be the one who could help us the most."

"I understand that. And I'm glad you called me," I reassure them. "But you still need to talk to the police about it. If you are really sure someone was in the workshop and something is wrong, you need to file a police report about it. This could have something to do with the murders, but it also might not. Either way, there needs to be a formal record of what happened."

They look at each other with grim looks on their faces. I make the call and wait with them until the officers arrive. I don't recognize either of them, so I introduce myself and give them a brief overview of the situation before leaving them to speak with Lois and Shawna. While they give their statements, I go to look at the sampler blanket hanging on the wall. My eyes scan over the stitches, trying to catch patterns beyond just the sections of different stitches making up the overall piece. I wish I'd taken pictures of the stitch sequence Xavier showed me.

I consider video calling him, but I rethink it. I don't want the women, or the officers, to overhear us talking about the possibility of what Xavier may have uncovered. This isn't something I can come right out and ask about. Instead, I roam around the shop, looking at each of the samplers hanging on the walls and the pieces set up as examples in different corners of the space. I take pictures of them, sending them to Xavier. I try to note different colors and patterns that stand out to me. Pieces that seem oddly placed or that seem like that don't exactly make sense. I don't know nearly as much about this stuff as Xavier does, so I'm sure there are things I would never notice, but that in of itself feels significant. If I don't notice the things that he does, maybe others don't as well. And that could be the entire point.

The officers stop into the room where I'm standing to tell me they're finished and I thank them but don't walk out with them. Instead, I wait for Shawna and Lois to come in and find me taking in a smaller sampler blanket framed in the kitchen.

"It's beautiful, isn't it?" Shawna asks. "It's my favorite."

"Did you make it?" I ask.

She laughs. "Oh. No. That's a bit more patience than I have, I'm afraid. I'm far more of a simple stitcher myself."

"Don't sell yourself short," Lois says. "Shawna makes wonderful hats and has started doing adorable little toys to hand out to children."

"Did you make the squishy little turtles?" I ask.

Her eyes light up a little and she nods. "Yes. I love those."

I smile. "A whole bag of those ended up at Sam's office. They've been bringing them to kids in the hospital or their 911 calls. He's planning on bringing more of them to a community event that's coming up in a few weeks and handing them out to the kids. They are so adorable."

"I'm so glad to hear that."

She seems thrilled by the compliment, though she's trying to keep it down. It has the effect I was going for, putting her at ease and priming her to talk more about From Heart to Heart. I don't want to reveal anything, but also want to give enough suggestion that if there is something more happening within the ranks of stitchers, they'll have an idea I know something. I want it to act as an invitation for them to tell me more.

"It must really be nice knowing you help people with all you do," I say. "All of you."

Both women nod.

"It's rewarding," Lois says. "And I love doing crochet so much that it feels almost selfish. I remember one time a neighbor of mine was talking about all the volunteer work he did and for a moment I just stood there admiring him so much because he did so much good. I was thinking to myself that I should really get involved in something like he did because I wanted to do good for other people, too." She laughs. "I really didn't think about this. I enjoy it so much, it feels like I was doing it for myself."

I laugh along with her. "I can see that. I'm sure you all help even more than people realize. People see the new babies that have blankets and those who live on the streets able to stay warm because of handmade hats. Scarves. But it's more than that. There's so much benefit to what everyone does here."

I wait for a reaction, even the slightest one, that would suggest they know anything that hasn't yet been said about the donations or a code within the stitches.

"It's why we do it," Shawna says. "Even if they don't talk about it much, I believe every person who contributes here has a very personal reason for doing it that's more than just wanting to do something for other people."

"I agree.," Lois says. "Making something with your own hands, everything we put into each item, just… means something."

The conversation is uncomfortable, but I don't know if I'm the only one in that place. The other women look at me with emotion-softened eyes and seem to feel like they've found a cozy spot to nestle down in, something that they can talk about without having to keep delving into the horror of the murders or the fear that the same thing could happen to them.

"It does," I say. "And I really admire you all so much for continuing on. It takes courage and dedication to keep going in times like these. Remember when I said that killings are often done to send a message? This sends a message, too. But I also need you to remember that you should be cautious. It's important that everyone take steps to keep themselves and the others safe. There are still so many questions, and until they are answered, no one should be at the workshop at night. I noticed you haven't changed the locks or added any extras, and you really need to do that. I would even consider putting up security cameras as an added precaution.

"I want you to remember that officially there is still no indication that the workshop itself has anything to do with the crimes. But considering the nature of the victims' involvement here, and the apparent break-in tonight, it's important to cover all the bases. I can help you in any way you need me to. I happen to have a fairly considerable amount of experience with the need for security."

I meant it as a lighthearted comment, something to lift some of the fear, but my own words fall heavy into the pit of my stomach. Even with all of the security measures, I still wasn't safe in my own home.

"We will," Shawna says. "Thank you for everything you're doing for us."

"Is there anything else we can do?" Lois asks.

I'm about to tell her there isn't, but I shift. "Actually, do you have anything else that Sherry or Tricia made that hasn't been donated yet? Like you said, when something is made by your own hands, it means so much. I think having items that they created around will really help us feel connected to them. It will help keep the investigation focused."

CHAPTER SEVENTEEN

WALK BACK OUT TO MY CAR WITH THE FEELING OF EYES TRACING
down the back of my neck. It isn't Lois and Shawna. They're ahead
of me, already in Shawna's car. I watched them lock the doors to the
workshop and then go to the car to make sure they got there safely. But
now I can feel someone watching me.

Shaking off the feeling, I put the tote bag full of stitched items in
the passenger seat of my car and climb behind the wheel. The first thing
I do, just like my father taught me when I was barely starting to drive,
is lock the doors. I don't remember him ever giving me a reason. I only
remember him telling me I should always look through the windows
into the back seat before I get in the car, then lock the doors immediately. Before putting on my seat belt. Before starting the car. Before
anything.

"Ass down, lock down," he would say.

My mother would not have appreciated him saying that to his fifteen-year-old. But they probably would have laughed about it when I wasn't in the room.

With the doors locked, I glance in the rearview mirror. I don't see anyone. But the feeling is still there. I drive away from it, waving at the ladies as I go, heading home.

Xavier is still at the table when I get there. Dean is asleep on the couch and I hear water running upstairs. Sam's home.

"What happened?" Xavier asks.

"Someone broke into the workshop," I tell him. "Actually, they didn't break in. Shawna left the door unlocked when they left for the evening and someone just went in. They didn't damage anything and as far as I know nothing was stolen. I wasn't there when they were giving their formal statements to the police. But they did go through the rooms and toss stuff around."

"Like they were looking for something," he says.

"That's what it seems like. Do you think there's something there worth looking for?" I ask.

"My understanding of the code isn't perfect. I've been trying to piece it together. You were absolutely right. That sampler blanket is a cipher. But it's incomplete. There are still gaps," he says.

"Gaps?" I ask.

"The sampler does reveal pieces of the code. But as I was working it out, I realized what was being spelled out doesn't make sense. Which means there's more to the code than just that blanket. The other samplers might have something to do with it, but I'm still trying to work it out."

"Maybe these will help." I put the tote on the floor beside the table and pull out a couple of the things Lois and Shawna gave me. "These were made by Tricia and Sherry. Not too long before they were murdered, I'd have to guess since they were still at the workshop."

"Where did they get them?" Xavier asks. "Did you see where they were kept?"

"Just in the distribution room," I say. "A couple of things were in the bins like everything else. This one," I pick up a shawl, "was in a box that was being packed for a recipient. Apparently, Sherry made it. Shawna knew because she helped her pick the yarn out. And then this one," I show him a scarf.

"Tricia," he says.

"Mmhmm. It was on display next to the white board in the front room."

"Right where anyone could have seen it or taken it," he says. "Exactly."

The sun is starting to come up when I finally crawl into bed next to Sam. Some of the smell of soap and shampoo is still clinging to his skin and I nuzzle close to breathe him in for the few seconds before I fall asleep.

I only let myself sleep for a few hours and when I get up Xavier is back where I left him next to the table.

"Did you sleep?" I ask.

"Some," he says.

It's the only word I hear from him for the rest of the day. While he continues to examine the items and compare them to what he has already deciphered, I turn my attention to digging deeper into From Heart to Heart. I realize what I know about them and everything they do is only surface level. It's the glossy information sheets kept in a basket on the front desk and the professional website that encourages anyone interested in the fiber arts to come and stitch with them. I know it's a façade. At least some of it. I just don't know what's behind it.

I bring up the list of recipients and clients the group works with so I can delve further into each one of them. I need as much detail as I can get so I can try to find links, inconsistencies, anything that might start answering some of our questions. The list has everything I would expect.

Battered women's shelters, homeless shelters, halfway houses, homes for families of children in the hospital, hospitals, hospice centers, treatment clinics, schools, community centers...

I read everything I can about the groups, the people in charge, and their connection to the charity. Names that appeared on the guest books from the memorial services stand out to me and I take note of them, finding as many pictures as I can so I can identify them in the pictures and remembrance footage. But one name that rises up out of the description of a community center doesn't correspond to either of the lists: Margaux Lennox.

It seems so familiar, but I can't place it. It's an unusual name, something that would catch attention, but it isn't just that. I know that name. I say it out loud, hoping the feeling of it on my lips will remind me of saying it before. Nothing comes to mind and I drop my head forward into my hand. The sound of the door opening makes me lift it again. Sam comes in carrying two large paper bags. The smell of Thai food makes my stomach growl. I can't even remember if I'd eaten since breakfast.

"Hey, babe," he says. "I called you a couple of times."

"Oh," I say, reaching for my phone. The screen is cluttered with missed notifications. "I'm sorry. I've been so lost in this I must have just blocked it out. I hope it wasn't important."

"Not from me. I was just checking to see if you wanted me to bring something home for dinner. I figured when you didn't answer that meant you were doing something, so that probably meant yes," he says. "I hope Thai sounds good."

"It sounds amazing," I tell him, scanning through my notifications to make sure I didn't miss anything critical.

I know if there had been anything especially urgent there are other ways to get in touch with me. But I don't usually miss calls or texts. Too much can happen too quickly. Other than a couple of texts from Bellamy about wedding planning she probably isn't expecting a response to and an email with more footage to go over, the other notifications are mainly throwaways. I let out a heavy breath and toss the phone onto the table.

"Where are the guys?" Sam asks.

"At a movie," I tell him. "Dean said Xavier hadn't blinked in four hours and was starting to worry about him. He didn't say anything on his way out so I can't fully guarantee he actually knows where he is or what's happening, but it will do him good to get away from all this for a little while."

Sam takes my hand and pulls me up off the floor, leading me into the dining room. He sets the bags down and I unpack them while he gets plates and drinks.

"You know, it might not be the worst idea for you to take his lead on that," he says.

"Not knowing where I am or what's happening?" I ask.

"Maybe not that part. But getting away from that for a while."

"It's my case, Sam. I'm leading the investigation. Getting away from it really isn't an option."

We dish up food and sit down, choosing the seats beside each other rather than across the table. It feels like I've spent so little time with my husband since all this began. It feels good just to sit next to him. I wish I could say it's without distractions, but that's far from the truth.

"Has anything else come up?" he asks.

"I had both McGraw and Coolidge run records checks to bring up any crimes or reports that have any connection to the recipient organizations that work with From Heart to Heart. There were some, but they were all easily explained away. A couple of angry husbands. Mental disturbance. Maybe a petty theft or public intoxication from a homeless resident of a shelter. Nothing that would make any sense to connect to these murders. Neither Tricia nor Sherry had anything to do with any of those criminals or the cases. There's no connection," I explain. "I want to say that's good because at least they weren't murdered because of their involvement in something they loved."

"But it's not good because it still leaves you with all the questions," Sam finishes for me.

"Exactly. I'm getting beyond frustrated. These two murders are clearly linked. They have to be. Yet, there's nothing to go on other than what Xavier has started to uncover with this code. But even that leads me nowhere. Knowing about it is a start, but until we know what it says and why it exists, there's nothing I can really do with it."

Sam cups my face with one hand and rubs his thumb across my cheek. "You're going to figure it out. I know you will. I mean, come on. You know who you are, right? You're Agent Emma Griffin. This is what you do."

I chuckle at his pep talk. I want it to make me feel better, but I just feel like the questions and blank spots are piling up so much in my head it's going to split if I don't start finding ways to get them out.

The next morning I'm sitting out on the porch sipping coffee and breathing in the cool, damp air of the earliest hours when Xavier comes out to join me. He's carrying a blanket he drapes over both of us and sits silently staring across the street for a few minutes. I don't know if I'm waiting for him to say something or not. Sometimes he sits with me like this and then gets up and leaves after a while without saying anything at all.

But this time he looks over at me.

"The smaller sampler blankets are pieces of the larger cipher. They work together like gears," he says.

"Like gears?"

"One moves the other, which moves the next, making the entire thing go. What one does dictates the next. The messages are coded in layers that have to be deciphered one bit at a time and they don't always work within each individual piece. Meaning some of the messages are larger and have to be pieced together with several different items, likely using different versions of the cipher for each." He takes a breath. "Something is happening in that workshop, Emma. There are words and phrases that suggest a covert operation and I haven't figured out yet what it is."

"A covert operation?" I ask. "Like a crime ring? Money laundering? Smuggling?"

He shakes his head, still not looking at me. "I don't know. But there's something happening. And it was enough to kill for."

CHAPTER EIGHTEEN

THE FEELING OF BEING WATCHED COMES BACK AS I'M DRIVING TO A nearby women's shelter. I've made appointments to go in and talk with as many of the recipients of recent donations as I can. Some of them have been extremely reluctant to get involved. I tell them I understand even though I don't. They express such gratitude for what the organization does for them and gush about how much the donations are appreciated, but aren't willing to stand up for the same people who brought them those donations.

I was able to convince them to send me lists of the donations they have received most recently and I intend on continuing to ask for their participation in the investigation. But since I have no evidence that indicates any of them are involved or would have any information that could reasonably suggest involvement, I cannot compel them to do or say anything.

The sense that I'm being tailed stays with me throughout the drive. It doesn't have the aggressive, dangerous feeling as when the still-unidentified green car followed me, but there is the distinct sense that there's someone nearby. It's a familiar feeling, one that reminds me particularly of the years before I moved back to Sherwood. In those days, before I knew the darkest of my family secrets, before I really understood where I came from and why I am who I am, there was a near perpetual feeling that someone was watching. I was never really alone. I know now why, but the eeriness hasn't left me.

I don't necessarily feel threatened by it, but I don't like not knowing who is around me or why they're invested in knowing where I am and what I'm doing. I pay attention to the cars around me and watch to see if any of them are still close when I park outside the shelter. I don't see anyone around, but I stay vigilant as I head inside.

The woman I speak with is visibly shaken talking about Sherry's death. She was her contact with the organization and always accepted the donations from her. She tells me a little more about her, giving me insight into her personality and the strong hint that what Shawna said about the people who participate in this charity are doing it for a more personal reason than just helping others. Sherry did this for a purpose that went deeper than just the desire to provide comfort and support.

I try the same technique I did with Lois and Shawna, asking leading questions to try to draw out any hidden details she might be able to offer, but she gives me nothing else and I leave, making my way directly to the next recipient on my list.

The feeling of being tailed stays with me throughout the rest of my appointments and as I make my way back home, but I don't see anyone follow me into the neighborhood. As I drive down the street, I notice Janet across the street in her front yard getting her mail. She waves and I roll down the window.

"Hi, Janet! How are you?"

"Emma! It's so good to see you up and about," she says, coming toward the car with a handful of envelopes and magazines.

"I've been getting out more and more," I tell her.

"I'm so glad. You look fantastic."

I doubt she's telling the truth. My hair is thrown up into a ponytail and the slight amount of makeup I put on this morning can't cover the exhaustion and stress I'm feeling. But I'm alive and the signs of my injuries have faded, so I suppose it's relative.

"Thank you. We need to catch up soon."

"Absolutely. How about a game night next week when Paul gets home from his trip?" she suggests.

"That sounds great."

"Looking forward to it." She steps back from the car and holds up her mail. "I noticed the driver deliver a package to your porch. I hope it's something fun!"

"A package?" I ask. "I don't know. Maybe Sam ordered something. Thanks. I'll make sure I grab it. Have a good day!"

I drive the short distance to my driveway and pull in. From there I can see the box sitting on the porch. Dean and Xavier must not have come out of the house since it was delivered. Just opening the door would have hit it. I scoop it up before opening the door, noticing there is no return address.

"What's that?" Xavier asks when I walk in the house with the box.

"I don't know. It was delivered today. It's addressed to me, but I didn't order anything. There's no return address."

"Maybe you shouldn't open it," Dean says, coming in from the kitchen. "Considering everything that's been going on."

"USPS doesn't deliver package bombs," Xavier says in complete seriousness. "They tend to be sensitive about that sort of thing."

"Thank you, Xavier," Dean says.

I take out my phone and call Sam.

"Babe, there was a package on the porch when I got home. Did you order something under my name?"

"Yeah. Those shirts for the bowling fundraiser, remember? I used your account so I didn't have to make a new one. They were supposed to come today," he tells me. "How big is the box?"

"I mean, it's not small," I say.

"That must be it, then."

I give Dean a knowing look. "Alright. Thanks, babe. Are you going to be home soon?"

"Should be another couple of hours, but then I'll be there."

"See you later. I love you."

I hang up and relay the explanation to Dean. Setting the box down on the dining room table, I take a pair of scissors out of the sideboard and slit the tape on either side. Instead of the packing slip I'm expecting on top of a layer of plain brown wrapping paper, I find a white notecard.

"What's that?" Dean asks.

I shrug. "It just says 'D.W.' and then 'M' in parentheses." I flip the card over before handing it to him. "It's blank on the other side." I move the layer of wrapping paper and the breath streams out of my lungs. "Holy shit."

"What?" Xavier asks. He comes to the side of the table and looks into the box. "Are those..."

"The donation items from Tricia's car," I say. The letters on the note-card click in my head. "D.W. Dennis Wicks. That's the name Detective Coolidge said was on the sign-out sheet from when her personal property was claimed."

"What's the 'M?'" Dean asks.

I shake my head. "I don't know." I reach into the box and start pulling out the clear plastic bags the items were placed in before being shipped. "What the hell? Who is this person? And why did they send these things to me? They know who I am and where I live, obviously. Why didn't they just approach me?"

Xavier opens one of the bags and takes out a stack of acrylic squares. "There isn't a single doubt in my mind that Tricia didn't make these. Which means she either brought decoys for some reason, or the real items she brought were swapped out."

"Her scarf," I say. "Like you said, she didn't just happen to have it under her outfit. There is far more significance to it than that. Tricia wasn't just wearing it. She was *hiding* it. Whoever killed her was probably looking for that scarf. And I think that's exactly why these things were swapped out. If she brought them herself to throw somebody off, who? And why? And is the person she intended to throw off the same one who killed her?"

CHAPTER NINETEEN

Meeting place
Protection
Arrangements have been made
Three in the delivery
Down by the water
Pivot, iron fish swimming left now
Avoid blue and purple. Rx Thursday
Lost.

THE LIST OF WORDS AND PHRASES DECIPHERED FROM THE CODED pieces, written out on pieces of butcher paper taped to the wall, is getting longer. It's the easiest way to organize them and keep them visible, but I don't like them being there at night or if the house is empty. If we're not going to be actively using the list, I make Xavier take the paper off the wall and roll it up so it can be stashed away rather than remaining easily visible to anyone who comes in the house. Not that it would mean anything to anyone who didn't already know what he's doing.

But I can't be too cautious.

I'm still keeping this detail confidential. Over the last two days I've spoken with several more recipients of From Heart to Heart's work, as well as talking over the break-in with Pat, but have kept all mentions of the code or my suspicions about the workshop to myself. It's far too significant and impactful to share when I don't know who I can actually trust, or even what is truly going on.

I can't help but think about the dual realities that seem to be in place. Something is so very clearly going on behind closed doors at From Heart to Heart, but the women I've spoken to haven't given any indication they know of anything beyond their stated public mission. It seems not everyone is privy to the true nature of the group, which leaves me wondering who among them is involved and who isn't.

During a break from rewatching security footage and having video chats with recipients who prefer not to have in-person meetings, I sit in the living room with a forgotten sandwich and stare at the messages starting to fill the paper. Many of them hit close, reminding me of under-cover work and stings I've orchestrated throughout my career. Others pull at my heart, making me think of my father and my late mother, and their vital work in rescuing women from brutal, horrible situations and delivering them to safety.

The thought of my mother makes something suddenly click. I go to my office where I left the notecard and look at it again. Taking out the lists of guests from the memorial services, I see a pattern I hadn't paid attention to before now. Several of the attendees signed with just their first name and last initial. When I first looked through the names, I noticed these but was aggravated by the lack of last name because it didn't allow me to effectively research the guests.

But now, I noticed something else. In both instances, two guests signed the book with a first name and the last initial "M." One signed it Dan. The initial stands out to me. D. As in D.W. It's incredibly tenuous, but I grasp onto it. Sitting down in front of my computer, I pull up the pictures Pat sent me and find the one that shows the strangers at the edge of Sherry's graveside service. Then I open a file that has several seconds of footage I clipped out of the remembrance recording.

I watch the clip three times, focusing in on the man I believe was at both services. The man with the heavy limp. Each time I watched the footage before, I noticed something at his neckline but wasn't sure what it was. It seems to slip out of his shirt for a second and he moves it back out of the way. I look more closely at the video, then zoom in on the still image. It's not sharp or perfectly clear, but there's enough detail for me to believe beyond a reasonable doubt that the man is wearing a necklace. And on it is what looks like a dog tag.

Encouraged, I take out my notes about the recipients of the donation items again. At the top of the page is the name that hasn't left my mind but I haven't been able to place. Until now.

Margaux Lennox.

For a brief moment, I thought maybe she was the reason behind the "M" on the notecard, but that's out of my mind now that I remember her. And know why the men stood out to me so much.

The last time I saw her name written was among the thick folders I pulled out of the casket buried in a grave in Florida bearing my mother's name. Those folders contained the names and case information of the women my mother had a hand in saving during her service to the organization known as Rescue prior to her death.

Now I know why the men struck me as so familiar. It's not that I knew who they were as individuals. I knew who they were as people. Those men are Rescue handlers.

"Are you busy?"

"Never too busy for you, honey. What's going on? You feeling alright?"

Hearing my father's voice is always comforting. I never let myself forget how it felt not hearing it for so many years. I can't take for granted that now he's usually just a phone call away. Despite everything that happened to him, Ian Griffin is not one to back down. He likes to try to tell people he had a brief foray into thoughts of retirement after returning from his deep undercover work investigating his own brother, but I don't think he was ever really serious about it. I got my work ethic, drive, and determination from him. He will continue to fulfill his role to the absolute best of his ability until he no longer has that ability.

It means sometimes there are days or weeks when I can't get in touch with him, but I know he's there. He finds ways to check in with me. And it makes it even more important when I can so easily connect with him like I am now.

"I'm fine. Much better than I was. I actually need to talk to you about a development in the case that I'm working." I describe the man at the services, the appearance of the items on my front porch, and the notecard. "I know the notecard was from one of them. The name he put on the sheet when he was signing out Tricia's personal items was Dennis Wicks, D. W., but it's the 'M.' That was a message to me. On the guestbook, it says Dan M. But I was never able to find anybody with a name like that. I'm sure it's whoever this Dennis Wicks person is. That M. It was meant for me. Murdock."

Just saying the word sends a slight shiver along my spine. It took years after seeing it for the first time for me to learn that it wasn't being used as a name but as a title given to the highly skilled handlers who protected the agents of Rescue. Every one of them would use it, concealing their own given names in a sign of foregoing themselves for the good of Rescue. Behind that title they were not individuals but tools designed to watch, shield, and protect. By whatever means necessary.

In the graveyard where the records of all the lives my mother saved are buried beneath a stone engraved with her name, another grave sits inches away. On that stone is the name Elliott. I knew him as Ron Murdock, the man who spent his life watching over my mother and then me, then lost it on the front porch of a quiet cabin in the middle of the woods. He was the epitome of what these men stand for. And I believe I've just encountered more of them.

"Rescue is still very active," my father confirms. "I just met with some of the former agents a few days ago. I haven't heard anything about the murders you're investigating. But I will reach out to Christine and find out what I can about any involvement they have with From Heart to Heart."

"Thank you."

I allow myself a few minutes to talk to my father just about life and to plan for the next time we'll have a chance to see each other before hanging up and immediately starting another call. This one is to Pat. I ask her to activate the phone tree and get everyone she possibly can to the workshop in two hours.

"Is everything alright? Did something happen with the case?" she asks.

"I'll fill everyone in later," I say. "Right now, I just need to get as many volunteers and members together as we can. It's important I talk to everybody today."

CHAPTER TWENTY

B Y THE TIME I GET TO THE WORKSHOP, IT'S ALREADY BUSTLING. IT doesn't look like as many of the women are here as were before, but there's enough. And I see the faces I wanted to. I don't waste time. As soon as I get inside, I take my place at the front of the room and lift my hands up to get their attention.

"Hello, everybody. If you could just quiet down and turn your attention to me, I would appreciate it. Thank you so much for coming out here at such short notice. I promised all of you that I would keep you up to date on developments happening in the case, and that's why I'm here today. I wish that I had more answers to give you, but for right now we are still finding our footing and following up on every lead and possibility that comes our way.

"I know that's not what you want to hear. Especially considering the incident that occurred here the other night. I want you to know I have been in touch with the police who responded and that this is being taken very seriously. They have increased patrolling in the area and have also spoken with the other businesses to ask them to be vigilant. Both the Empanada Market and the hair salon willingly turned over the footage from their security cameras. That footage didn't produce anything valuable, but you should take the fact that they volunteered the footage as a very good thing. You have supportive neighbors willing to be there for you and help keep you safe. That's the goal for all of us."

I pause to see a smattering of nods and encouragement, but it's not much.

"Which brings me to asking you for help again. In the course of our investigation, we have come upon some names that could be important. They could not be. What we want to know is if these names sound familiar to any of you and what you can tell us about them," I say.

"Where did you get these names?" one of the women asks.

"The sources are allowed to remain anonymous when providing potentially sensitive information in an investigation," I tell her. "Revealing those identities could compromise the case and cause significant risk." She looks satisfied, if slightly unnerved by the explanation, which was my goal. When she sits back as if to withdraw from me, I look out over the rest of the group. "Alright, if you'll just listen closely to the names I'm going to read out and think hard about whether they mean anything to you.

Mel Foster. Cooper Daniels. Maris June. Phillip Creed. Do any of those sound familiar? Think about versions of the names. For example, instead of Mel, maybe Melanie or Melissa. Phil instead of Philip. Maybe Mary." None of the women react. They shouldn't. Those names have nothing to do with the case. They're fake names I'm using to make a baseline. "Alright. How about Dan Murdock?"

Coming right out with the name is meant to be a shock, to startle any of the women who do know him. But there's no reaction.

"Daniel Murdock?" I prod. "Danny?"

A few of them exchange glances with the people around them like they're looking for any sign of who knows these people. They shake their heads and murmur their inability to help.

I try one last push. "Maybe try initials. D.J. Murdock. Or maybe M.J. for Maris June."

But there's nothing. I smile, but I'm sure the disappointment shows on my face.

"Is that bad?" Carlie Chambers asks. "Should we know those names?"

"No," I tell her. "It isn't bad. Like I said, these are just names that have come up and I wanted to find out if any of you know of them. But

I need you all to understand that the work I do and that my team does is only as good as the information that's given to us. This investigation will not succeed if you are hiding anything from me. This is not the time to try to maintain confidentiality or flex your loyalty by not telling me something you know would matter to this case.

"I know I said earlier to not worry about wasting my time—but if you know something, that *is* a waste of my time. Precious time that could be vital in catching the person responsible and putting them behind bars. Do not hold anything back from me. And don't assume you know what is meaningful and what isn't. That's my job. If it even crosses your mind, it's worth mentioning to me."

The women gathered in front of me still look confused. A couple of them look stung, frightened by my words.

"Ladies," Pat says, stepping forward, "are you listening to Agent Griffin? Do you understand what she's saying? If any of you know anything, or even *think* you know anything, you need to tell her. Even something very small could be significant."

"That's right," I say. "Thank you, Pat."

"I think it might help if everyone takes a few minutes to share what they remember about the days leading up to the murders. Talk among yourselves and compare your thoughts. Did you interact with Sherry or Tricia? Did you hear anything, see anything? Strange phone calls? Cars that seemed to hang around too long? Anything you can come up with." She turns to me. "While they're talking, Agent Griffin, I have those turtles you requested for your husband. If you'll come back here with me, I'll get them packed up for you."

Without waiting for any response, Pat turns on her heel and walks down the hall toward the distribution room. I remember talking to Shawna about the turtles and saying how much the children who had received them love them, but I don't remember asking for any more. Sam has been the one keeping his inventory of toys and other items stocked. Curious, I follow after Pat. In the time it takes me to weave through the women in the front room to get to the hallway and through the yarn room, Pat is already in the distribution room. As soon as I enter, I see Shawna is here as well.

"Hello," I say, looking back and forth between the two women. "What's going on here? Because if I don't miss my guess, this isn't actually about more turtles."

Pat shakes her head. "No. It isn't. But I didn't want to create any suspicion among the other women. There's something we need to talk about."

My heart skips a little. "Alright. Go ahead."

"Dan Murdock," she says.

I nod, not showing any emotion on my face. "Yes."

They exchange a look. In that single glance is a thousand questions and a kind of fear that can't be put into words by anyone who has never felt it closing in. Pat meets my eyes again.

"It isn't a name," she says.

This is enough to confirm what I already suspected.

"I know that," I tell her. "What I want to know is how the hell you know that."

Pat draws in a breath. "*Spaseniye.*"

She nearly whispers it and her accent changes the flow. It sounds less like it is truly pronounced and more like the phonetic coverup used in every context from real estate ventures to business contracts to conceal who is actually behind them. I've seen it many times before.

Spice Enya.

Spaseniye. Russian for salvation, for rescue.

I draw myself up and take a moment to compose everything in me before I allow myself to react. Anger has started to tingle at the tips of my toes and burn the backs of my legs. I'm trying to stay calm.

"I need you to tell me exactly what you mean by that," I say in a steady, quiet voice.

"You already know," Pat says.

"Are you trying to tell me that From Heart to Heart has been working with Rescue?" I ask.

Now that I've said it, both Pat and Shawna seem to relax and get more tense at the same time. Now it is undeniable that I know what they're talking about, but it also means they've revealed themselves and their connection to the intensely protected covert group.

"Yes," Pat says. "We made a connection with them about a year ago. Maybe a little less. We've been working with them since."

"Are you fucking kidding me?" I ask, my voice rising up, then dropping back down to try to keep the women from the front room from coming down here to find out what's happening. I step closer to Pat. "It's been three weeks since Sherry died. I've been involved in this investigation since then and now I'm leading the federal investigation into it, which has included me coming here and asking for help over and over. And you never thought you would bother to inform me that you are working with a group that saves women from abusive marriages, sex trafficking, slavery, oppressive governments. You didn't think that mattered?"

"I'm sorry," Pat says. "I know you're upset."

"That doesn't even begin to express it," I tell her.

"Emma, please. You have to understand. Not everyone in the group knows about our efforts. It isn't like we started as a way to do this. There are far more of us that know nothing about it than do know about it, and it is critical we keep it to ourselves," Shawna says.

"That's all well and good for them," I say. "I can understand not bringing in everybody that's in the group. But how could you not be open and honest with me from the beginning? In fact, I'm going to turn your own words right around on you, Shawna. You told me you didn't call the police the night of the break-in because I'm FBI and already investigating the murders. That was the whole point in thinking I would be the better choice to help you that night.

"So you thought it made sense to bring me all the way out here because somebody came in through an unlocked door, but you didn't think to tell me about the organization's side hustle getting women out of the grips of life-threatening situations. Including, in case it slipped your mind, rescuing them from entities who would very happily kill in retaliation for what they see as theft."

"I'm sorry," Shawna says. "I tried. I tried to get you to understand that something else was going on."

"We understand how frustrated you are," Pat says. "We know you're upset and angry. You feel like we held something back from you that could have swayed the investigation thus far."

"Of course, it would have!"

"But please step back for a second and think about this from our perspective. You know the position we're in. You know it would have compromised our mission and countless lives if we had just come right out and told you. We have no idea who knows what we're doing and who doesn't, who we can trust and who we can't. From the very beginning, we thought you might already know what was going on here. We were waiting for you to say something. But then you didn't and it made us unsure. Until we had confirmation that it was safe to talk to you, we couldn't take that risk," she continues.

As angry as I am, I know she's right. This isn't actually an unusual situation. There's a common misconception that all members of all government law enforcement agencies know everything that is going on within the myriad of organizations and networks that provide logistics and intelligence. There's the thought that if people are helping others and working toward a greater good, they must all be a network cooperating together.

This isn't the case. It is actually extremely rare that agencies freely exchange information and talk in full detail about everything they are doing, and there is very little involvement with grassroots organizations such as Rescue. Even if there's awareness, there's little, if any, comingling.

Even within the Alphabet Soup agencies—the FBI, CIA, NSA, and others—there are covert groups, deep undercover operatives, and ultra-classified efforts not to be discussed with anyone else.

"We honestly believed you were chosen for a reason," Shawna says.

"For a reason?" I ask incredulously.

"Not some celestial reason," she clarifies.

"Because of your mother," Pat says. "We know who you are, Emma. We've known since Xavier first started talking about you. We thought you might have been specifically chosen to investigate because of your mother."

"No," I say, shaking my head. "No, that's not the case. I am at the head of this investigation largely because of my personal involvement. I became connected with From Heart to Heart through Xavier, who was already involved for a couple of months. He thought I would benefit from doing something that would remind me that there's good in the world and revive what I started my career based on. After the FBI decided to investigate Sherry and Tricia's deaths, I was brought in because I was already connected. It didn't have anything to do with Rescue. I didn't even know about the link."

"Sherry and Tricia had information they didn't share with anyone else," Shawna tells me. "They were working closely on a very important mission and didn't share access to it. We don't even know what they were doing. They died before it could be completed."

"We're worried about the integrity of the mission," Pat continues. "It could go very wrong and there's nothing we can do to stop it. We wanted to share everything we know with you so you can."

"I will do everything I can, but waiting has cost us a tremendous amount of time. I need you to get together everyone else who knows about these efforts and find out if there are any details they can share…"

"That's just the thing," Pat says. "We can't."

"Why not?" I ask.

"It's just us," Shawna tells me. "We're the only ones left."

"It was just the four of you?" I ask, stunned.

"There were two others, but they both passed from natural causes. Now the two of us are all that's left. But like we said, we weren't privy to most of the details. We were utilized for deliveries and construction of some of the coded pieces."

"You know about the code," I say.

They nod. "But only to the extent that we could construct pieces based on patterns and instructions. We knew it was a code, but not what the code was. Not what was being sent," explains Pat.

I don't tell them about the scarf. I want to know what it says before I talk to anyone about it. Even with these women coming to me and revealing the connection between the organizations, I'm not sure who and what I can actually trust.

"Have you found out anything else? Has there been any progress in finding the murderer?" Pat asks.

"There isn't anything concrete right now. We're working through some information we've found and evidence that has come up. I hope it brings us closer very soon. And with the new information you gave me, maybe it will get us there even faster," I say.

Them coming forward about the code in the pieces and working with Rescue haven't made me waver on my decision to keep the details of the case confidential. Their admission that they have contacts with Rescue and that is how the code is used does give me some relief. It means the covert group within the organization is doing good things. But it doesn't mean that they need to know all the information I do or be aware of every one of my movements.

"There's more we can give you," Shawna says. "We don't know everything, but we can provide you with all the information we do have and show you everywhere we think Tricia and Sherry could have hidden additional information. We have been discussing it, and there are some files and further ciphers we think could be important for you to see. We can also give you contacts they worked with. But we can't do it now."

"Like we said, not everybody knows about this. We're the only ones left and we don't want to compromise everything that Tricia and Sherry worked so hard for. We need some time to get everything together and if we want to talk to you about it privately," Pat says.

"Absolutely. Let's meet tomorrow," I say.

"That works. We'll contact you with details."

I thank them both and leave the workshop, stunned by the new revelations and how they've changed the investigation. I was already concerned that I was right on the edge of investigating a serial killer. Now I realize this is something much more.

CHAPTER TWENTY-ONE

A T HOME, I SIT IN FRONT OF THE STRANGE ASSORTMENT OF acrylic squares spread across my table, my brain churning through everything that's happened. I wonder why the man calling himself Dennis Wicks, whether that's his actual name or not, claimed these items and sent them to me rather than simply telling Pat and Shawna that I could be trusted. The handler clearly wanted me to know what was going on, but it would make sense that he would then let those within the group know they could come to me and tell me about the connection to Rescue.

Instead, I'm left with faceless contacts and endless questions. It creates a sense of distrust and makes me wonder why things are unfolding the way they are. There's a reason he didn't want to turn that information over to anyone else but specifically to me.

It means something. Nothing the Murdocks do is by accident. They've dedicated themselves completely to protecting the agents within Rescue, and by extension, anyone working with them. It makes me think of Elliot and how painful it was for him when my mother was murdered. I didn't know any of it until I was an adult, but now I can look back on my childhood and see how much he did for her. Then after she died, how much a part of my life he continued to be even though I didn't know it.

The fact that Dennis Wicks was at both memorial services but with different groups makes me wonder if Tricia and Sherry were recognized as agents within the group and assigned their own handlers, or if those men were just part of the larger organization and there as representatives with Wicks as their primary contact. Though I know now Pat is pretty adept at keeping things from me even in moments of tremendous stress and pressure, she truly didn't seem to know who the men were when I asked her. I wonder how much she and Shawna really know.

I need to speak with Margaux Lennox. She's going to be able to provide me with the most insight into Rescue's dealings with From Heart to Heart and why Tricia and Sherry might have been targeted. I use the contact information on the shelter's website to send a message to Margaux. It's brief and surface-level, simply asking that she get in touch with me about an important matter and signing my name. She'll recognize it.

The next day, I haven't heard back from Margaux by the time Pat reaches out to me to tell me to meet them in the parking lot of the workshop. They'll lead me from there. It's more secure than giving out location details over the phone. I agree and hop in the shower. As I'm getting out, Jeffrey calls with details about the case and then Bellamy clicks in with urgent questions. By the time I'm finished with both of them, I'm already running late. I throw everything I need into my satchel and as I'm grabbing my travel mug of coffee, Xavier comes into the kitchen.

"Emma, I need to talk to you."

"We'll talk when I get back. I'm running late, I can't stop right now," I tell him.

"It's really important."

"I'm sorry. I shouldn't be long."

I get a glimpse of him standing at the door as I drive away. His face is dark, but I don't have the time to stop and talk with him right now. I can give him as much time as he needs when I get back, but for now, I need to get to the workshop and find out what more Pat and Shawna can tell me. I'm more than halfway there when my phone rings. I see Pat's number on the screen and answer it.

Before I can say anything, I hear what sounds like a heavy thud and a cry.

"Pat?" I ask.

There are more sounds, distant voices, something that sounds like a scuffle, and muffled screams. Just before the sound cuts off I hear a single word.

"Lois!"

The line goes dead and I call back. It doesn't even ring. I call for emergency backup, sending the police to the workshop. I don't have Shawna's number, so I continuously call Pat's phone, hoping she'll answer. She doesn't pick up.

I beat the police to the workshop. My tires scream as I turn into the parking lot. There are no cars parked in front of the building, so I take my gun from my hip and run around to the back. Two cars are parked close to the back door to the workshop, one with its driver's door standing open. Lying on the ground beside it is Pat.

My heart drops to my stomach as I hear sirens wailing in the background. Flashing lights splash color over her face, glistening on the blood dripping down her head and down the side of her neck.

CHAPTER TWENTY-TWO

"THIS IS PAT LEDGER. SHE TOOK OVER AS HEAD OF FROM HEART to Heart after the death of Tricia Donovan. I was coming here to meet with her and another member to discuss some information they might have regarding the recent murders."

"And the other member? Where is she?"

"I don't know. She wasn't here when I got here and I don't have her contact information," I say.

Almost as though I have beckoned her into being, I hear Shawna's voice calling my name from around the front of the workshop. I jog around, ducking under the crime scene tape being guarded by two uniformed officers. Shawna looks frantic, trying to push back another officer stationed in the lot. The other businesses have been evacuated and blocks have been put in place to prevent anybody from getting into the area.

"What's happening?" she demands.

"Where were you?" I ask. "You were supposed to be here with Pat."

"I know. My husband had an emergency at work and I had to go to the hospital to make sure he was alright. I tried to call Pat, but she didn't answer. What is going on? Where is she?" she asks.

Her voice is trembling and her eyes flicker to the door to the workshop and the crime tape to the side. I reach out and take both of her shoulders in my hands.

"Shawna, I need you to listen to me. Have you heard from Lois today?"

She looks confused. "Lois? No. I haven't spoken with her since yesterday. Why?"

"Pat has been murdered. I found her behind the workshop."

She lets out a wail and I lift my voice to overcome it. "Lois's car is there. I got a phone call from Pat's phone when I was on my way here and I heard screaming. Somebody shouted Lois's name. It might have been Pat, but I can't be sure. She isn't here and we can't locate her. We've searched the workshop and the surrounding areas, and there's no sign of her."

"Oh, my god," Shawna says, looking like her knees are giving out and she might be sick. "Oh, my god, what happened to her?"

"Did you know she was going to be here today?" I ask.

Shawna shakes her head. "No. The whole reason we wanted to meet with you here is because we didn't think anybody else was going to be here. We wanted to bring you to a couple of places we think might be significant. No one else was supposed to be here."

"I need you to go home," I tell her firmly. "Don't talk to anybody. Don't leave. Give me your contact information and I will be in touch when I can. I'll have an officer bring you."

I put her phone number and address into my phone, then ask one of the uniformed officers to give her a ride. He will drive her car and another officer will follow to bring him back to the scene. I duck back under the crime scene tape and jog back to the crime scene. CSU is processing the scene, trying to piece together the bits of evidence available to try to understand what happened.

Lois's car has blood smeared across the inside and a chunk of hair caught in the door. Pat had been dead only a matter of minutes when I arrived, telling me I just barely missed whoever did this.

"We need an immediate bulletin. Lois Keegan was abducted and is presumed in extreme danger."

One of the responding officers immediately whips out his phone to make the call. "Yes, Agent."

Fear rolls in my stomach. This is a change in the process. Tricia and Sherry were both killed by three gunshots. No signs of struggle. No one else involved. I don't know Pat's cause of death yet, but I don't see gunshot wounds. The damage to her head could be it, but I won't know what happened until I get confirmation from the medical examiner.

This shift in operation is extremely concerning. Not only does it mean we can't rely on the pattern anymore, but Lois's abduction changes everything. Her life is in severe danger right now and I have to wonder why they didn't kill her immediately.

"She wasn't supposed to be here," I tell Detective McGraw. "I was meeting with Pat and Shawna. No one else was supposed to be at the workshop today, but Lois apparently showed up."

"Maybe that's what changed things," he says. "The killer may have intended to target Pat or even both of the other women, but then Lois arrived and the plan changed."

"I'm going to go talk to Shawna. Keep me updated on anything you find out."

I start toward my car and he calls after me. "Agent Griffin?" I turn around to face him. "Why were you meeting with the women today?"

I stare back at him without emotion. "Keep me updated."

When I get back to my car, I pick up my phone and see I have a message from Xavier. I open it and see only two words.

Roman Cleary

An image beneath it shows a close-up of a segment of Tricia's scarf.

Abandoning my plan to go to Shawna's house, I instead call her and let her know I'll be coming to speak with her soon. I give her another warning not to leave the house or talk to anyone, then drive home as fast as I can. Xavier is waiting for me when I walk in the door.

"Roman Cleary? The FBI agent who disappeared?" I ask. "That's in the scarf?"

He shows me the pictures of the scarf and the paper where he has deciphered different patterns of stitches.

"The scarf contains a message coded using four different machinations of three ciphers. It's complex and would require someone really knowing what they're looking for to be able to understand it. It's still fractured. There are pieces of it I haven't been able to completely interpret, which tells me there's either another cipher or another version of one of the existing ones. What I have been able to uncover is a message about the agent and the mission that was underway. It included where he was meant to be and the failsafes that were put into place to protect the mission in the event of something like this happening," he tells me.

"That means From Heart to Heart wasn't just involved with Rescue," I say.

Xavier shakes his head. "This is much bigger than that."

"I need to find out more about him," I say. "I'm going to call Eric."

I start up the stairs.

"Emma."

"Hmmm?"

"Whose blood is on you?"

I look down at the blood spread across one leg of my pants and on the cuffs of my sleeves. My hands shake as I lift my eyes back to him.

"I'm sorry."

I wait until Dean is back to keep Xavier company before I call Eric. I feel like the world around me is on fire. There's so much coming at me from every angle and I don't know where I'm supposed to turn next. For now, I settle on finding out everything I can about Roman Cleary. I need to know who he was, what he was doing, and what happened to him. If his name was hidden in a secret missive, he must have something to do with what the group was doing, or at least have a connection to their efforts.

Someone has caught on to the work of these women and was trying to get to the information they had. They stopped them in the ultimate way, but I need to know why they had it in the first place. What did they have to do with the missing agent? And what happened to him?

"I've already told you everything I know about him," Eric says when I get in touch with him. "He disappeared after his flight and there hasn't been any sign of him."

"Has anyone checked with the failsafe measures?" I ask.

"What failsafe measures?" Eric asks.

I let out a heavy breath. "There's a lot more to this story than we realize, Eric. I need to see the surveillance footage from the airport."

"We've already reviewed it. Roman goes through the airport, through security, and out toward the private plane waiting for him. That's it. Security protocols don't allow footage of him actually getting on the plane, but we know the plane took off at the correct time and the crew gave no indication of anything being out of the ordinary about the trip."

"How much of a crew was there?" I ask. "Have they all been interviewed?"

"Almost none. It was a covert flight, Emma. Pilot and co-pilot, both of whom were in the cockpit the entire time. They've been questioned, but they didn't have anything to offer," he tells me.

"I still need to see the footage."

Eric doesn't argue. "I'll send it to you."

CHAPTER TWENTY-THREE

I T DOESN'T TAKE LONG AFTER GETTING OFF THE PHONE WITH ERIC for Margaux Lennox to get in touch with me. She's heard about Pat's death and asks me to meet with her. We choose a coffeeshop and I tell Xavier and Dean I'll be back soon.

"Be careful, Emma," Dean says.

"I will."

I see Margaux through the window of the shop before I go inside. She's hunched over the table, her hands wrapped around a cup of coffee she doesn't seem to remember she has. Her eyes focus on the surface of the table in front of her. The picture of her in my mother's file flashes through my head. The years have done kind things to the woman who looked gaunt, empty, and worn down in that image. She's more robust, and even from only seeing the side of her face, I can see pristine makeup on a lovely face.

It's the sadness weighing her shoulders down that aches in the center of my chest as I approach. She shouldn't have to feel any more of that. She went through enough of that pain at the hands of the people my mother saved her from and she shouldn't have to face any more of it. But it's inescapable. And the truth is, as much as it can feel hard to say, Margaux chose a path that would cause her more pain. Like my mother did.

Instead of choosing to accept the freedom and the new life my mother and the Rescue group gave to her, she decided to stand beside them. She wanted to give back, to contribute instead of just run. It would have been smarter to run. But she chose to fight.

"Margaux?"

She looks up at me and nostalgia floods her deep green eyes. She stands up and faces me.

"Emma Griffin," she says softly. "Can I hug you?"

"Of course."

She takes me into an embrace and I feel like she's wrapping her arms around my mother in the same moment.

"You look just like Mariya," she says when we step back from each other. Worry darkens her expression and the corners of her mouth tug down. "I'm sorry, I'm sure you..."

"It's alright. I like to hear it." I look over to the counter. "I'm going to get some coffee. Can I get you anything?"

She shakes her head and I go to order a drink and two croissants. I set the plate down between us and sit down.

"I'm so glad you reached out to me," she says.

"I'm sorry it's under these circumstances," I say.

She nods, looking down into her coffee again. "I made contact with From Heart to Heart about a year ago. I'd been following the work they did and I thought they could be extremely helpful in our efforts. It's harder now than it ever has been. The threats are more sophisticated, and their resources are extensive. The ability to track people, trace movements, intercept communication. It has all become so much more advanced since your mother's era. "We needed something that would change that. A way we could take advantage of something that already existed and would go without notice. The work we've already accomplished is nothing short of amazing." Tears well in her eyes. "But now..."

"Do you know anything about what happened to Tricia, Sherry, and Pat?" I ask.

"No. I am devastated about their deaths, but I don't have any information to offer." She pauses as two people walk by the table. When they're out of earshot again, she leans slightly across the table so she can lower her voice. "We haven't received any threats and we have no idea who could be involved. I feel so incredibly guilty. They've lost their lives and it could be because of the work they were doing with us."

I shake my head. "You can't let yourself think that way. Working with this group is a risk. Anybody who agrees to do it knows that. They were proud of what they did, and you should be, too. Right now, we need to think about Lois Keegan. She's another member of From Heart to Heart. She was abducted when Pat was murdered."

Margaux's hands come up to cover her mouth. "That's horrible. I wish I could tell you something. All I can do is offer you information about all the clients we've worked with since getting the ladies involved."

"That's a start. Thank you. Is there anything else you can tell me? Anything that might be valuable? Missions that have particularly stood out to you? Contacts that might be more complex or impactful than others?"

I don't want to mention Roman Cleary, but I want to give her the opportunity to tell me if they were doing any more than just rescuing Russian women and their children from bad domestic situations and other pressing risks. I don't see anything in her expression that says she's hiding anything. She has no reason to. She knows I can be trusted. I'm confident she has nothing else to tell me. I go home glad to have spoken with her, but disappointed I didn't get any further.

"Emma, you know what I'm going to tell you," Sam says later that night while we're getting ready for bed.

"That I shouldn't be so sure she isn't lying to me?"

He shakes his head. "No. She knows you and your legacy well enough to have complete trust in you. She would have every reason to want these murders solved. What I'm going to tell you is that there's no such thing as coincidences. You didn't just happen to know those women. There's a reason you ended up in the path of this organization."

I feel like he's right, but I don't know what it means.

The next morning, I go see the medical examiner to find out the results of Pat's autopsy. This murder stands out from the others in several ways. As I suspected, cause of death was a blow to the head, but she also suffered a gunshot wound to her back. There are some defensive wounds, unlike Tricia and Sherry, suggesting she might have been trying to either defend herself or Lois.

"Did you find anything that might give any insight to the killer?" I ask.

"No. No hairs, no fiber evidence. Nothing that stands out. But I did find something while examining her clothes."

"Her clothes?"

My thoughts immediately go to the scarf Tricia wore, but I know Pat wasn't wearing one when she died. I didn't notice her wearing anything that was stitched.

"Yes. I don't know if it's significant, but I put it aside." He reaches into his drawer and offers me a small piece of paper. "I found it sewn into a small pocket inside the waistband of her pants. Does it mean anything to you?"

The paper is covered with a series of small markings. I shake my head. "No."

Smoothing the paper onto the desk, I take several photographs of it, then hand it back to the medical examiner so it can be submitted as official evidence. As I leave the office, I stop to speak with Gene, telling him about the paper and warning him that it's not to be discussed with or released to anyone, not even family. He agrees and I make my way back home.

CHAPTER TWENTY-FOUR

THE FOOTAGE FROM THE AIRPORT IS WAITING FOR ME WHEN I GET home. There are several surveillance cameras set up around the airport, so there are files of footage from all of them. He's given me a list of time stamps to indicate when Roman Cleary is visible. I watch through each file and see exactly what Eric told me. The agent walks from the parking deck into the airport. Another camera picks him up walking inside and going to the self-service kiosks. I watch his progress through the airport and out onto the tarmac. Nothing seems unusual. He's not upset or worked up. He doesn't seem particularly rushed or like he's anxious about his day. He barely even acknowledges the people around him.

I watch it a few times before I realize something so blatantly obvious I feel like an idiot not having noticed it before. I call Eric.

"Did you watch the footage?" he asks.

"I did," I say.

"Then you see what I meant," he replies.

"I did," I admit. "But I also noticed something else. Watch the footage from the fourth camera. The one that shows Cleary go out to the tarmac through the private access door."

"Give me a second." I wait while he pulls up his own screen of the footage. "Alright. There he is. He walks through, goes outside."

"Cleary's not the only person who uses that door that night," I point out.

"Well, of course not. There are a lot of private flights that go out of that airport. There's lots of people going through that door."

"Right. In particular, a man in a dark suit very much like his. If you go back about fifteen minutes in the footage, you'll see him go through that door and out onto the tarmac," I say.

I wait while he watches it.

"Alright. So somebody else who was dressed like him went out the private access door close to him. I mean, he's a tall white guy wearing a dark suit. Could be any businessman or politician or whatever."

"That's true. But now I want you to go back to the second camera angle. The one that shows Roman going into the airport and walking through to security. Scan back about twenty minutes from when you see him enter."

"That's the same man coming in," Eric confirms.

"Yes. And what does he do?"

"He goes to the self-service kiosk," he says.

"Right. He goes to the ticket kiosk. Then gets on a private flight."

There is silence on the other end of the line for a few seconds as he processes what I've said.

"He wouldn't need to get a ticket," he says.

"No, he wouldn't. There's no reason for that man to need to go to that kiosk. And he spends a pretty considerable amount of time in front of the machine. He even prints out a boarding pass. You can see it come out of the kiosk. Which means he did purchase a ticket on a commercial airline of some kind. But that's not what stands out to me the most. Watch carefully as he gets his boarding pass and walks away."

I pause while he watches the footage. He makes a sound that tells me he noticed the same thing I did and scans back to watch it again.

"He took that woman's suitcase."

"Yeah. You can watch her come in, go to that kiosk, and print out her own boarding pass. But then that man comes and takes her suitcase and she takes his. Then she walks to the airport, goes through security, and heads toward the gates. Like nothing happened. But that wasn't just some careless mistake. Those suitcases were sitting next to each other, but he had to reach his hand over in a different direction than he had when he put the suitcase in place. He intentionally took hers. That has to mean something."

"It's definitely worth looking into."

"Great. In the footage you can see which gate she goes to, which means you can get the flight information. If we can access the passenger manifest, we can find out who that woman is and where she was going. I would be very curious to find out what happened to her after she got on that flight."

"I'll get the team on it," Eric says.

Not long after getting off my call with Eric, my phone rings again. Thinking he might have noticed something else, I grab my phone, but it isn't his name on the screen. Instead, it's Detective McGraw. My heart rate increases and my mouth goes dry.

"Agent Griffin," I answer.

"The alarm system at the workshop has been activated," he tells me without greeting.

I groan. "I'm on my way."

Immediately after Pat's murder and Lois's abduction, I made sure an alarm system was added to the workshop that would immediately contact emergency services if it was tripped. It has only been in place for a day and already I'm racing to get there. I'm terrified of what we might find. Everyone in the organization was already warned not to return to the workshop and not participate in any deliveries or other related activities until further notice. But that doesn't mean they're listening.

The rest of the shopping center is still closed, but there are several cars parked in the lot in front of the workshop. I get out and run over to where Detective McGraw is standing. There's no ambulance or sign of CSU, but I don't let myself feel hopeful until he looks at me and I notice no tragic news in his eyes.

"What happened? Is everyone alright?" I ask.

"Everyone's fine. Responding officers swept the entire building and didn't find anyone. Nothing seems out of place. But they did find this."

He holds out an envelope with my name written across the front. A pit settles into my stomach at the sight. What is it now?

"We haven't opened it. It's been photographed."

I nod, both appreciating the sign of respect and wishing I would have at least somewhat of a warning of what I am going to find inside. Stepping away from the detective, I open the envelope and pull out a slip of paper. On it is a link and a message.

"Your choice."

CHAPTER TWENTY-FIVE

I JOG BACK TO MY CAR AND TAKE OUT MY TABLET. CAREFULLY INPUT-ting every character, I call up the link in my browser. When it opens, my stomach turns. A livestream shows a closeup image of Lois, her face dirty and streaked with dried blood, her expression terrified. She appears to be in a wooden box and looks nothing short of frantic. She lifts a hand to claw at the wall of the box beside her and I notice blood on her fingertips. Streaks on the wood tell me she has been trying to dig her way out. As she lifts her head, something in the corner of the box moves and I realize it's a rubber tube coming down from the lid of the box.

I can only assume it's there to occasionally provide water. Lois's desperate cries and frightened whimpers come through, but there's no way for me to communicate with her. I can only watch her struggle, not let her know I can see her or try to provide any comfort.

Jumping back out of the car, I get Gene's attention and show him what's on the screen.

"Oh, god," he mutters.

"This is an extremely serious situation. She hasn't just been abducted. She's being held prisoner and whoever has her expects something."

"That note. It came with the link. What does it mean?"

"All it says is that it's my choice. But I don't know what the hell that's even supposed to mean. There's no other information. I'm going to reach out to the Bureau and tell Eric what's going on. He might be able to trace the footage or the IP address and find out who's doing this."

"And after that?" Gene asks.

"After that I figure out what I'm going to do next." I start back toward the car to call Eric and a thought comes to me. "Have somebody reach out to Shawna. Make sure she's still at home and nothing has happened to her."

I tell Eric everything as fast as I can and send him the link so he can look at the livestream.

"I'll do what I can," he says.

"Thank you."

I watch the stream for a few more moments, not wanting to look away. Lois is locked in that box alone somewhere, and as ridiculous as it sounds, I feel like I'm abandoning her if I stop watching without knowing what I'm meant to do next. She sobs as she pounds on the sides of the box, causing dust to fall down onto her face. I can't see the lid to determine the dimensions of the space, but from the way the tube is hanging, it seems like it's not much bigger than a coffin.

I swallow down that thought and look at the note again, hoping to see something I didn't notice. The thought of invisible ink goes through my thoughts like a fevered flush just before something right behind Lois's head catches my eye. Each time she shifts, a message written on the wood appears. I keep watching, my body shaking in frustration at the helpless feeling of not being able to move her out of the way and see it. I can't sit still anymore.

I finally get out of the car and start pacing around the parking lot as I continue to watch the stream. Finally, she moves enough for me to see the message. I type it into a note on my phone as soon as I see it.

TXT 25152118195126

"Did you get something?" Gene asks, jogging up to me.

"Look at this. This should be a phone number. It should be telling me to text this number. But there are too many digits. Even if it was an area code and the phone number, there are still too many numbers. So how am I supposed to know which is the actual phone number so that I can text it?"

"Maybe that's it. Look for an area code. Then that will tell you what numbers to use," he suggests.

It sounds simple enough to work, reminding me of the first step in deciphering a simple code, which is to look for regularly repeating patterns in sets of two or three that could correlate to the most common words, such as "of," "the," and "is."

But it's not that simple. None of the area codes from around here appear in the sequence of numbers, either beside each other or with a regular set of numbers in between. I look at the video again. Lois has her hands over her face and I can hear murmuring as if she's deep in prayer. If she's been in that box since her abduction, her condition could be deteriorating rapidly. Even with the assumption that the tube is providing some water to her, she's not going to be able to withstand the dehydration, starvation, stress, and other factors for very long. I have to find a way to get her out of there.

"Did you notice that?" Gene asks, pointing to the screen. "There are other numbers."

I look where he's pointing and see "07734" written on the side of the box.

"That's not enough digits to be a phone number," I say. I look at it again. It looks familiar. "I know that sequence. Why do I know that?"

I try to think of what it could be. A date. An address. A zip code. None of them fit. Lois has started to go still. She's no longer praying and her hands have slid down to rest on her chest. I can't tell if she has fallen asleep or passed out. Depending on where the box is being kept, the temperature inside could be very high, making it even more dangerous.

"07734," I whisper to myself. The feeling I got watching the footage of the airport, the fluttering, shuddering feeling of something so obvious passing by me hits as I realize exactly what I'm looking at. "07734. Hello."

"What?" Gene asks.

"Those numbers. That's what they mean. I was researching a cold case that involved pagers. Back in the '80s they used shorthand to communicate. Because there could only be numbers put on the screen rather than letters, there were some standard ones, like 07734. It's just like a calculator in math class." I type the numbers into my phone's calculator and flip it upside down. "Hello."

"So you're supposed to flip that sequence of numbers upside down and it means something?"

"I don't think so. I think what it means is that those numbers aren't the actual numbers, but they need to be deciphered."

"How are you supposed to know how to decipher them?"

"The simplest answer is often the right one. Basic alphanumeric code, just like when people used pagers."

It takes me a couple of seconds to go through the numbers, determining which are single digits and which are double. I finish and Gene looks over my shoulder at what I've typed onto my screen.

"Yourself?"

"That's what the numbers spell out."

"They want you to send a text message to yourself?"

My hand dips into my pocket and I pull out the envelope that had the note in it. My name is written across the front, but at the very top of the "E" is a tiny pound sign, so small and nearly integrated into the letter I didn't notice it at first.

"No. But I know what they want."

I realize now they're not looking for an actual phone number. Whoever this is has used a text app to create a number to receive messages. I translate my name into numbers, input it into my phone with the pound sign in front of it, and send a text.

"Hello."

It goes through immediately, setting my teeth on edge. Aggravation and simmering anger take over as I feel myself being drawn into another sick game. I hate this. I hate the manipulation. I hate being toyed with. But there's no question what the stakes are in this game. As the note says, it's my choice. I either do this, or I leave Lois to die.

The response to my text takes far too long to come through, but it finally does.

Hello, Agent Griffin. Now you know what you're in for. This is the way it's going to be. You follow what we tell you and do what we want you to do, and we will keep Lois alive. If you please us, we'll eventually lead you to her. But remember. The choice is yours.

CHAPTER TWENTY-SIX

I T TAKES ERIC ONLY A MATTER OF MINUTES TO CONFIRM THAT HE can't trace the number I texted. The app is untraceable, not linked to any specific individual. There's no way to know who downloaded it or to what phone the messages are being sent. For right now, I am totally at the mercy of whoever is on the other end of that number. I could say no. I could say I'm not going to play along with them and that I'm just going to figure out who they are in order to save Lois. But I know I have no way of doing that. At least not quickly enough to feel confident I could save her life. And they know it, too.

I'm going to have to get more out of them. I'm going to have to do what they want for now. This is going to take all of my skill and instinct, and my time is limited. Every second puts Lois's life in more danger and increases the risk that someone else close to her and the other women will be the next target. My mind flashes to Shawna. I haven't heard anything about her. Calls have gone unanswered. Officers have been dispatched to go to her house and check on her, and I'm waiting for them to call with an update. I don't know which thought pains me more. That she might have already become the next victim? Or that she might be involved?

I text the number again.

What do you want?

This time, the response comes within seconds.

A picture of the sampler blanket on the wall.

I'm wary of the simplicity of the request. It almost seems like a test, just to see if I will actually do what they tell me to. But I also feel the weight pulling down on me. They didn't just ask for a picture of any random item from the workshop. They want one of the sampler. They know about the code and the cipher contained within the stitches. At the very least, they know there is something meaningful about the piece and want to see it for themselves.

I still have the pictures I took of the blanket on my phone, but I don't send them. I don't know if I'm being watched and am very aware that I could be being judged on every one of my movements. I have to play by their rules even if they haven't told them to me yet, and I have a feeling they want to know I took the picture now.

The door to the workshop is still open and I rush inside. I go straight to the conference room and take a picture of the sampler but hesitate. They only asked for a picture of the sampler on the wall. They didn't specify which one, or which room. The test they are actually giving me seems to become clearer. Maybe it's not whether I will do as they say, but what I know. Instead of snapping a picture of the main sampler hanging on the wall, I go to one of the smaller pieces and take a picture of that. I purposely zoom in to avoid showing the outer dimensions of the blanket while making it look like I am providing a clear view of the stitches.

I send it and wait.

Thank you. We will be in touch.

The false courtesy of the message crawls across my skin.

What now? Tell me what you need next.

Lois doesn't have long. I don't have the time to wait patiently for them to communicate with me when they want to.

You will hear from us soon.

I check the live stream again and see Lois still struggling. Her eyes are open again and she has her hands above her head, seeming to press upward on the lid. Every time she pushes, dust and debris tumble down on her. It suggests the box is made of plywood or pressboard. I wonder where they have her. If she's just in a room somewhere or locked in a storage container. I don't want to entertain the thought that she could be underground. If she is, the danger is even worse. The weight of the dirt pressing around the box could cause it to collapse, crushing her at any moment.

I watch her for a little while longer, hating the helpless feeling it's giving me, but needing to feel like she isn't completely alone. It makes me sick to see her there suffering and so obviously afraid, but there's nothing I can do.

CHAPTER TWENTY-SEVEN

"I T SAYS TO GO ALONE."

"I don't give a damn what it says. You aren't going alone."

Sam tries to stand in my way so that I can't go out the front door, but it doesn't do him any good. I push past him and walk out.

"This is what I have to do."

"Emma," he says, grabbing me by my arm.

I spin around angrily to face him. "I've spent two days running all over doing a fucking deranged Easter egg hunt for these people. I've gathered rocks in a pile. I've thrown paper airplanes in a field. I have found specific colors of yarn and wrapped them around fucking trees, Sam. Tell me what good any of that has done? Shawna is so traumatized, she won't speak. All she was able to give me was the address of a ware-house that is empty and hasn't been used in a year. Which tells me she knows absolute shit and was more or less a mule. I have to do this."

"Why?" Sam asks. "Why do you have to do this? Like you just said, it isn't doing you any good. You aren't getting closer. But all those things were stupid games. They were just arbitrary things to keep you wasting time so you weren't focused on anything else. This is dangerous."

"Then I guess I'm done wasting time."

I start to turn and he takes me by my wrist to turn me around to face him again. "Please, Emma."

I fix him with a glare. "Sam, I have to. I have my gun. The unit will be nearby. I have to do this."

He sighs and finally relents. "I know you do."

I get in my car and pull up the stream of Lois, still trapped in the box. She looks sweaty and desperate. Her lips are chapped and her hands are covered in blood. Sometimes she sings to herself or whispers long prayers and her voice has gone quiet and dusty. A couple of times when I have finished one of the ridiculous tasks they've sent me to do, they've sent water down the tube into her mouth. It's been enough to keep pushing me forward.

Turning off the tablet, I set my phone in its holder on my dash and set the GPS to the address that came through the last text. The instructions told me to park three blocks away and enter from the back. I make sure there's nothing of value in the car, putting the tablet in a lockbox installed in the trunk. I don't have a lot of hope that the car will still be here when I get back, but taking precautions is the best I can do.

Wanting to take my gun out but following the warnings of the text that said not to touch it, I set off down the dark street. It's littered with refuse, empty lots between derelict houses acting as makeshift dumps. They smell of waste and decay. This is one time when I want to feel the eyes of someone watching me so I can know I have backup. But I don't. I told Margaux to call off the handler trailing me. I appreciate the offer, but that only complicates things. All she was able to tell me about Dennis Wicks is that he was assigned to claim Tricia's personal belongings and send them to me to ensure they would be safe.

She didn't know they were decoys.

That revelation threw me off balance. I assumed she would have at least some idea of what Tricia was doing. I hoped she would be able to tell me who she was trying to help or why she was in Maryland, but she couldn't offer me anything. The only active cases Tricia was working were in the Mount Percy area and had nothing to do with any of the items in the car or the hotel where Tricia was found. It leaves me with a burning feeling in the pit of my stomach. There's still more. Tricia had more secrets, and she paid for them with her life and the lives of Sherry and Pat. And if I don't figure this out before the people on the other end of the phone finish with their fun, Lois as well.

The house where I'm going looms ahead. It was once beautiful. Like the rest of the neighborhood, it was once a lavish home where a family lived, where children grew up in hope. But that was a long time ago. The beauty of the houses on this street is long gone. The hope faded. The people who had lives here are now somewhere else, bringing with them any chance for meaning and a future.

What's left behind is the carcass of a neighborhood, ravaged by drugs and gangs, taken over by squatters. As the hope left, what was leftover by society took over. It happens all too often. An area looks promising, filled with optimism and possibility. Then priorities change. Economies collapse. That place that was once so desirable becomes destitute. It collapses under the weight of its own failure and all that's left is bones to be picked by the people whose paths have led them to embody the same abandonment and despair.

I walk up to the house and follow what was once a fence line to the back. Where the door should be is a large hole that leads down a set of steps into a basement glowing with blue light. A tall, imposing man stands halfway down the steps, his arms crossed over his chest. I wonder if he knows he's a living cliché. I doubt he would care.

He holds up a hand and looks me up and down when I cross the threshold.

"You best be on your way," he says. "You've got the wrong house."

"I know where I am," I reply. "I was sent here."

Another man shows up in the doorway several steps below. A shock of green hair lays across his forehead, concealing some of the tattoos that cover nearly his entire face. Only his eyes stare out from circles so pale it's like all the blood has been drained from his body.

"What's this all about?" he asks.

"Says she was sent here," the man on the steps tells him without looking away from me.

"Who sent you?"

"Gideon sent me," I say. That's the name I was provided. I know it's meaningless. It's a codename. But that doesn't matter right now. I need to get in and out.

A smile crosses the man's face. "Alright. Come on."

I take a step down and the man in the middle of the steps holds up a hand to stop me.

"You've got a gun."

"Of course I have a fucking gun," I say. "You think I'd come here without one?"

He looks taken aback by the snap in my voice, but I don't back down. This might not be a place I'd ever choose to be, but it doesn't scare me.

"Psycho," the man says, and I have to hold back the scoff that comes up my throat. "Chick's got a gun."

The green-haired man I'm now assuming is known as Psycho looks me up and down. He sucks his teeth in a way that makes my fingers flex and my spine straighten.

"You fixin' to shoot me?" he asks, the laughter in his voice saying he doesn't actually believe that to be an option.

"Not if you don't give me reason to," I say. "Can we move this along? I'm not here to do any bonding. You know what Gideon wants."

"Let her through, V," Psycho says.

V steps to the side and I walk past him, going down the steps to the landing leading into the basement. Psycho steps the rest of the way through the door, forcing me backward so I'm between him and the wall, with V blocking the steps.

"You make a habit of doing deals out in the open like this?" I ask.

We're not exactly exposed where we are behind the house, but I don't like being cornered and the tensions are starting to run high. I have to keep it together. Lois is looking worse. She's barely getting water and I haven't seen her eat anything since the livestream started. The person behind the messages has made it very clear they are controlling her fate. They will do with it as they please at any given moment, but they always frame it as being my choice. If I choose to do what's demanded of me and I give them what they want, she continues to live a little longer. They dangle eventually earning her release in front of me like a carrot.

I despise them for it.

But she can't be punished for what they do. I have to keep playing along. It didn't take long for them to demand another picture of the sampler. It tells me they know something about it and what they are looking for, even if they don't know exactly what it means. They've sent me to accomplish a list of silly tasks and meaningless stunts. They demanded crime scene photos of Sherry and Tricia. That one was harder for me to fulfill. I didn't want to give them to them. It felt disrespectful and tasteless to hand over images of their bloodied bodies, knowing they wanted them for trophies.

But I gave them to them. Lois got more water. For a short time, she seemed more restful. It wasn't enough to get her out.

Now I'm here. I don't know the purpose of it. There has to be one. Even the ridiculous tasks that seemed like nothing more than busywork were exactly what Sam said: distractions. Meant to keep me away from doing anything else to investigate. If I was out collecting stones or making videos of myself throwing paper airplanes, I couldn't be digging deeper into the murders or following their trail.

This doesn't feel like that, though.

"Someone is eager," Psycho slithers.

"Maybe she's a cop," V grunts behind me.

"I'm not a cop," I say. Technically, it's the truth.

Psycho licks his lips. He's twitching slightly, his eyes unblinking. The smile on his face is constantly moving, shifting and changing like it's under its own control.

"Well, you wouldn't say so if you were, now, would you?" he says. "I think we should check to make sure you aren't wearing a wire. I can't let my business be at risk. It would just be irresponsible."

He lets out a sickening laugh as he takes another advancing step and his hands catch either side of my ribcage. They slide around, then up over my breasts, squeezing as he laughs.

"Have to be thorough."

"Give me what Gideon wants," I growl between tightly clenched teeth.

Psycho runs one hand over my breast again, then steps back with a sickening grin.

"She's clean."

He walks into the basement without invitation. I follow him, trying not to react to the thick, grotesque smell that suddenly wafts over me. I'd caught a whiff from the stairs, but it had been manageable. Now I feel like it's burrowing its way into my hair and my clothes and every pore of my body. It's a combination of body filth, rot, and age. Every surface of the room is covered in discarded fast food containers, molded glasses, and paper plates used so many times they have dissolved away in places. Several mattresses stained with various fluids clutter the floor on one half, several blankets tangled in a pile nearby. An almost inaudible scratching sound tells me something else has made its home among the refuse.

The men come into the room seemingly unaware of the disgusting conditions of the room. V closes the door and I shake my head.

"Open it," I say.

He gives a short laugh and makes no move to open the door again.

"Relax, lady," Psycho says. "You're here as my guest. I want you to feel welcome. Doesn't seem very friendly if the door is standing open, now, does it?"

"Open the door," I demand.

He looks at me for a brief second, then turns away and walks over to a dented, rusted metal cabinet on the wall. He pries it open and I see several guns piled on the top shelf. V shifts his weight toward me, almost taking a step. The weight of my own gun on my hip is reassuring and my fingertips tingle with the desire to wrap my hand around it. It's like it knows. Like in this moment it is not an inanimate object but an extension of myself, somehow already aware a situation like this would usually warrant my weapon being in my hand and focused firmly at the man in front of me.

But it stays where it is. For now, I am still playing along.

Psycho stands in front of the cabinet with his back to me, but positioned so it's obvious I can see the guns from my vantage point. He wants me to see them. It's a flex, a show of his confidence and power. I say nothing and he takes a small bottle off another shelf and closes the cabinet doors. The smell of the room around me is burning my throat. It's familiar in a way I don't want it to be. I don't let it show on my face, but I subtly sweep my eyes through all the area of the room that I can see.

I almost missed it. It takes a second look for me to know what I'm seeing. Not twenty feet away from me, near one of the grotesque stained mattresses, a leg sticks out from under a pile of filthy laundry. Already discolored, it clearly belongs to someone who has been here for a while. Blood tinging fabric bunched at the top of the thigh suggests the person didn't have a gentle way out of this world.

"Let's get this done. I have other places to be," I say.

"Still so eager," Psycho says, that morphing smile coming back to his lips. "You should relax. Hang out a while. I bet you'd find we could be…" his fingertips slide down the front of my neck and briefly dip into my neckline. He might think he's smart and still be checking for surveillance equipment. He might just be an ass. "Friends."

"I'm not really in the market for new friends right now," I reply tersely. "I'm here because Gideon sent me and I'd like to get what they want and be on my way."

His eyes flicker over to the body under the dirty clothes and he tosses me a grin like I caught him with an untidy living room and is trying to brush it off.

"This one got in a little over her head," he says. "No worries. Come on." He opens the bottle and tips something granular into his palm. He dips the tip of his pinky into it and touches it to his tongue. "Try a bit."

"Just here for the shopping, not the samples."

He laughs. "I like you. You should stay. Party with me."

He's getting increasingly close to me and I'm very aware of V behind me, creating a barrier between me and the door. I have a feeling this is far from the first time they've played out this dynamic.

"Too bad these aren't my dancing shoes," I say.

"Oh, that's alright. You can take them off. In fact," he reaches out to take hold of my shirt. "Why don't you go ahead and take all of it off."

I struggle away from his grasp, but make sure to not make any sudden movements. "Get your hands off me."

"What happened to being so eager?"

His flashing eyes and undulating smile have become menacing.

"I told you I am here for one reason and one reason only," I say. "Give me what Gideon wants."

"And what do I get in return?" he asks.

"Here."

I reach into my pocket for the bundle of cash taken out of my own bank account this morning. It's not enough to make much of a difference to me, and I'm willing to do it to help Lois, but the principle pisses me off. Psycho watches the stack of bills drop to the sticky top of a nearby table, then looks back at me.

"Maybe Gideon wasn't clear about what I was offered," he says. He gets close enough that I can smell his stale breath and feel the heat radiating off his body. "Why don't you get a little more comfortable?"

"Don't touch me," I say. "I don't care what you think Gideon offered you. Take the money, give me the damn bottle, and let me out of here."

Psycho waves his finger and tsks like he's disciplining a child. "Ah-ah-ah. You haven't figured it out yet, have you? You don't leave until I've decided I got enough. And you *really* don't want to try me." Something dangerous flickers in his eyes and he lowers his voice. "I know you saw the guns in that cabinet. I'm happy to take them out so you can get a better look at them, but they don't like to be taken out unless they're going to be used." He nods toward the body under the dirty clothes. "Maybe I should just give you some time down here with my friend over there. She can tell you all about what happens when people think they're more than they actually are."

"Seems like you'd be the one to tell me that," I counter.

He briefly bites his bottom lip, his gaze dropping as he lets out a chuckle. In one swift movement, his head pops up and his fist swings around to punch me in the side of the head. The blow drops me and it takes a second to be able to see straight again. I shake my head, trying to get my bearings.

"Get her up," Psycho says. V reaches down and grabs me by the arm, wrenching me up off the floor. "Take her gun."

The large man reaches for my hip to wrangle my gun out of its holster. That's enough to break through any daze. I slam my elbow up into the underside of his chin and follow it up with a hard kick to his gut. He stumbles back, breaking through a flimsy wood table and smashing his head on the cement floor. Psycho lunges at me, but I'm already going for him. His nose crushes under my fist and his body buckles with a sweep of my leg around his knees. I drop my elbow into the middle of his back to flatten him, then kneel with my knee between his shoulder blades.

Wrapping an arm around his neck, I yank his head up so my mouth is beside his ear.

"No one touches my gun," I snarl. "If you were actually going to *use* one of those weapons you have in the cabinet, you would already have it when I came in here. If I don't miss my guess, they don't even have bullets in them and that friend of yours died from badly cut drugs and a dirty needle."

V groans and starts to pull himself up off the floor. I take out my gun and point it at him. "I suggest you just keep resting. This isn't for show. It is loaded and I am very familiar with how to use it." V stays on the floor.

I put my face down again. "Just a tip, calling yourself Psycho makes you sound like a pansy-ass piece of shit. Choose something else before you try to go play with the big boys."

I release his head and snatch the bottle he'd dropped. I make a point to stand on his back for a step as I walk out of the basement and hurry up the steps. As I make my way back across the yard and around the side of the house to the street, I notice a bike leaned up against the wall. There's just enough light coming from the moon overhead for me to see bright green paint streaked across one side of the frame. Putting that in the back of my mind, I jog back to my car. One of the back windows is smashed and it looks like someone started to take one of the tires off but gave up.

It's better than I thought it would be, and I take the tablet out of the lockbox, check the backseat, and get inside. The doors locked and my gun visible sitting on the dashboard in front of me, I put my phone in the holder so I can get directions home. Before I can start the car, I get a text.

You know the deal. No cops, Agent Griffin.

I snatch the phone and message back.

Bullshit. No deal. I have the address of a flop house and the drugs you offered me up as payment for.

A response comes through immediately.

And I have Lois.

Another message contains a video clip. I click on it and see Lois gripping the rubber tube above her head, screaming into it. A gush of dark brown water comes down the tube and into Lois's mouth. She sputters and more muddy water splashes onto her face.

Go ahead and call the police. They won't find me. And you won't find Lois.

I shake with rage and slam the steering wheel.

Your choice.

CHAPTER TWENTY-EIGHT

What do you want?

IT'S THE FOURTH TIME I'VE TEXTED THE UNKNOWN PERSON SINCE the day I left the drug house. The only communication I've gotten since then is instructions for where to leave the bottle I took with me. I expected to find something in the hollowed-out area under a rock where I was instructed to go immediately after leaving the neighborhood. I thought there would be a note or some kind of clue the way there has been during other similar tasks during this messed-up game.

But there was nothing. I put the bottle under the rock and stayed nearby until the sun came up and a security guard told me I had to leave. Showing my shield wouldn't have mattered. Without good reason for me to be there, a legitimate case I'm working I can reference, pulling my weight will only cause disruption and bring attention I don't need. I was tired, dirty, and aching from the run-in in the basement. As frustrated as I was not to see someone come and pick the bottle up, I needed to get home.

After a couple hours of sleep, I checked my messages anticipating the next instruction but found nothing. I get a call from Gene early in the afternoon.

"I just thought I'd let you know we've finished canvassing the apartment complex behind the store where Sherry was murdered. A few people mentioned seeing someone running away, but the descriptions varied so much it seems to me one or two of them might have actually seen the killer, but the others probably just saw someone who lives there taking an evening jog or something. A couple people told us there were visitors in the complex because of a big birthday party, but we were able to track them down. I interviewed that young couple again and they gave the same information. And I spoke with a woman who matched the description a couple of people gave for someone they didn't recognize in the neighborhood, but she was there visiting her sister and was just getting there when it happened."

"That's not a lot to go on," I say.

"No, it's not. We've talked to Sherry's children and grandchildren, but it didn't turn up anything else. You know Tricia didn't have any family. We talked to a couple of her neighbors and they all said she was more energetic than people half her age, was always getting into something, and always stopped to talk to anybody she saw around. Every Christmas she made baskets of treats and left them on porches. Even though she lived alone, they said she was rarely actually by herself. There were constantly people visiting her."

"Anyone in particular?" I ask. "Did they notice someone who came frequently?"

"I don't know," he says. "They just said they saw people coming to see her often."

"Find out," I tell him. "I need to know if there was anyone who came regularly. Get me a description, a car make and model, anything."

"Got it."

I end the call and immediately open my phone again to call Shawna. She's still reluctant and her voice trembles as she talks, but she agrees to meet with me and bring me to the places she and Pat were going to the day Pat died. I tell her I'll be at her house in an hour and get ready to leave. Before I get in the car, I check on Lois. She's almost completely still, her eyes closed and her hands folded on her chest. For a second, fear jumps into my heart, then I notice her eyelids fluttering and relief settles over me. I wish I could say something to her. Even if I don't know where she is and can't get to her right now, I wish there was a way she could hear my voice and know I'm trying.

A message pops into my texts as I pull out of my driveway.

Stop investigating the murders.

I stare at the message, stunned at the request. For the first time, I can't just go along with what the faceless person on the other end says.

I can't do that. I'm a federal agent. I can't just walk away from my assignment.

Even if I could, there's no way I would. I'm driven to find out who this person is and why they killed Sherry, Tricia, and Pat. No threats from them will stop me. I'll do what I can to find Lois alive, but my willingness to play along stops at stepping aside in the investigation.

Then send me all your evidence. You have twenty-four hours.

Frustrated and angry at the demand, I don't bother to respond. They are giving me twenty-four hours, so I'm going to take some time to think about how to handle it.

When I arrive at Shawna's house, I notice a car parked in the driveway and another in front. They both look familiar, but it isn't until I'm walking up the front sidewalk that I know why. The door opens and Shawna steps out onto the porch with Macy. The bright sunlight brings out the gold highlights in Macy's auburn hair. She and Shawna are two of the youngest members of From Heart to Heart. I don't know their actual ages, I'd say probably ten or fifteen years older than me, but Shawna's straight blonde hair and rounder body make her look the younger of the two.

Macy takes a step down from the porch before she notices me.

"Hey, Emma," she says. "Shawna mentioned you were coming over. I don't mean to interrupt. I just wanted to stop by and check on Shawna and see how she's doing. I know this has been a lot for her."

"It's been a lot for all of us," Shawna says.

Macy hums her agreement and pulls Shawna into a hug. "If you need anything, call me. I'm ten minutes away."

"Thank you."

Macy manages a tight smile as she walks toward me. "I'm glad you're here. She's been having such a hard time. I think it will make her feel safer to have you around."

"Safer?" I ask.

Macy's eyes narrow slightly like she isn't sure how I missed her meaning. "She was supposed to be there that day. The only reason she wasn't was because she got delayed. We don't know what could have happened if she had gotten there on time. She might have been killed. She feels like she has a target on her. You'll make her feel better."

"She isn't alone, though. Her husband's here with her."

Macy shook her head. "He's a trucker. He's away most of the time."

"Emma?"

I look over Macy's shoulder at Shawna. She's still standing on the porch, her arms wrapped around herself tightly even though it's a relatively warm day.

"You be careful, too. Keep your eyes open. If you see anything…"

"I'll get in touch."

I nod and she heads to the car parked in front of the house. I walk up onto the porch and Shawna and I go inside.

"It was nice of her to come by."

Shawna smiles slightly. "A couple of the ladies have. It's good to feel like part of a community. Especially when Carl is away."

"I didn't realize he was away from home a lot," I say. "The day you were supposed to meet me at the workshop you said he had an emergency at work and you had to go to the hospital to be with him."

I keep my voice casual, trying not to sound suspicious.

"He gets a couple of days off for every week that he drives. He had a heart attack on his way back out on the road. He's been in a cardiac rehab center since." She shifts her weight and looks down at her feet. "The other ladies at the workshop don't know. I figured they already had enough to worry about, they didn't also need to worry about Carl and me. The only one I told was Pat when I realized I wasn't going to be on time."

"But you shouldn't have to be worrying about this alone, Shawna," I tell her. "You deserve support. I wish you had told me."

"Of all people, you certainly don't need anything else on your mind. He's going to be alright. The doctors didn't hesitate when I told them I was going to be gone for a couple of hours and came out to the workshop. I feel selfish wishing he was home with me so I wasn't alone."

"That's not selfish," I say. "You aren't the only one who is afraid. And I'm doing everything I possibly can to end this."

"You will. I know you will." She draws in a breath and lets it out in a resolute sigh. "And I'm going to try to help you. Let's go."

As we drive toward the warehouse, Shawna tells me everything she knows about the work of the covert group within the organization. It isn't much. She already warned me that she didn't have as much involvement or knowledge as Tricia, but she apologizes again as she largely reiterates things I've already learned. She's in a strange place, balanced between knowing she is the last remaining tie to Rescue in the group and because of that has information no one else does, and the disappointment of knowing she doesn't have all the answers even still.

I already have some familiarity with the warehouse because of the research I did after I first found out about it. Officially the space is owned by a company that went out of business years ago and hasn't been utilized since that company moved out. There's some graffiti, and every now and again teenagers trespass to get some sort of street cred, but other than that, it's essentially just been a hunkering old cement building. At least to those who just walked down the cracked sidewalk in front of it or drove past barely noticing it on their way to better things.

They don't know the warehouse is one of a handful of hubs used by Pat, Tricia, Sherry, and Shawna to conceal what they were doing. Rather than keeping everything centralized in just one location, according to Shawna, they met, worked on projects, and stored things in these different places. That way everything wouldn't be compromised if one location was somehow breached.

She brings me into the warehouse and through several doors to a room with a hatch in the floor. It opens into a pit, reminding me of the deep wells garages sometimes have that let mechanics get beneath a vehicle without having to lift it up. Alarm bells start to go off in my head as Shawna gestures for me to go down beneath the building.

It hasn't escaped me that she is the only survivor of the group, the one person who has this knowledge still. She could be feigning ignorance, pretending she doesn't know as much as the others supposedly did in order to throw off the natural suspicion.

At the same time, I am also very aware that even if she is telling me the truth, we have still walked into a potentially dangerous situation. The person responsible for murdering the three women, and who still has Lois held hostage, knows something about what's going on. The extent to which they are aware is still a question, but it's obvious they want to know more. If they've found out about this place, we could be walking straight into the lion's den.

"We need to take a step back," I tell her. "I'm going to call for some extra support."

"Extra support?" she asks.

"To ensure we're safe and that any situation that may arise can be handled," I say.

Shawna shakes her head. "I'm not supposed to talk about these things with anybody other than you. I can't break that confidence." She sounds nervous, almost frantic, as if she worries that something could happen to her if she shares too much. "That's why I didn't call the police the night of the break-in."

"I'm not calling the police. At least, not Detective McGraw and those investigators. I'm going to call my husband and cousin. You've met them, remember? My husband is a sheriff and my cousin is a private investigator. They've helped me with a lot of cases. You can trust them."

She nods and I make the call. The night at the drug house looms large in the back of my mind. It was by far not the first time I've been in an environment like that. It wasn't even the first time I've bought drugs and tried to ignore bodies. I tucked that all away in my mind, knowing there will come a day very soon when it all goes to McGraw so he can do what needs to be done. It eats at me that I haven't done anything with it yet. But it's the choice I had to make, and unfortunately there are times when it becomes necessary to choose a living person over a dead one, to be able to look beyond a corpse and not acknowledge its humanity in order to do everything possible to save someone still breathing.

I walked into that house knowing there was a unit less than a mile away. They didn't know why. I didn't give them any details about what I was doing or even where I was going to be. An app on my phone had been programmed to send out an emergency alert with details of how to find me if I didn't deactivate it within a set amount of time.

But I don't have that measure in place today. I came to meet Shawna without thinking of the potential risks and now I realize I need to be more cautious. Not just for myself, but for everyone else involved in this.

When they arrive, Xavier isn't with them. He's still at the house, deciphering the codes. There's something missing. He's been able to unlock most of it, but there's a final key somewhere that controls what he believes will likely be the most important missives. The complexity of the code looms in my thoughts. There's something there. It feels off, but I can't place it.

Dean and Sam follow us down into the room beneath the main floor and we find ourselves in what looks almost like a bunker. If it wasn't for the clearly modern lighting and how clean the space is, it might pass for a bomb shelter. Instead, it feels like a repurposed space. It was once something else, but has since been converted into a room that could be used as both an office and rudimentary living quarters.

"This is where they would come when they were working on some-thing especially sensitive," Shawna tells us. "I was never at those meet-ings, but I would help them set up and then after would help with deliveries. There are documents stored in a hidden lockbox, but I don't have the key."

"Where's the box?" I ask.

She shows us how to move a piece of furniture to reveal a panel in the wall that then slides out of the way to reveal a safe.

"Did they keep a key here?" I ask.

It's a long shot. Going to so much trouble to conceal something only to stash a key within reach of it would be a tremendous oversight. And yet, at the same time, so simplistic and seemingly ridiculous some-one might do it thinking no one would actually realize what they were seeing.

"No," Shawna says. "As far as I know, only Tricia had one. Pat might have, but I never saw her use it. I only saw the lockbox opened once and that was to put a file into it. I never saw what was inside."

I look over at Dean. He's smart and intuitive, but his thought pro-cesses aren't why I asked him to be here. I figured I might be in use of some of his more specialized skills. I don't have to say anything. He nods and reaches into his pocket for the slim black case he almost always has somewhere on his person. It takes him a few minutes, but he manages to get the lock open.

"Tricky, but not impossible," he announces as he stands up. "I guess they thought there were enough layers of security already in place they didn't need to go too extreme in locking the box. It's actually kind of refreshing to see people choosing manual locks again over these fancy new computerized ones. They might be more convenient in some ways, but they are also buggy as hell and can cause a world of trouble if they malfunction."

He steps aside and gestures at the box with a dramatic sweep-ing hand.

"Thanks," I say as I shine the tiny flashlight kept on my keys into the box.

I learned a long time ago not to just go sticking my hand in places without looking first. A fairly simple lock could mean not going the extra mile to secure something. It could also mean a trap.

The beam of light falls on several stacks of files. I pull them out and bring them over to a table where I open them. One is filled with images of crocheted and knitted items without context or caption. Several of the other folders are almost exactly like the ones I found in the coffin beneath my mother's gravestone. They detail the cases they worked with the Rescue group and the exact role they played in the process of saving the desperate women.

Another folder holds a stack of glossy photos. Like the pictures of the stitched pieces, there are no explanations behind the seemingly random assortment of objects, landscapes, and vehicles. There are a couple of drone images that show what look like the same locations from different angles and others that appear to be schematics and blueprints. We spread everything out on the table and try to scour each of them for any indication of what it could all mean.

"Any of this ring a bell?" I ask Shawna.

She shakes her head. "I don't know. I'm sorry."

"Don't be. This stuff is very complicated," I tell her. "I know the Rescue group. I am very familiar with what it does. And I know a lot goes into it, but what you're telling me, all these pictures with no explanation, and what I've seen with the coded pieces… it goes so far beyond that."

"Emma," Dean says.

He's holding another folder open in his hands. I stand beside him to look inside.

"That's an official seal," I say, touching my fingertips to the document at the top of the stack. "CIA."

"Someone has redacted almost all of it," he says. "All that's left is some dates and a couple of code names."

I take the folder from his hands and go through the documents. "More CIA. USAID. State Department. Oh, my god."

Dean points to a seal I don't recognize. "I've seen that. During my SEAL days. It's a highly classified group some people don't even believe exists."

"Holy shit, what is this?" I whisper. I flip another couple of pages and pull one out. My eyes burn as I scan over it. Like the others, most of the document has been blacked out, undoubtedly by Tricia or Pat after the information was used and no longer needed but still required protection. But what's left is still recognizable. And I know the seal like I know my name. "FBI."

CHAPTER TWENTY-NINE

"WHAT WERE THEY DOING?" SHAWNA WHISPERS, HER EYES wide as they sweep over the papers.

"We need to go," I say. I gather up all the documents and files and carry them with me back up the metal ladder onto the main floor. "Sam, call Eric. Find out if he's got anything on the woman at the airport. Tell him I'm on my way there."

"Got it. Be careful. Call me."

"I will," I say, getting into my car and ushering Shawna into the passenger's side. "I love you."

"Love you."

My phone blinks with another message.

What do the messages say? What has he found?

I don't have time to answer right now. Instead, I quickly check on Lois. Her head rocks back and forth slowly and she licks her lips. Her hair has become matted from lying there for so long. She searches for the rubber tube and tries to suck something out of it, but it's dry. I turn off the video and head for Shawna's house.

"I'm going to drop you back at your house. Just like I told you before, I need you to stay inside and not speak with anyone. Listen to me, Shawna. Anyone."

"I won't," she says.

"If you want to go see your husband, please arrange for someone to bring you, preferably someone not in From Heart to Heart."

"I will."

"You have no idea how much you've helped," I tell her.

"I wish I could have done more."

I look over at her to try to comfort her and see that she has a piece of paper in her hand and is looking at it intently.

"What's that?" I ask.

She turns the paper toward me to show me a sequence of markings, lines, and curves stacked on each other in a way that seems to suggest shapes but nothing specific.

"I found this tucked in with some of the other documents. There are a few of them," she says.

"Another code?" I ask.

"No, it's a crochet pattern done in a chart," she explains. "You learn what stitch each of the symbols corresponds to and then all you need to do to learn a new pattern is look at the chart. Some people hate them, but others swear by them. My grandmother never used a written pattern. If it didn't have a chart, she didn't make it. She knitted, but it's the same concept."

"What are the different colors for?" I ask, nodding at the paper to indicate the sections of symbols written in different inks.

Shawna shakes her head. "I'm not sure. It's not something that usually shows up on charts like this. Some people highlight their charts to help them follow along more easily, but this was actually written in those colors. This is a continuous pattern. The five colors don't correspond with anything about the pattern that makes sense. It's not the individual stitches or different sections or special techniques or anything. That's really strange."

We arrive at her house and Shawna sets the folders down in her seat. I watch her go into her house and the minute I know she's safe, I head for the airport. My phone rings while I'm barreling down the highway. It's Eric. The airport is just on the outskirts of DC, so I have a drive ahead of me, but I need to get there.

"Please tell me you have good news, Eric."

"Hey. I've got some info on the woman from the airport. According to the passenger manifest, her name is April Sheridan. Does that mean anything to you?" he asks.

"No. It doesn't sound familiar. Damn. Anything else about her? Anything that might make a difference?"

"No. She got on a plane to East Texas, and that's it," he tells me.

I let out a sigh. "Alright. Thank you. I'm headed to the airport now to see if I can talk to the pilot. Did Sam fill you in?"

"Some. What the hell is going on out there?"

"I don't know. But I'm going to find out. I'll keep you updated," I say.

I end the call and my eyes flash over to the papers sitting on the passenger seat. I see the stitch chart and realize why it looks so familiar. I pull off the road so I can pull up the picture of the small piece of paper found folded up in the waistband of Pat's pants. The markings look almost identical. For the first time, I realize the markings are in blue ink, the same shade as on the larger pattern.

I send the picture to Xavier with a voice message attached explaining what it is. My mind churning, I get back to the drive.

The pilot who flew Roman Cleary's private flight is eating in one of the restaurants just outside security when I finally track him down. I walk up to the table with my shield already in hand.

"Christian Smith?" I ask.

A bewildered expression on his face, he wipes his mouth with a napkin and nods. "Yes. Is there something wrong?"

"I'm Agent Emma Griffin with the FBI. I have some questions for you about a recent flight. Can I join you? Or would you rather speak somewhere else?"

He gestures at the seat across the table from him. "Please. Sit. I don't have long. I have a private flight in an hour."

"This won't take long. Has anyone spoken to you about the passenger Roman Cleary?"

He takes another bite of his sandwich and nods as he chews. "Yes. I spoke with an officer who needed me to confirm that he did get on the flight."

"And he did?"

"Yes. But I didn't see him. My copilot and I were given strict instructions that neither of us were to emerge from the cockpit after half an hour before takeoff and until half an hour after landing. We're accustomed to piloting flights for special agents and other sensitive passengers. Political figures, law enforcement, military leaders. We're held to the utmost scrutiny, so this wasn't all that unusual a request," the pilot tells me.

"Was there anything else unusual about the flight? Any other instructions you were given?" I ask.

"I was warned that there would be a point during the flight when the side door would be opened and that all proper safety precautions would be taken. Again, the specific craft I was flying is designed for the doors to be opened from the inside. Similar to what you might see with skydiving. I expect if a passenger has secured that specific type of air-craft they have a reason for it. I don't need to know that reason. All that matters is we do as we are told so we don't compromise the needs of the passenger, and that's what we did. The agents on board needed those specifications to be upheld, so we didn't question it."

I take note of his wording. "Agents?"

"Yes. That flight had two passengers. I don't know the second man's name. Again, not information I need in order to successfully captain a flight."

"Is there anything possible you could give me about him? Even a physical description?"

He shakes his head. "No. We didn't even see their faces."

I thank him for speaking with me and go out into the bustling termi-nal again. It's a smaller airport compared to the massive, congested ones closer to the heart of the city, but it's still busy, especially at this time of day. I watch as people hurry to get to the next step in their traveling process, getting tickets, checking bags, going through security. As I'm standing near the security line, I watch a man take a zippered plastic bag out of his bag. Rather than containing the expected toiletries, it has doc-uments. One item looks like a birth certificate. He looks at an ID card and then sifts through the papers in the bag. Apparently made confident by what he sees, he heads into the nearest security line.

I'm back on the phone with Eric as soon as I get to the parking deck.

"There was someone else on the flight," I tell him.

"What are you talking about?"

"I just spoke with the pilot from Roman Cleary's flight. I wanted to find out if there was anything unusual about the flight or if Roman was acting strangely during it. But according to Captain Smith, he didn't even see him. Not before the flight or after."

"We already knew that. Like I said, Roman got off the flight at the destination, but then didn't reach his contact. We're still looking into the failsafes that were in place, but as far as we've been able to find out, he didn't utilize any of those, either. All we know is that he did get off that flight," Eric tells me.

"We know somebody got off that flight. And if it was only one person, that says a lot," I say.

"What do you mean?"

"The pilot confirmed that everything was done according to the needs of the agents onboard. Agents, plural," I emphasize.

"He must have misspoken. Roman Cleary was the only person on that flight."

"No. He didn't misspeak. He specified that there was a second man on the flight. He didn't see either one of them, but there were two."

"I don't know what to tell you, Emma, but that flight was booked for one agent. Roman Cleary. Nobody else should have been on it," Eric says. "Is there anything else you need me to look for?"

"Try to find out more about April Sheridan. There has to be something we're missing."

I hang out feeling frustrated by his pushback. I understand the plans for the flight only included Roman, but the pilot was very clear. He said agents. Plural. And then he specifically confirmed that there was a second man on board. That's not something he's going to just imagine. And if two men got on that flight and only one got off, something very serious happened while they were in the air.

And Tricia and Pat knew about it.

CHAPTER THIRTY

"It's the last piece of the cipher," Xavier confirms later by phone while I'm on my way back to Sherwood. "It's brilliant. Rather than just relying on finished pieces, a pattern can be far more easily distributed and transported, and the markings themselves easily manipulated so they look perfectly normal to someone who doesn't know what they are looking at."

"But guides the version of the code to those who know," I say.

"Exactly."

"This is so much bigger than just Rescue," I say, feeling antsy as the traffic in front of me slows and I feel trapped among the cars. "I thought they were just involved in domestic activities of the Rescue group. But it was too much. It was too complex. Now with the link to Roman Cleary and everything that we found in that warehouse..."

I take a breath, barely believing what I'm about to say. "These women are involved with international operations groups. Intelligence groups. They're not just dedicated to helping domestic abuse sufferers or people seeking asylum from oppression. The covert group within From Heart to Heart was a relief organization, but it sounds like they were…"

"Spies," Xavier finishes.

"And whoever's behind all this knows what the women do and want to get their hands on the information."

"Someone is working for the other side."

The cars in front of me are slowed to a near-stop. I turn my wheel sharply to pull out of the line of traffic and off an exit that leads to a rest area.

"Xavier, give me to Sam, please."

I tell Sam I'm going to stop for a little bit while traffic calms down, maybe grab a snack at the rest stop. He reminds me I've been going non-stop all day and there would still be a couple of hours of driving ahead of me before I get home. He convinces me to check into a hotel, at least for a few hours, and get back on the road when I'm rested and he can know I'm driving safely.

There's a pocket of hotels and 24-hour restaurants not much further down the exit, so I continue on and pull into the parking lot of the first one I reach. Grabbing the overnight bag I always keep ready in the trunk of my car and all the files from the warehouse, I go inside and get a room. A hot shower does me good and I sit in the middle of the bed waiting for food from a nearby diner to be delivered as I check on Lois. It feels selfish and indulgent to be comfortable the way I am while she looks so miserable. She has her head turned to the side and several strands of sweaty hair stuck to her cheek, almost looking like blood.

Have you made your choice, Agent Griffin? You're not going to try anymore?

The message puts my jaw on edge and twists my stomach.

I don't know what you want.

If I play dumb, I might be able to draw something out of them, encourage them to make a mistake.

Yes, you do. The messages, Agent. The deciphered ones. I want them.

I can't get them to you now. I'm not at home.

In the morning, then. Get them to me and get your men to back off. And maybe I won't have to punish Lois again for your misbehavior. I'm running out of patience, Agent Griffin. And Lois is running out of time.

The messages stop and I go back to watching the feed of Lois, trying to see any signs of her condition. I see the TXT message on the side of the box and look for anything else that might be there that I could have missed. There could be another hint, intentional or not, that could tell me where she is. I watch until my food arrives, then pause to eat. I fall into a fitful sleep with chaotic thoughts bouncing off one another, trying to form themselves into ideas that feel just beyond my reach.

When I check out of the hotel the next morning, I notice the car beside me looks like it's recently been involved in an accident. A streak of white paint mars the black surface of the back passenger door and along the rear. The image immediately sparks a flash of memory. Bright green paint streaked across the frame of a bicycle leaning up against the drug house.

Tossing everything into the car, I jump in and get on a call to Sam.

"I need you to get in touch with all the body shops throughout Mount Percy, Sherwood, and the surrounding areas," I tell him. I describe the bike and the paint on it. "It was like the transfer that was on my car after being hit by the green car. We haven't been able to track down the green car, but we haven't been asking about anyone getting a paint job fixed after hitting a bike. There might have also been some damage to the undercarriage."

I'm not even halfway home before he calls me back.

"Superior Auto Body and Detailing on Clover Road just outside Mount Percy worked on a bright green two-door that had an unfortunate run-in with a bicycle about a month ago. Messed up the paint job and did a little bit of damage to the muffler, but nothing serious."

"Did they give you the VIN? Can we trace it?" I ask.

"Already done. It's registered to a Ted and Lacy Carter of 2319 Pine Forest Road," he says.

"You are amazing. I'm headed there now. I love you."

I know it's a long shot to hope that the green car will be sitting outside of the house when I arrive, but I'm still a bit disappointed when I don't see it. I walk up to the front door and ring the bell. A pleasant, perfectly conventional-looking woman I would place in her early fifties answers.

"Can I help you?"

"Hi," I say with as bright and disarming a smile as I can manage. "I'm sorry to interrupt your day. My name is Emma Griffin. I'm with the FBI. Are you Lacy Carter?"

"FBI? Is something wrong?"

She looks frightened but not necessarily surprised.

"Honey? Who's at the door?"

A man a few years older than her who perfectly corresponds with her in appearance comes up behind Lacy and slips an arm around her waist. Khakis, a pastel sweater set, and a dusty blue polo make them a pristine picture. They should be smiling out from a silver picture frame in a high-end department store somewhere.

"She says she's with the FBI," Lacy tells her husband.

He extends his hand to me. "Ted Carter. Is everything alright?"

"Emma Griffin. I'm sorry for upsetting you. I am just here to ask a couple of questions."

"Come on in," Ted says, stepping back and gently guiding his wife along with him.

They bring me a few feet into the house, but not all the way into the living room. I can understand. An FBI agent showing up on their front porch unsolicited isn't something most people would welcome cheerfully.

I ask them about the car, avoiding talking about it running me off the road or the bike I saw. Instead, I suggest it was described as being near the scene of an incident and that I was looking for a potential witness. This seems to put Lacy at ease.

"Yes," Lacy says without hesitation. "That car is registered to us, but it belongs to our son. We bought it for him as a gift a few years ago."

"Was there any damage to the vehicle recently?" I ask. "I just want to make sure that I found the right one."

"Yes, Clinton backed over his own bike." Ted shakes his head but gives a good-natured chuckle. "I wonder about that boy sometimes."

Despite the laugh, these words seem to sting Lacy. She forces a smile but it trembles. This is a mother who has dealt with her son's shit for years and is used to carrying the burden of worry while her husband deludes himself. I can imagine the kinds of thoughts that likely went through her head when I introduced myself. It's impossible she isn't aware of her son's drug use and likely many kinds of erratic, dangerous, and criminal behaviors. I won't elaborate on it for her. She'll know it all soon enough.

"And do you know if he was on or near Blue Bell Road on the sixteenth of last month? Particularly the gas station at the corner of Sweetwater?"

I'm pulling names out of my memory of looking over a map of the area. They at least seem familiar with what I'm talking about and exchange questioning looks.

"Possibly," Ted says. "He had a friend who lived over in that area when he was younger. Did he do something?"

"No," I say, shaking my head and brightening my smile. "Not at all. He just could have seen something helpful. Or maybe not. We just always like to follow up on everything we can."

They nod and I can see the gears turning in their heads as they start to wonder why the FBI would be involved in something so apparently minor they hadn't even heard about it.

"If we see him, we'll certainly let him know you were asking. Do you have a business card I can give him?"

I take one out of my pocket and hand it to her. If he ever gets a chance to see that card, it won't be in his last days of freedom. But I would like to see the look on his face when he sees my name.

"Well, I think I've taken up enough of your time. Thank you for your help." As I'm turning to leave, I notice a crocheted shawl draped over the back of a chair. I point to it. "That's lovely."

"Thank you," Lacy says. "A friend of mine made it for me."

"Good friend. Thank you, again. Have a good afternoon."

I had asked Sam to handle another round of inquiry phone calls while I went to meet with the couple, and by the time I get home, he has answers for me.

"We called every rental car agency in the area. None of them have rented out a maroon van in the last couple of months. But then I contacted Rent Used, that place over near the old movie theater. The one that rents out the old cars other agencies don't want. They don't require a credit card and accept cash payment. It took a little bit of prodding, but I did finally get the owner to admit that sometimes when someone agrees to pay cash, with a little extra, they'll even rent them a vehicle without recording their identification."

"And they rented out a maroon van recently?"

"Just before you saw one following behind you," he confirms. "He didn't have a name to give me, but he said he'd never forget renting to the guy. He said he was a tall, scrawny dude with tattoos all over his face and bright green hair. He said he didn't understand why the guy wouldn't want to leave his name or an ID. It isn't like anyone could miss him."

The description is exactly what I'd expected: my good friend who calls himself Psycho. The one whose parents bought him a car that matches his hair and try really hard to hang on to loving their child even as they watch him spiral.

"Was there anyone else with him when he rented the van?"

"The owner said he thought he saw someone else climb into the back of the van, but they weren't able to describe them."

"Can you get a warrant for the van and have CSU process it?" I ask. "I'm sure it's been cleaned since it was rented, but there might still be some kind of trace evidence available."

"I'm on it."

"Thank you, babe. Where's Xavier?" I ask.

"The gym," Sam says.

"The gym?"

That doesn't sound like Xavier. It makes more sense when I get to the back room Sam converted a few years ago and find Xavier has set up several large banquet tables and has all the evidence laid out on them. The butcher paper list of words from the code is now hanging over the mirror on the wall and another piece beside it has a frenetic storm of words scribbled all over it.

"Anything, X?" I ask.

"I'm getting there," he tells me. "Do you have the charts?"

I give him the documents and his face tightens.

"What's wrong?"

"The colors," he says. "They're just bothering me. I don't understand why they're there."

"The chart Pat was hiding is in this same shade of blue," I point out. "Maybe the number itself means something? Have you seen any other references to the number five in any of the messages?"

"No. The only numbers I've found are references to 'two' and then a couple of 'three.'"

"Alright, keep trying."

I leave the gym-turned-office and call Eric. He's already deep in the midst of trying to contact the departments and organizations that Tricia and Pat were clearly working with to try to get more information about what they were doing. I want to be surprised that none of them have reached out to assist the murder investigation, but I'm not. It's an unfortunate reality that the preservation of the mission takes precedence over the individuals working on the team. If they were to get involved in the murder investigation, it would mean having to reveal the work the women were doing and compromise what I believe is a very large, complex network.

This isn't something new. This work has been ongoing for years and a slip could cost countless lives. They will look into the murders in their own ways, but it will be more important for them to ensure the work the women did is secure and everything isn't revealed. I know that means they are aware of my involvement. They know I've been assigned to the case and at this point may even be in contact with my father. It will all unfold soon enough, but right now my focus is to stop any more violence.

My next conversation is with Dean. I tell him about the man I saw getting ready to go through security at the airport and the bag of documents he had with him.

"It made me wonder if he was using those documents to supplement identification that had something wrong with it. I know there are steps in place to try to deal with situations when people don't have their ID, it's expired, there's wrong information on it, any of those things. In the footage of April Sheridan going through security at the airport, she hands the front desk her ID, but then also another piece of paper. The camera isn't close enough to show what it is, but I wonder if she could have been using alternate identification."

"Because her boarding pass and her ID didn't match," he says.

"Exactly."

"I'm on it."

"Thank you."

My whirlwind morning of phone calls isn't over yet. Taking just a minute to check on Lois—thankfully, she's still alive—I call Shawna and ask her about the other locations she was going to show me.

"The warehouse isn't the only place they went, you said. There were others."

"Yes. There's a house out in the country that's been in Pat's family for a couple of generations. Sometimes she would go spend weekends out there or have gatherings. But then it turned into a space for the group. A lot of the coded donations were stored there. I don't know for sure since I wasn't involved, but I think that's where they met with their contacts as well."

"Can you send me the address?" I ask.

A stop by the police department gets me Pat's keys that are still being held. Then I head out to the house. Shawna wasn't kidding when she described it as out in the middle of nowhere. It's far beyond the city limits, past lush farmland and sitting in the middle of a large plot of land covered primarily with large trees and a winding creek.

The house looks like a painting as I approach. The tranquil scene is a stark contrast to the tension I'm feeling. I scan the area carefully before walking up to the door and trying each key before I finally unlock the door. I look around but don't find any further documents or communications. In the living room I find a large assortment of items ready to be delivered. Blankets, acrylic squares, and shawls are spread out next to a deep pile of hats.

I run my hand over the stitches of one of the hats. It's smooth and simple, just the same stitch comprising the entire hat. That tells me not everything here has some kind of hidden meaning. These are items meant for From Heart to Heart's main mission, not the clandestine secrets they kept. As I look over the hats, I notice quite a few made with a soft, deep blue yarn. This stands out to me and I take a picture of a couple of them.

Dean calls me as I'm looking through the other items, trying to find ones that have the patterns I've come to recognize.

"You were right. The name on her boarding pass was April Sheridan, but that is her married name. She's divorced now and back to her maiden name of Garth."

"Is her middle name Macy?" I ask, feeling a knot tying in my stomach.

"It is," he says.

"Thanks, Dean. Do me a favor and take some pictures of the crochet charts I gave Xavier, then send them to me," I say.

"Sure. What do you need them for?" he asks.

"Bait."

CHAPTER THIRTY-ONE

WITH THE KNOWLEDGE OF WHO SHE ACTUALLY IS IN MIND, I watch the footage of the woman walking through the airport again. Now that I have her name in the back of my mind, I can see that who I have been calling April Sheridan is actually the Macy I know. She is wearing a very good wig, extra makeup, and clothing I would never imagine her in, but I can recognize her. Something is very wrong. There's no reason she should be at that airport, and she certainly shouldn't be exchanging suitcases with an FBI agent. Or, at least, someone posing as one.

When the images of the chart come through, I stare at them for a few seconds, then text them to the mysterious number. Taking a second to steady myself and swallow down the anger and betrayal I'm feeling, I also send along a picture of the scarf Tricia was wearing when she died. It's one that doesn't show the entire piece. Just enough to give the impression.

You might want this.

Several minutes pass without any response. My chest starts to feel tight. Just when I'm starting to feel like my gamble hasn't paid off and might have just put more people in danger, I get a message back.

Well done, Agent Griffin. You finally made the right choice. I'm impressed. Sherry did a lovely job designing that. And just as I promised.

Another message pops up with a picture of the gates of an old military cemetery and a plot number. I look up the cemetery and find out it's closer to Sherwood than it is to here. I send an old map of the plots to Sam and call him to explain.

"We're on our way," he says.

"I am, too," I tell him. "I'll meet you there."

Locking the door to Pat's house behind me, I run out to my car. As I'm driving toward the abandoned cemetery, the words of the message and what Xavier told me about the numbers in the code filter through my mind. I keep driving as the thoughts twist and bend, forming conclusions that vaporize nearly as soon as they develop only to come together into something else. With the footage of Lois playing on my tablet, I reach over to dig through the glove compartment until I find the papers Tricia had given me the first day I visited the workshop.

A brochure and flyer tell me the history of From Heart the Heart and introduce me to some of the volunteers. Beneath that are several sheets with printed patterns. Each has the name of the designer in tiny letters beneath the title of the pattern. Sifting through confirms my suspicions. Some of them are underlined in different colors. When I first saw that, I thought it indicated the upper volunteers. Now I realize it's something else.

I glance at the screen to see Lois looking terrified and desperate. My phone rings.

"We're at the cemetery," Sam tells me. "We're almost at the plot."

"I'll be there in just a few," I reply. "Don't wait for me. Just get her out of there."

"I can see something," Dean's voice says in the background. "It looks like disturbed dirt."

"I think we found it," Sam reports. "We're almost there. There's something sticking up out of it. Like a narrow pipe."

Horror rushes through me.

"Sam, stop!"

Before I can say anything else, the sound of an explosion makes the phone fall from my hand.

CHAPTER THIRTY-TWO

SOMEHOW, THE LAST FEW MINUTES OF MY DRIVE TO THE CEME-
tery both stretch on for what seems like hours and pass in the blink
of an eye at the same time. I don't bother pulling into a parking
space. I just skid to a stop on the side of the road and I'm leaping over
the fence before I even cut off the engine.

"Sam!" I scream, my heart pounding as I pump my legs faster than
ever before.

"Emma, over here!" comes a voice. I'm already turned and running
in that direction before it registers that it's Dean.

"Are you okay?" I call out. As I get closer, I see Dean helping Sam to
his feet, and I want to break down. There's no blood. No indication of
any major injury.

They're alive. Holy shit. They're alive.

I finally reach them and double over on my hands and knees,
wheezing.

"We… we were…" Sam huffs, "far away enough that we didn't get caught in the blast." He cradles his shoulder, which is covered in dirt. "The blast blew us back and I hit that tombstone, though. Knocked the wind out of me."

I straighten up and throw my arms around him. "I thought I almost lost you," I whisper through tears."

"I know. Believe me, I know."

The EMTs tell me Sam and Dean are both going to be fine. Both have mild burns and scrapes, and Sam has a pretty hefty bruise on his shoulder from being blown into the tombstone by the backdraft. But they're going to be okay.

It's only because I know they are both safe that I'm heading back to the house in the country. I've already called for backup. Their ETA is fifteen minutes. Mine is less than five.

The livestream has gone dark so there's nothing left to check. All the texts from the mysterious number have disappeared, deleted within the app by the sender. But I'm still left with the knowledge that there is corruption within the efforts Tricia believed in so deeply. Betrayal, secrets kept from the wrong people, dirty agents. All building up to murder and the terrifying prospect of what intelligence they'd gathered falling into the wrong hands.

Those words made my teeth grind together. I heard them twice during this investigation. Now I look back and hate myself for not catching on faster.

I walk into the house and immediately smell coffee. Someone is here. My gun drawn, I walk cautiously through the living room, glance left and right at the windows, before turning a corner into the kitchen. Macy stands at the counter, pouring coffee from a pot into a mug. She hears me and turns to face me. A smile flickers to her lips.

"Hello, Agent Griffin," she says. "Nice of you to stop by. I was wondering if I'd see you today. Good thing I just made a fresh pot. Let me pour you a cup."

She takes another mug from a display on the counter and fills it.

"Put it down and go sit at the table," I tell her.

Macy looks at me with the kind of expression a preschool teacher gives a child at the brink of a temper tantrum. She walks slowly across the large kitchen toward the table in the breakfast nook.

"Now, Emma. Can I call you Emma? We're friends here. You don't need that."

"Put it down." She rolls her eyes and sets the mug down. "We are not friends, Macy. And if you make a wrong move, you're not going to be anything. You're going to tell me everything you know. Did Tricia, Sherry, and Pat die because of what happened to Roman Cleary? Or was one horrific crime just not enough?"

Another smile tilts her lips as she takes a sip of her coffee and sets it down.

"The colors on the chart. References to two and then three. Psycho was a nice touch. Was the plan to have him kill me, or just for me to be traumatized and withdraw from the case? But it was carelessness that sealed it. I want you to know you're going down because of a blue hat."

She looks confused. "A blue hat?"

"Sherry was supposed to work on that project. She was the one heading it up. She even came up with the patterns. Patterns with her name on them highlighted in yellow. Just like the yellow chart piece I'm sure will stitch up to make the scarf Tricia was wearing when she died. A little slip in that message. No one knew about that scarf or who worked on it, but you did."

Her eyes flash, but I continue.

But it's those hats. The ones stacked up in the other room. The yarn they're made of couldn't have been bought after her death. She bought all of it from the store. Which means the yarn was bought in a fairly large quantity before her death so they could still be made even when she was gone. Just before, I would say. A matter of an hour or so. That gave time for you to leave without running into Sherry and still be in the area ready to ambush her in the parking lot. After all, the project still had to be finished. And she's nothing if not dedicated."

Macy's eyes narrow. She knows now. Her chin lifts in defiance, but I take a step closer.

"Where's Lois?"

CHAPTER THIRTY-THREE

MACY'S EYES FLICKER SLIGHTLY, AND THE HAIR ON THE BACK OF my neck stands up. For a split second, time freezes, and my thoughts race.

Then, the crash seems to fill all the available sound in the world, and I find myself being pitched to the right and down, my legs useless to hold me up.

Hundreds of tiny shards of broken glass fly through my slow-motion vision of the world as I fall. Each piece glitters in the light, some still clinging to the dark brown liquid drops of coffee. A bubble of morphing shape flies behind them, hot, brown and sticky as it spills over the coffee table, the counter, Macy. It spreads as it accelerates through the air, and by the time I feel my elbow crashing into the wooden floorboards, the hazelnut-flavored projectile has covered most of the kitchen.

My head crashes into the leg of a chair and the world speeds back up.

Pain sets in immediately and is followed by a burning sensation. My left eye is suddenly blurry, and I feel scratches across my cheeks and forehead. Warm, sticky fluid covers the back of my head, and I reach back to place my hand over it. It comes back brown and red.

Coffee and blood.

My legs don't want to get back under me, and I am a sitting duck for Macy as she dives on top of me. Behind her, Lois is throwing the handle of the coffee pot toward the sink, her teeth gritted as she watches the fight unfold.

I try to get my arms up to block the first punch. I miss.

Macy doesn't.

My head rocks back as her fist buries itself into my cheek. Another rains down on my chin from the other side. She is wailing at me as I try to get my arms up.

I buck my hips and roll hard to my right. My feet slip on something sticky, but the momentum carries Macy off me and off balance. I use the opening to swing an elbow high and wide. It's a wild shot, but it connects. I feel her back up. Getting to one knee, I try to find her with my one good eye, squinting the other shut as liquid runs down my face and I give up the hope that it isn't my own plasma spilling everywhere.

Macy rebounds, getting to her feet and rearing one leg back. She swings a soccer kick into my stomach, and I absorb the blow, grasping at her leg. She cries out in surprise as I wrap my arms around her and dive for the floor, taking her with me.

With no idea how to defend an anklelock, Macy flails at me and I twist hard on her foot. I hear a snap, followed by a scream so piercing that it makes me wince.

I let go of her limp leg and roll to my feet, standing just in time to see Lois turning back toward me from her place in front of a drawer in the kitchen counter. She has drawn another weapon.

A butcher's knife.

Macy is rolling on the floor between us, screaming and grasping at her ankle in horror. Lois draws up as tall as she can and runs, diving at me after her second step, swiping the knife diagonally across her.

I dodge at the last second and Lois smashes into the wall. Ramming against her, I press her face-first into the wallpaper and slam my hand against her wrist. It's just enough to get her to drop the knife. It clangs to the ground and I kick at it, sending it away a few feet.

Lois tries to spin around, to face me, but I yank her down by the collar, pulling one arm behind her back and pressing my elbow to the back of her neck. She hits hard and grunts, the wind clearly knocked out of her.

I reach into my back pocket and pull out the handcuffs, slapping one over the wrist in my hand, then pulling the other arm back before she can get her strength back. She kicks and squirms, but I hold her down long enough to cuff her.

Eventually, she stops fighting, exhausted and crying, heaving deep breaths in defeat. Blood is trickling from her mouth and a cut above her eye. But she's done.

Macy is curled up in the fetal position, holding her leg and whimpering. She's no longer a threat either.

Scooting back, keeping my eyes on both of them, I press my back against the counter and reach up, blindly searching until my hand finds what I'm looking for. As the door bursts open and backup arrives, I take a deep sip of the black coffee and wave them in. Blood trickles down my face and into my lip, where I wipe it away before taking another gulp.

One of the officers stares at me. I shrug and hold the mug in the air as if to toast him. A drop of blood falls from my chin and lands in the mug.

"Damn it. I got blood in my coffee."

The arrests go smoothly as I rattle off everything I suspect the two of them of doing, then I yet again find myself loaded into an ambulance and whisked to the hospital. This time, I don't argue. They let Sam and Dean come to my room after I've gotten settled in. Xavier has called Bruce for a tow and should be here soon.

I explain how tiny details building up over the course of a few days led me to the realization that what I believed to be a livestream of Lois was actually a series of pre-recorded segments, set to play whenever I clicked the link. It was expertly done, not a surprise considering the connections I now know Lois has. But she hadn't been careful enough. After the footage of the mud coming through her rubber tube, an effort to make me feel guilty and try to force me to play along, there were several times when she was dirty, but then the next time I checked in, there was no dried mud around her and her hair was no longer matted. They'd lined up the clips out of order.

"And you think Tricia was involved?"

"Not purposely. She brought Lois in to help them handle a new case. She trusted her. She hadn't told the others yet that she'd been working with them. I think she suspected a mole. She didn't realize she was bringing in a snake. I believe Lois at the very least orchestrated those murders to protect the double agent she's been working with. And she brought Macy in to help. There's still so much to unravel. I don't think we've even scratched the surface of what they were doing. But for now, the one responsible is in custody and we can start the process of healing the damage she's done."

EPILOGUE

A WEEK LATER I FINALLY MAKE IT TO JANET AND PAUL'S HOUSE FOR game night. Eric took all the information I was able to get him and they searched the area of the plane's flight path, eventually finding Roman Cleary's body, unceremoniously thrown out of the plane into a body of water. There are still so many questions to be answered. We don't know why he was targeted or the identity of the man who killed him. We will. It's just a matter of time. At least he's home now.

The note from the airport—*"You'll never find me"*—turned out to be what we thought it least likely to be: a game. We finally found out a little boy on a very long layover was playing with this sister and his favorite action toys and came up with the idea of a villain escaping into the night and leaving a mocking note behind. The villain's name was Robo Carnage. A bit intense for an eight-year-old, but at least it explains away the initials.

Sam still says it isn't a coincidence. No such thing. It's the same answer I give when Janet asks if I think all of this had anything to do with my attacks. I know it didn't. What I still don't know is who attacked me and why.

But tonight, I'm going to only think about Scrabble and possibly an ill-advised visit with my old nemesis Mr. Boddy.

"Fill me in on everything that's been happening," I say to Janet as we get started on the massive spread of snacks we always have at the ready for these gatherings. "I feel like I've missed so much."

"That's because you have," Sam says.

"Well," Janet interjects with a laugh, "it's Sherwood, so there isn't ever that much to miss. Did Sam tell you about that weird fog the night you were attacked? It was the strangest I've ever seen. It rolled in like a mist, then settled over the town and just stayed there. It's a miracle there weren't car accidents all over because of it. Then by morning, it was just gone."

"Wasn't there fog the day I woke up?" I ask.

Janet and Paul exchange glances.

"Come to think of it, there was," Paul says.

"But the most excitement came from all the cold cases that got solved," Janet says. "It was amazing watching the news and seeing so many stories about families finally getting the answers they needed. The Village Square Mall massacre. That poor little girl whose bones were found in the school after so many years. I know that has to make you feel so good. Especially the capture of Holden Gray."

She's describing cases I've been researching for years. Intense, devastating cold cases no one has been able to solve.

"Holden Gray?" I ask. A flash of a summer camp drenched in blood flashes through my mind. "From Camp Hollow?"

"Yes," Janet says, looking surprised I don't seem to know what she's talking about. "He was arrested two days before you woke up after being on the run all this time. There was evidence he was planning another spree."

I shake my head in disbelief. "How? How did all these cold cases get solved?"

"Didn't Sam tell you?" Janet asks.

"Tell me what?"

I look at my husband. There's a tinge of red on his ears.

"I, uh. I thought you already had enough on your plate right now. I was planning on telling you at the right time."

"Tell me what?" I repeat.

"I found your files," he admits. "Dean and I were trying to find anything that might help us figure out who had attacked you and we found the cold cases you were working on. We ended up reading through them. You did incredible work, Emma. None of us had any idea you were even working on those cases."

I shrug. "I guess. It was just something I did when I needed to clear my mind of the cases I was working. I work murders right after they happen, but there are so many killed and missing that never get their stories told."

"But you told them. You had already laid out everything. You had those cases solved."

I frown. "I did?"

"Yes, you did. We just had to take the final step. You solved the massacre at Camp Hollow. You caught the Village Square killer. You solved all of them."

"But how? I didn't have all the answers. I was still looking for evidence."

He shrugs. "Maybe just because you were always focused on current cases, you couldn't see the forest for the trees. But they were completely conclusive. Open and shut. We, um..." he chokes out an emotional laugh, "we were saying that you were solving these cases even while in a coma."

That makes me grin. "Wouldn't that be something."

"There are people who want to make a series about you and these cases. But I told them, and Eric, and everyone else no one was to approach you about any of it yet. I'm sorry if I stepped on your toes or took liberties I shouldn't have. I just saw that work and knew it needed to be out there," Sam says.

"Don't apologize. I'm glad you did. The families deserve to know. I just didn't know if the evidence was ready yet."

"It was," Sam says. "There's still work to be done on some of them. But it will get there."

I suddenly remember the name of the theme park I'd been researching. The vivid dream I had about it rolls through my thoughts.

"The theme park," I say. "Trinity Pointe. What happened?"

"He confessed," Sam says. "You'd written in the files that you believed Michael Channing was severely traumatized by everything that happened and might not even be aware of what he was doing when he attacked the teenagers at Christmas. Xavier suggested approaching him where his mind was and giving him the apology he'd never heard. It worked."

"Where was he?"

"A hospital," Sam says.

"Not the theme park?"

He looks at me strangely. "That park has been closed for years, Emma."

"But there was a survivor," I say. "Michael tried to kill him, had him captive."

"No. Michael wasn't there that night. The survivor was found, but just barely."

"Caleb Portier," I say. Sam nods. "He's a medical examiner now."

"I know. You had newspaper clippings about him in the file."

All the details come flooding back to me now. It's been a long time since I've worked on those files, so long much of it had faded in my memory. But now I remember them. I stop.

"Did you talk to me while I was in the coma?"

"Every day," he says.

"Did you talk to me about this?" I ask.

"A little. Not much. I didn't know how it would affect you. Why?"

"I... dreamed the whole time I was under. I was experiencing those cases as if I was investigating them when they happened. I was there at Camp Hollow, at the mall. I was there when... wait. Did Xavier talk to me?"

"All the time. He read you stories at night. It was his special private ritual with you."

The lightbulb that goes off in my head as I finally put it all together. "Did he read me stories or *tell* me stories? Did you ever actually see a book?" I ask.

"I saw him with a big binder. I thought he'd maybe printed some stories." Realization comes over him and he sighs.

"Damn it, Xavier."

I laugh. "At least it was entertaining. It's really strange, though."

"What is?" Janet asks.

"One of the dreams I had... I can't remember having a file on it. That hotel. With the peacocks everywhere. An extremely wealthy philanthropist had sold the opportunity to murder people to bored, over-indulged rich people."

Sam gives me a quizzical look. "Babe, I don't know what you're talking about. What hotel with peacocks?"

My mind wanders back to the week at the retreat, the voices I heard that seemed to come out of the walls, how I felt like I was both there and not.

"I guess it was just that place between awake and asleep."

They go back to eating and start getting the games set up. I walk over to the window and look out over the street in front of me. I can see my house and I peer through the window to where Xavier is sitting on the couch, a massive bowl of popcorn in his lap, jars of sourdough starter around him. The newest, Luke Ryewalker, is tucked up close to his side. Dean is off to the side. I occasionally see his arm reach for something on the table or Xavier turn to look at him.

Xavier's eyes suddenly focus on the window. There are blinds on Janet's window, so I know he can't actually see me. But he doesn't look away and smiles.

AUTHOR'S NOTE

Dear Reader,

Thank you for choosing to read *The Girl and the Deadly Secrets,* the first installment in this new season of the Emma Griffin® FBI Mystery series.

I have to admit, saying goodbye to the *Emma Griffin® FBI Mystery Retro-Limited Series* was bittersweet. I mean, who doesn't love a good flashback to the totally tubular '80s? But, let me tell you, I am stoked to bring Emma back to the present timeline and dive headfirst into the overarching mystery that I have planned for this new season. Trust me when I say, there are plenty of clues to uncover, heart-pumping thrills, and answers to discover for Emma this season. And I am thrilled that you are joining me on this journey!

I owe Emma and the rest of this beloved cast of characters to your unyielding support and enthusiasm. So, if you could take a quick moment to leave a review for this book, I would appreciate it enormously. Your reviews allow me to keep living my dream as an indie author and bringing you the thrilling mystery stories that you love.

While waiting for the next Emma Griffin book, I invite you to experience the first installment in my brand new series, *The Girl in Paradise,* featuring FBI forensics specialist Bella Walker in the stunning landscapes of Hawaii! Bella finds herself investigating the most head-scratching, bizarre case of her career, with six rich elites brutally murdered on sacred Maoli land. She's up against some tough obstacles, including police corruption and the dangerous Yakuza crime syndicate.

I promise to keep bringing you heart-pounding, mind-bending mysteries that will keep you at the edge of your seat, and coming back for more!

Yours,
A.J. Rivers

P.S. If for some reason you didn't like this book or found typos or other errors, please let me know personally. I do my best to read and respond to every email at mailto:aj@riversthrillers.com

P.P.S. If you would like to stay up-to-date with me and my latest releases I invite you to visit my Linktree page at *www.linktr.ee/a.j.rivers* to subscribe to my newsletter and receive a free copy of my book, Edge of the Woods. You can also follow me on my social media accounts for behind-the-scenes glimpses and sneak peeks of my upcoming projects, or even sign up for text notifications. I can't wait to connect with you!

ALSO BY

A.J. RIVERS

Emma Griffin FBI Mysteries Retro - Limited Series

*Book One— The Girl in the Mist**
*Book Two— The Girl on Hallow's Eve**
*Book Three— The Girl and the Christmas Past**
*Book Four— The Girl and the Winter Bones**
Book Five— The Girl on the Retreat

Ava James FBI Mysteries

*Book One—The Woman at the Masked Gala**
*Book Two—Ava James and the Forgotten Bones**
*Book Three —The Couple Next Door**
*Book Four — The Cabin on Willow Lake**
*Book Five — The Lake House**
*Book Six — The Ghost of Christmas**
*Book Seven — The Rescue**

Dean Steele FBI Mysteries

Book One—The Woman in the Woods

Bella Walker FBI Mystery Series

Book One—The Girl in Paradise

Other Standalone Novels
Gone Woman
* Also available in audio

Made in United States
Orlando, FL
21 May 2023

33352519R00138